# CRASH COURSE

## SCOTIA STORMS

## CATHRYN FOX

# COPYRIGHT

Crash Course
Copyright 2022 by Cathryn Fox
Published by Cathryn Fox

Discover other titles by Cathryn Fox at www.cathrynfox.com. Please sign up for Cathryn's Newsletter for freebies, ebooks, news and contests: https://app.mailerlite.com/webforms/landing/c1f8n1
ISBN ebook: 978-1-989374-54-2
ISBN Print: 978-1-989374-53-5

# 1

## PIPER

I n Nova Scotia, April showers bring...snow. I'm not just talking about a light dusting here—like the weatherman called for. I'm talking thick, heavy flakes that are weighing down my hair and piling up fast beneath my Jimmy Choo's. Having grown up in Baddeck, a small town on Cape Breton Island, where they get even more snow than they do here in Halifax, you'd think I'd know better than to wear expensive shoes in April. But I had to talk to my fashion design teacher over at the community college and I always like to appear put together and professional. But you'd think I'd know to carry my shoes and put them on just before my meeting.

I trudge across the street, my feet and ankles freezing, and note a few cars swerving as they take the corner. I guess they took their winter tires off too soon. At least I know better than to do that, and I'm glad I walked to the campus this afternoon instead of driving, even though only a fool would be traipsing outside in this kind of weather. I snort at that. I suppose I've been called worse...

I hurry across the street, on my way to my friend Kennedy's house, and as I approach Beckett Moore's Jeep in the driveway, I roll my eyes, because yes, he's the one who's called me worse. Not to my face, of course, but I'd heard things back when we attended Baddeck High together. Who would have thought we'd both end up at the same college in Halifax? I probably should have figured it out though, considering he's an amazing hockey goalie, and much coveted by the Scotia Storms, the academy's kick ass team.

Beckett and I even shared a few business classes our freshman year—keeping our distance in the classroom, of course—and while I'm enrolled in the business management program, I'm also taking design classes at the community college because fashion is my passion.

I put my hand on Beckett's snowy Jeep to steady myself as I navigate around it, not wanting to land on my butt as my feet slide, but the second I make the turn—big fat snowflakes blurring my vision—Beckett comes sliding out from underneath the vehicle, the dolly's wheels getting stuck in the snow.

I gasp at his sudden, unexpected appearance, and try to jump out of the way, but I slip and contort, hurting my back, and end up with my legs wrapped around his head, as I straddle his face. Wait, is he grinning?

"What the hell, Beckett!" I try to stand, but only end up wiggling and gyrating, and dear God, never in my entire life did I imagine I'd be sitting on Beckett's face—or that I'd be enjoying it. Okay, maybe I did once, a couple months ago at our friend's wedding, when he accidently smudged cake on my cheek and dress, then accidently swiped at my breast when he tried to help me clean it off. Ridiculous, right? Especially considering the fact that I hate this man with every fiber of my being and would like nothing more than to wipe that smirk from his face. A man as horrible as Beckett should not be gifted with such adorable dimples.

"Need a hand?" He puts his big, rough hands on my hips to still me.

Ohmigod, he has no idea what his touch is doing to me. Or maybe he does. There isn't a girl on campus besides me who is immune to his charm. In my current predicament, as snow falls onto his face, his mouth so close to the needy juncture between my legs, I'm not convinced I'm immune to it either.

"What were you doing under there?"

"What are you doing up there?" he counters, and I'm pretty sure his hands are holding me in place.

"I'm trying to get off."

Ohmigod, kill me freaking now.

"Is that so?"

I give a fast shake of my head, and my wet hair clings to my cheeks. "It's not...I mean, I didn't mean it that way."

"You didn't mean you're not trying to get off me?"

"Yes. No."

I'm going to kill him for twisting my words, although maybe I'm the only one thinking they sound sexual. How could I think otherwise when I'm talking about getting off as I wiggle on his face?

He lifts me, easily moving me around, until I'm on his waist, and he sits up. His face is right there, inches from mine, and his gaze drops and takes in my mouth as I try to plant my shoes on either side of him. To anyone looking, I'm sure they think we're dry humping in the driveway, except I'm wet, and it's not from the snow.

What is going on with my body?

I put my hands on his shoulders for leverage, and he helps me lift myself off. "Good?" he asks as I get to my feet, my sex once again right there in front of his face. I grumble under my breath and keep my hands on his shoulders as I carefully lift one leg over him and set it down on the ground beside the other. Once I'm stable, I let go of his shoulders, and try not to think about how his muscles moved beneath my fingers. But seriously, the last thing I want to do is fall on him again.

Okay, maybe it's not the last thing.

I shake my head and shut down that ridiculous inner voice, making a mental note to give myself a good hard lecture later. We hate Beckett.

He jumps up from the dolly and snatches it up. "What are you doing?" I ask.

"I was fixing the muffler hanger. It was loose and rattling, making a terrible noise."

"In the middle of a snowstorm?"

His gaze leaves my face, leisurely traveling over my light stylish coat, tight jeans and ruined shoes. His brow arches in question as his gaze cuts back to mine.

"Yeah, okay."

I turn from him, and nearly face plant as I try to make it up the sloped driveway. I windmill my arms, nearly losing my backpack off my shoulder, but before I fall, his hand is around my waist, anchoring me to his body. I'm sure the touch is as painful to him as it is to me. I've heard the things he'd said about me our senior year in high school, although he pretty much stopped speaking to me after my seventeenth birthday, walking around our high school like I didn't exist. I'm not really sure what I ever did to him. The morning after my party, my car was vandalized. Someone had spray painted "slut" on the driver's side door.

Everyone assumed it was Beck, and when my parents confronted his parents and Beck was call downstairs to answer questions, he vehemently denied doing it. Funny thing is, I believed him. Even after the cold way he treated me, I still believed him.

Our parents didn't associate with each other before the incident; they didn't really like each other. Probably because mine own and run Baddeck's elite golf and ski resort, and his are blue collar workers, and yes, it's also true—and sad—that my parents think they're way better than everyone else, and didn't want me associating with those from the other side of the tracks. After the graffiti incident, both sets of parents despised each another.

He might not have put that word on my car, and while I don't for one-minute think he thinks I'm a slut, he no doubt assumes I'm a pampered princess, which in a way I am, but I don't hold the same beliefs as my parents. He just can't be bothered to see me as anything else, and because of it, I can't be bothered to show him. So now we're enemies, despite the fact that we share the same circle of friends.

"Thanks," I tell him, despite our past. He's helping me walk, and I'm grateful.

"Sure."

He helps me up the stairs, and pulls open the front door. Kicking snow off his boots, he wipes his face, leaving a big streak of grease on his forehead.

"Oh, you have..." I reach for his face and he flinches back. "Grease."

"Yeah, I know. I don't want you to touch it and get dirty. You're dressed so nicely."

Appreciating that, I nod, and he waves his big hand, a gesture for me to enter. I step inside and moan as the warmth envelopes me. Our friends Kennedy, Matt and their little girl Madelyn moved into this downtown house last October, and Beckett moved in with them shortly afterward, so I'm used to seeing him here. Or maybe a girl could never get used to seeing Beckett, especially since he likes to walk around without a T-shirt.

"Piper," Kennedy yells as she comes running down the hall, a dish towel in her hands. "You're soaked."

"I fell," I explain and steal a fast glance at Beckett, hoping he's not about to give the gory details of me riding his face.

"Come on, let's get you out of these clothes." I start shivering almost uncontrollably as I take off my ruined shoes, and set my backpack on the floor. I hope the fabric inside isn't soaked. Matt agreed to be my model for my final clothing design project, and I don't want to drape him in wet fabric.

Kennedy glances at Beckett's wet clothes and hair and shakes her head. "Did you fall too?" Before he can answer, she says, "Get changed, you're dripping all over the floor and I don't want you to catch your death of cold."

"Yes, Mom," he teases with a smirk, and Kennedy gives him the death glare. Honestly, they get along like brother and sister, and from what Kennedy tells me, he's amazing with her daughter. Me? Not so much. As an only child, I'm not used to siblings and I never really babysat. Nope, any spare time I had, I was working at the family's resort. My parents have been grooming their only child to take over for as long as I can remember. Too bad I hate the idea. Maybe even more than I hate Beckett.

I'm too afraid to tell my folks, though. They've been so good to me, and they pay for everything, from my food and rent to my education and extracurricular activities. Heck, they even sponsored a brand new Olympic sized pool for the academy, simply because I love to swim. I even have my own key to the facility, and can use it any day, at any hour. I owe my parents, and the lodge has been in the family for generations. It's only right that I take over when they retire. I've consoled myself with the idea that I can design clothes on the side, but let's face it. Who has time for such things when running a golf resort and ski lodge year-round?

"I just have to put this in the garage," Beckett says and holds up the dolly.

Kennedy nods and asks, "Did you get your Jeep fixed?"

"Yeah, and I'll get to your spark plugs once the snow lightens."

"No hurry on that. I'm not planning on driving anywhere in this." She glances out the door, shivers and hugs herself.

"You're always so cold," Beckett says, and puts his free hand on her arm, and rubs up and down to create warmth with friction. She smiles up at him, her gaze full of warmth and it's easy to see they have a special bond.

"Thanks."

"Good now?"

"Yup."

I don't like the guy, but it's so nice how thoughtful and caring he is with Kennedy. It's so damn sweet. But is it odd that I have this weird knot of jealousy tightening in my gut? Yeah, I think it is. Honestly, I've had male friends and casual boyfriends over the years, but I've never experienced a real closeness, or a special bond with any guy.

With that he nods and disappears back outside. Kennedy loops her arm in mine and takes me toward the stairs. We head up, and I say, "You and Beckett really get along well."

"Yeah, he's a sweetie." I almost snort, but don't want to be rude. "We really like having him here. He's handy too, and always willing to help out with anything we need."

If I spent the night, would he help out with the ache between my legs?

Dear God, what am I saying?

Kennedy frowns. "I'm a little worried about him, though."

"Worried? Why would you be worried?"

"I think he's working too hard. I haven't seen him with a girl in...forever."

"You mean he's not parading them in and out of here every weekend?"

"Nope." We reach the landing, and she puts her fingers to her lips to let me know Madelyn is sleeping, and I breathe a sigh of relief. It's not that I don't like Madelyn, I'm just a bit nervous and uncomfortable around her. I never know what to say. All I do know is that I'm not a natural around children.

Inside the master bedroom, Kennedy grabs me a pair of sweats, a T-shirt and sweater, which I probably won't need because it's super warm in the house. "I have an extra pair of boots for when you leave, or you can stay over if it gets too bad out there. Hey, the four of us could make a night of it."

Stay over, and be forced to spend more time with Beckett. No. Thank. You.

"Thanks," I say. "I'm sure I'll be fine."

"At least stay for dinner."

"Sounds great."

"I'll leave you to get changed. Meet me downstairs when you're done. I'll put on a fresh pot of coffee."

Ever so grateful, as Kennedy makes the best coffee ever, I listen to her footsteps on the stairs and glance around, feeling a little uncomfortable getting changed in their master bedroom. I quietly open the door, and tip toe to the bathroom, shutting the door tightly behind me. I glance at my face in the mirror, and shake my head. With mascara dripping down my cheek, it's a wonder Beckett didn't scream in horror when I sat on his face. The girls I've seen him with would never be caught dead with their makeup running. Although I must say I haven't seen him with anyone since he's moved in here.

God, I sound like a jealous fool, when I'm anything but.

I peel off my coat, and damp sweater and wiggle out of my jeans. Not an easy task when they're wet. I bend forward and grab the tub, having a hell of a time getting my ankles through the skinny jeans, when the bathroom door swings open. I gasp, straighten, spin around and lose my balance as my gaze lands on a bare-chested Beckett, his T-shirt draped over his shoulder, in that sexy way that teases every eroge-nous zone in my body.

He falters backward a bit. "Oh, ah...sorry."

"I...I was trying to get off..." I hop around on one foot stuck inside the leg of my jeans, and that's when I realize I'm only in my bra and underwear, about to faceplant again.

He closes the distance between us faster than a world elite sprinter, and the second I'm in his big arms, his dimple appears as he smirks and teases, "Again?"

## 2

# BECKETT

"**B**eckett!" Piper screams at me, and I turn around, fast, to give her privacy as she hops around on one leg. Okay, maybe not that fast. The sight before me is spectacular, and I could make fun of her since we hate each other, but I don't want to. I'm not much into revenge—even after she invited everyone in our high school class to her fancy-schmancy birthday party, except for me—and maybe my brain is too caught up in her near nakedness to think of some witty comeback.

Honestly, I'm not bitter about being left out. Much. But way to make the boy from the wrong side of the tracks feel like a real loser. At the time my parents told me, the only one who can make me feel less valued is me.

They were right, I know that, but as I sat my seventeen-year-old ass in my bedroom, with my best friend David, who refused to go to the extravagant pool party because I wasn't invited, it was hard to rationalize the truth behind my parents' statement. I might be older and wiser, and I hate to admit this, even to myself, but sometimes I still feel like that young boy who came from nothing, who always had to prove his worth. And then to get blamed for some graffiti I was not responsible for. At least my family believed me, but it just showed what others thought of me. I know I'm the number one goalie at the academy, and have no trouble finding someone to help warm my bed, but it can be hard to shake the deeply rooted feelings of insignificance.

But I refuse to prove it to Piper and her stuck-up family.

"Get out!" she shrieks again.

"Oh, right," I say her shrill words pulling me back to reality. "I was coming up to get changed and Kennedy asked me to grab her phone on my way back down. She left it in here earlier, and I didn't realize you were changing. Sorry."

"Here it is, just don't turn around." I reach behind me, and her cold hand touches mine as she places Kennedy's phone in my hand.

"There's this thing on the door," I begin, trying to be funny. "It's called a lock. It's a pretty new invention so I understand if you didn't know about it. I can show you how it works later, if you like."

"Just go, please," she mumbles under her breath, and there's something in her voice. A kind of shaky vulnerability I never expected to hear from the princess who's been pampered her whole life. I step from the room, shut the door behind me, and come face to face with Kennedy. She's standing in the hall, her mouth ajar as she stares at me wide eyed. Across the hall, in her bedroom Madelyn is awake and calling for her mom.

I cringe. "I guess we woke her, huh?"

"Yeah, but it's okay." She gives a dismissive wave of her hand as she grips Madelyn's doorknob. "It was time for her to get up anyway. What's going on?"

I gesture to the closed door. "I sort of walked in on Piper changing. I didn't realize she was in there."

"She was in my room changing when I went downstairs. I didn't realize she was in the bathroom either."

I throw my hands up in the air. "See, not my fault. Oh, here's your phone."

She takes it from me. "Speaking of seeing..."

I glance down, almost sheepish. "Yeah, she was half dressed."

"Ugh. That couldn't have gone over well."

I stare at Kennedy. Is that a smirk playing with the corner of her mouth? Can't be. She knows we hate each other, and no way would she ask me to grab her phone if she knew Piper was changing in the bathroom.

The washroom door creaks open, and Piper's face is red as she stands there in Kennedy's clothes. I never thought that a T-shirt and sweats were sexy before. She has a sweater draped over her shoulder as her wet hair drips, leaving the T-shirt a bit damp.

"I'd better get Madelyn," Kennedy says and opens the bedroom door. "I'll meet you both downstairs."

Piper glances at me. "Do you have to walk around without a shirt on?"

"Does it bother you?"

"Yes...No." She shakes her head.

"Maybe you like what you see?" I tease, just to pull a reaction out of her.

Her blue eyes turn murderous. "No, I don't. It's just that it's cold out."

"It's cold out but it's not cold in here. Kennedy keeps this place hotter than an inferno. She's always cold."

"Fine, do what you want." She makes a beeline for the stairs and while I was going to put my shirt on, I decide to leave it draped over my shoulder. I stand there for a second and just shake my head as she leaves, grateful that our semester is almost over, and she'll likely be going home to the family's resort for the summer. My plans are to stay here and work at the campus cafeteria, and take on more hours at Mighty Auto Service Station.

I poke my head into the bedroom, and my heart swells as two-year-old Madelyn smiles at me. "Beck," she says and holds her arms out.

"Sometimes I think she likes you better than me," Kennedy says, and I hold my hands out to the wiggling little girl. Kennedy hands her over, and Madelyn kisses my nose.

"At least someone around here likes me," I murmur. I love the kid, I really do and even though Matt isn't her biological father it doesn't matter. He loves her like she's his own.

Kennedy frowns at me. "I like you."

"Okay that's two out of three females," I say as I head into the hall carrying Madelyn downstairs. I walk into the kitchen and find Piper at the kitchen table, a frown on her face. "Everything okay?" I ask.

Her head lifts and her smile is as fake as every puck bunny's social media profile picture. Come on, no girl wakes up looking like they just spent hours getting their hair and makeup done. While I appreciate the effort, and I've dated many of them, I'd much prefer a real girl over the saccharine ones who pretend their lives are perfect.

No one's life is perfect. Except for maybe Piper's. Or at least I thought it was, up until I found her sitting here looking like she might cry. My heart constricts as I put Madelyn in her highchair and tug on my T-shirt. Kennedy goes to the front door to greet her fiancé, and my very best friend, Matt. He was over at Kennedy's mom's place, helping her move some furniture.

"Hey, Piper. Are you sure you're okay?" I ask, keeping my voice low.

She nods again, far too fast and far too exaggerated for it to be believable. "Yes." She shakes her phone. "Just my folks, excited that I'll be coming home in a few weeks."

Holy shit, she doesn't want to go back to Cape Breton Island. It's all over her face. I stare at her, and for the first time in my life, I get the sense that all is not perfect in her world.

"You'll be helping out at the resort?"

She smiles, but it doesn't reach her pretty blue eyes. "Once again, I'll be in charge of scheduling activities, and giving tennis and swimming lessons. Things like that. Someday I'll take over the place." She snorts. "I've been groomed for that for as long as I can remember. I honestly don't know why I need a business degree. I already know how to run the place."

I stare at her for a second and while she's trying to put a positive spin on things, I can almost taste the resentment on her tongue. Why would anyone resent being handed a million-dollar business? I'm not sure I understand it, but I guess I can be dense like that.

"Tennis lessons, swimming lessons. Sounds like a hardship." I'm not trying to be an asshole here; I'm just saying that to see her reaction. What's to hate about inheriting a resort and why does she not want to go home? I know she's close to her parents. Heck, I love my family too and try to get back to see them every chance I get. I'm the second oldest, with two younger sisters who are both smarter than me and will kill it in the world when they're older, and one younger brother who is going to be a lawyer judging by his arguing skills. It was my older brother who taught me auto mechanics. I'm working hard to help pay my way through school, so my parents can put make sure my siblings get what they need growing up. I plan to kill it in the NHL so I can help my parents pay for my siblings education, and get them out of Cape Breton.

Don't get me wrong. I love where I grew up, but opportunities for careers are few and far between. My grandfather worked in the coal mines for years. My dad did the same until he got sick and took a mechanics course. With Cape Breton's economy heavily dependent on tourism, outside of that, there's a high unemployment rate, and I want my siblings to make something more of themselves.

"Not a hardship at all." She sets her phone down. "Will you be heading home this summer?"

"At some point I'll try." I don't bother asking if she wants to meet for drinks or dinner when I do. Hell, we live only minutes away here, and don't meet up for anything. Sure, we're always doing things together because we're in the same group of friends, but outside of it, we steer clear of each other.

"Matt," she says, her face lighting up as he enters the kitchen, and while I get she really likes him, I also get that she wants to end our conversation.

My phone pings, and I glance down and read a message from Dryden. He's one of the other goalies on the roster. He wants to know if I want to go practice, so I can critique him and help him get better, but I text back and let him know I'm busy. I'm all about helping the next guy improve, and I want him to be great to take over when I finish at the academy, but I'm about to eat, and it's a mess outside. I'm sure the rink is closed due to the storm anyway, and I don't want Piper thinking she upsets me so much that I always run the other way. I'd prefer it if she thought I was indifferent to her.

Matt says hello as he leans down to kiss Madelyn, and she blows bubbles on his cheek. "Hey, chicken nugget," he says, and pours himself a glass of water. Kennedy pulls a pot roast from the oven, the perfect meal for a cold day like today.

"You still on to be my model?" Piper asks Matt.

Matt laughs. "Sure."

I narrow my eyes and stare at my buddy. "Wait, you're going to be a model?"

"It's for my final assignment," Piper explains. "I have to design something fashionable, professional and affordable, aimed for a broke-ass male student who needs business work clothes." She turns to Matt. "You're still okay with walking the runway?" She puckers her lips. "I know it's a lot to ask, but you have the perfect body to showcase clothes."

Okay, not trying to take offense here. I am the epitome of broke-ass student. Though why would Piper ask me and what does she know about being broke?

Matt, modest guy that he is, laughs at that, and Kennedy hugs him. "It's true," she whispers, but we can all hear.

"Get a room," I say and roll my eyes, but there's a part of me that's jealous at what they have. I'm not against marriage by any means, I'm just busy working two jobs to pay for school and I'm the main goalie for the team, so I'm busy. Hell, I don't even seem to have time for girls anymore. Although I'm not sure time is the real problem here. I think maybe I'm just tired of the parties, and well...the fucking.

Holy hell, who am I?

Seriously though, it's all getting old. I was ecstatic when Matt and Kennedy found a place together and asked me to move in. It helped cut costs their costs and now I'm not subjected to the parties at the frat house every weekend. Okay, yeah, I really don't know who I am anymore.

"Wait, why are you designing men's fashion when you're a business student?"

She almost pales but responds with, "It's just a hobby. Something I enjoy."

When she doesn't say more, I nod and go to work on setting the table, putting out placemats, and cutlery and four glasses of water. I rinse Madelyn's cup and fill it with apple juice, bending to kiss her on the head as I give it to her. I glance up quickly to find a strange look on Piper's face.

"What?"

"Nothing," she replies quickly and turns to Kennedy. "What can I do to help?"

"Grab the casserole dish on the bottom shelf." Piper jumps up, like she's happy to be away from me, and sets the casserole dish on the counter. Kennedy plates all the food and Matt brings it to the table.

"Kennedy, this looks amazing," Piper says.

I dig right in. "She's a great cook." I wink at Kennedy. "She makes a mean lasagna."

Kennedy sets her fork down, and I sense something is going on as she and Matt exchange a glance. Matt sets his fork down too and I sit up a bit straighter.

"We were wondering," she begins, and my stomach knots. I don't think I'm going to like what she was wondering. Kennedy reaches out and takes Matt's hand. "We never had the chance to really celebrate our engagement, and we saved so we could book a resort on Prince Edward Island for a few days after our finals. Ryan Potter is from the island, and he knows the owner of the resort. He got us a great deal. He comes from a family of potato farmers. You know Ryan, don't you, Piper? He's a right winger on the team." Piper nods, and Kennedy frowns, and continues with, "Unfortunately, Mom can no longer babysit. She's taken on someone else's shift at the restaurant that week."

"I can help out," I blurt out.

"Thank you, Beck. We appreciate that, but we also know you hold down two jobs and can't be a full-time caregiver, but we were thinking, between the two of you, we could put together a schedule."

Jesus fucking, Christ. Is she kidding me?

Piper looks like they just asked her to go skydiving without a parachute when she asks, "You want me to babysit?"

"I mean, if it's not too much to ask."

She blinks, repeatedly, and I can't help but think she's looking for an excuse. "I'm expected home to help out at the resort."

Kennedy shrugs. "Oh, well if you can't. It's not a problem, we can probably find someone else to help out. Right, Matt?"

Before he can answer Piper blurts out, "No, no. I guess, I can postpone. You know if you really need me, and I owe you since Matt is being such a great sport helping me out with my class project."

Kennedy smiles. "It's settled then. We can talk details later." Kennedy focuses in on Piper. "Someday I have to visit your family's resort in Baddeck. Tell me more about it."

I can barely eat, and that's saying something as Piper talks about the resort—which she doesn't want to go home to. By the time she's finished—and I'm still freaking out that I'll be sharing this house with Piper—our meal is done. Matt and I do the dishes as the three girls all retire to the living room. I wash and Matt dries as snow continues to fall outside.

"Why do we live here again?" he jokes.

"Family," is all I say. "I realize someday I'll likely move far from Nova Scotia, but I like being close to family while in college. Are you sure Piper is the right girl to help with Madelyn?"

Matt gives a confident shake of his head. "Absolutely, and she has you to help."

I want to ask more, tell him I think it's a bad idea, but they're pretty close with Piper and I don't want to rock the boat, so I stay silent. We finish up in the kitchen and step into the other room. Piper has a worried look on her face as she glances out the window.

"I think you should stay," Kennedy says. "We can blow up the air mattress."

"You can have my room," I blurt out without thinking.

What the hell?

She turns to me. "I don't want to put you out."

Matt laughs. "Haven't you heard? Beckett likes to put out."

I laugh and shake my head. "It's not a problem. I want to shovel later when the snow stops and I'd just disturb you if you're sleeping down here."

"It's settled then. You'll take Beck's bed," Kennedy announces and jumps up. "Beck, can you watch Madelyn while Matt and I go downstairs and blow up the mattress."

"Yeah, no problem."

I scoop Madelyn up and note the way Piper is staring at me as we settle in to watch Madelyn's favorite cartoon. She has that same confused look on her face as she did when we were in the kitchen. Does she not think I know how to take care of a child?

When Kennedy and Matt return with the mattress, I stand. "I have some things to do in my room. I'll come down when you're ready for bed." I bolt up the steps and shut my bedroom door tight. The first thing I do is put fresh sheets on the mattress, then I settle on top of the bed, put my earbuds in and do some studying. Hours later, when I hear them all coming up the stairs, I open my door, mumble goodnight and make my way downstairs.

Since the snow is still coming down, I decide to shovel in the morning and drop down onto my make-shift bed. I lie still a long time, my thoughts on Piper, and living under the same roof with her for a few days. I toss restlessly, then decide a cold shower is in order.

No way am I going to lay on this air mattress and take my dick in my hand. One, I have no privacy down here, anyone could come downstairs and two, I don't want to think about stuck up Piper when I tug one out. No fucking way in hell. I push off my blanket, soaking wet because Kennedy keeps this house hotter than hell, and tip toe upstairs to the bathroom. With the night light casting enough light for me to see, I leave the light off, and jump into the shower. At first I turn it to cold, but it does little to put out my fire.

Unable to help myself, I turn the water to hot and the next thing I know, I'm quietly groaning as I take my dick in my hand, my thoughts on the girl sleeping in my bed as I stroke myself to satisfaction. Once done, I turn off the hot water, and pull open the shower curtain, just as the door opens, and the light flicks on.

"What the...?" I begin, my eyes adjusting enough to find a wide-eyed Piper standing there, staring at my still erect dick.

"Ohmigod..." She puts her hand up to block her vision, and damn if this isn't fitting after I walked in on her earlier. "I didn't...know...what...what..."

What the hell? Is she asking what I'm doing in the shower, so late at night? If so, I might as well admit the truth. After all, she should know who she agreed to spend a week with, right, and maybe this will change her mind and put me out of my misery.

"Um...getting off."

A moment of silence and then, "There's this thing on the door," she begins, her voice hoarse and low, and so damn sexy my dick stands up and takes notice. "It's called a lock. It's a pretty new invention so I understand if you didn't know about it. I can show you how it works later, if you like."

Okay, it's true. I deserved that, and I have to say, I kind of love her quick wit and nonchalant attitude. Go Piper.

## 3

# PIPER

I can barely keep my eyes from straying lower to take in the huge erection Beck's not even bothering to hide. Why would he, when it's that magnificent? I guess the rumors I've heard are true—he's the team's goalie, but he knows how to score, big time.

Because he's standing there like he doesn't have a care in the world, I refuse to let him know his nakedness is messing with my brain and my body, so I take a step into the bathroom, grab a towel and toss it to him. "Looks like you might be cold."

He grins, because he knows I'm referring to male appendages shrinking in icy water, and that's definitely not his problem. Not only is the house hot, the bathroom is steamy, and let's not even talk about the fire alarm going off between my legs.

Can Beck hear it?

Heck, I wouldn't be surprised if it woke the entire block. He takes the towel and dries his face and hair, leaving his cock on display. Once done, he wraps the fluffy cotton around his hips, and it hangs low, showcasing his delicious oblique muscles.

Delicious oblique muscles?

Good God, has the mere naked sight of him reduced me to a bumbling idiot?

*Yes, Piper, yes it has.*

He steps from the shower and plants his bare feet on the tile floor. "I'll just get out of your way and let you do whatever it is you were going to do." His voice is rich and thick, full of... arousal? No, I have to be mistaken. Nothing about me arouses him. I suppose he was in there thinking of some puck bunny, and that's why he sounds winded and distressed.

"I'm thirsty," I blurt out.

That grin that has girls handing over their panties appears and I resist the urge to do the same, when I suddenly realize panties are the only thing covering my ass. I grip my T-shirt and tug it lower when he says, "Oh yeah."

Oh God.

"Not like that," I say quickly, my insides flustered as I try to present calm and collected, but a theater student I am not.

"Not like what?"

"You know what I mean..." He stares at me, his brow furrowed. "I'm thirsty for water..." I wave my hand up and down his body. "Not for you."

"I wasn't thinking that. Funny you brought it up. Freudian slip maybe."

The man is insufferable.

I shake my head, and walk to the tap. I'm about to take a drink, when his hand lands on my arm. "I'll get you a glass of cold water from the fridge. These pipes are old, so we only drink filtered water."

I stand back up, and there's real sincerity in his eyes as he stares at me. "Oh okay, thank you."

"Head back to my room and I'll bring it up to you." As I stare at him—is he up to something—he snatches his clothes from the floor. "I meant to grab some clean clothes earlier. Do you mind if I grab some now?"

"No, sure, it's your room." Truthfully, I feel a little guilty for taking it, and forcing him to hide out in his room all night because I was downstairs with our friends. At least I managed to do some measurements of Matt. The deadline for my final assignment is approaching quickly. I glance over my shoulder. "I'll just go...wait for you."

He smiles, like he likes that idea and goes downstairs with his clothes in his hands. I tiptoe back to his room and flick the lamp on as I slide between the sheets. At least in the dim light I won't be subjected to looking at his body again. That was a real hardship...not. Needing something to do, I grab my laptop from my backpack and put on a stupid movie from a generation gone by. Watching something mind-numbing might help cool me down so I can fall asleep. I wasn't having much luck before I went to the bathroom. How could I with Beck's scent impregnating the blankets and sheets? I never realized how good the man smelled.

I listen as the fridge downstairs opens, followed by the cupboard, and a few minutes later, he's standing in the doorway, completely overwhelming my senses. "I'll be quick," he whispers as he hands me the glass, and I take a big gulp.

"Thank you." He stares at me as I lick some droplets off my lips and set the cup on the nightstand. Earlier, when I first came to his room, I tried not to notice anything, but that was like leading a thirsty horse to water and asking it not to drink. His room is pretty simple, much like him. I'm not saying that in a bad way. I just mean that he's not a very high maintenance kind of guy. There are no pictures, or posters, just a nice picture of an apple orchard. I assume Kennedy hung that. Do materialistic things not mean much to him?

"Your room is pretty sparse," I say, and wish I hadn't. I shouldn't be commenting on his things.

He tugs some clothing out of his drawer and turns to me. He gestures with a nod. "I have a picture." He walks up to it and smiles. "Do you like it?"

"I do. Is it...yours?"

He nods. "I saw it at the market, and it reminds me of home. We have that big apple tree on our property, remember?" We stare at one another for a second, as the scene on my laptop plays out, and that's when he remembers I've never been to his house. "Oh, right, never mind." He tugs on his sweats, under the towel and then unhooks it. Not bothering with a T-shirt he comes around to the other side of the bed. "What are you watching?"

"Nothing, it's stupid."

He narrows his gaze. "Is that Sex Drive?"

"Uh, yeah." Oh, God. I should have put on something that didn't have sex in the title.

"I love that show. It's so ridiculous."

"I started it earlier, when I couldn't sleep." I laugh and joke, "Strange bed."

"Hey," he says. "Don't talk about my bed like that. You'll hurt her feelings." He rubs his mattress and I do my damndest not to envision those hands touching my body in the same manner. What the hell is wrong with me?

"I guess she's not a stranger to having company?" Ohmigod, why would I say something like that?

His dimple appears. "For your information, I bought this bed when I moved in here, and she's a virgin."

Heat flushes my body, and while I'm not a virgin, I'm the closest thing there is to one. I lost my virginity to Noah Blackmore—one of the most popular guys at our school—at my seventeenth birthday party, and it was so horrible and messy, I just never wanted to do it again. Not that Noah wanted to do it with me again, either. The next time I saw him, he went the other way, and I'm pretty sure he was sporting a black eye. I have no idea what that was all about, or who he'd gotten into a fight with, since we barely talked again.

Honestly, I think I only did it with him in the first place because I was so hurt and angry that Beckett didn't show, and I had such a huge crush on him, I used Noah to...I don't know, get over Beck? Prove to myself that I was likeable... loveable, even? That I wasn't the snotty rich girl Beck thought I was?

"I'm sorry. I shouldn't have said anything about your bed. It wasn't right, and I didn't mean to sound like I was judging you." Heck, I don't want to judge. I'm judged enough.

"It's okay." The car scene comes on, and he turns his focus to the laptop. He laughs quietly, and as if forgetting we hate each other and that he's sleeping downstairs, he slides onto the bed, and adjusts his pillow.

We both fall quiet, and I shift so he can see the screen better, and this really strange sense of calm comes over me. Did Beck and I just make some kind of truce? I'm not sure but I hope like hell we did since we'll be playing house when we watch Madelyn, and life will be a lot easier if we're not up in each other's faces all the time.

I glance at him as he laughs, and there's just something about the way his smile lights up his face. The truth is, Beck is a happy, easy-going guy—a good friend to those he cares about —and a guy who doesn't need much and I kind of like that about him. Ha! Who would have thought I'd ever use Beck and like in the same sentence?

He shifts closer and I'm not even sure he realizes it, but our legs are touching—and it's sending heat zinging through my body. I don't move, though. There's something really nice about this shared moment.

"Can you turn the lamp off? From where I'm sitting there's a glare on the screen."

"Sure." I reach over and flick the light off, and the room goes dark, save for the light on the screen. I slide a little lower on my pillow and he comes closer. Half of his head on my pillow and half on his and wow, the scent of him on his bedding was one thing, but actually smelling his skin, that's all kinds of nice. I breathe deeply, and as his scent trickles through my veins, it brings with it a kind of need I've never before experienced. I steal another glance at him and take in the sharp angles of his face, which always soften when he's with Madelyn.

I can't help but think he'll be a good dad someday. He laughs again and I turn my attention to the screen. I stifle a yawn as my body relaxes, a warm contentment curling around me. The next thing I know, morning light is shining into the window, and I open my eyes, not at all sure where I am, until I turn to the right and spot a half-naked man asleep beside me.

Oh, crap.

I shift and try to slip from the bed, when I hear, "Fuck."

I go still, angle my head to find Beck running his hands through his hair as he sits up, his apologetic eyes locked on me. "I'm sorry. I don't know what happened."

"We both fell asleep watching the movie."

He nods, and glances at my laptop, the battery long dead. "It was just so warm…"

"And cozy," I add without thinking.

"Yeah."

"I guess she's not a virgin anymore."

His eyes go wide. "Did we—"

"No," I blurt out and half laugh, half groan. "I just mean, you had a girl in your bed."

"Yeah, I thought that was a dream," he says to himself.

"What?"

He throws his legs over the side of the bed. "Nothing."

"You said something about a dream."

"I'm just saying if I slept with you, I would have remembered." He checks the time. "Shit, I need to get moving."

"Me too. I need to get home and showered before class."

"You can shower here if you want."

"I need clean clothes."

"I can hook you up."

I laugh. "Can you imagine what people would think if I showed up to the academy in your clothes?"

His body stiffens, and his demeanor changes, becomes serious. "Yeah," is all he says.

God, what did I say? "I just mean I don't want people to think—"

"I know." He tugs on a T-shirt and opens his door. "I'll go clear the driveway and give you a lift to your place." I'm about to protest. Maybe we've already spent too much time together, but he cuts me off before I can say that. "I'm sure the sidewalks haven't been cleared yet and it will take you forever to get to your place."

He's right, so I nod, and he disappears down the hall. I wait for him to finish in the bathroom, and reach the main level before I leave his room. I make my own trip to the bathroom, and by the time I go downstairs, Beck and Matt are out shoveling, and Kennedy is running around getting Madelyn and herself ready for the day. I enter the kitchen and she goes completely still, her lids wide, her eyes full of questions as I stand there.

I hold my hands up. "It's not what you think."

She cocks her head. "What exactly do you think that I think?"

"That we slept together. We didn't do anything...you know, like make love."

She laughs. "Make love? If anything happened between you two it would be a hate fuck, and I know you're not into that."

"What?" I ask. It's true, I'm not into that, but why would she bring it up?

"You guys don't even like each other, right?"

"Right."

"That's why I asked both of you to watch Madelyn. I figured any other girl in this house...and well, Beck could get distracted from taking care of Madelyn. With you I don't run that risk."

Jeez, way to make me feel unlikeable. I realize she doesn't mean it that way but it still stings a bit and at least I know they weren't trying to set us up or anything stupid like that.

"Yeah, well he came in to get some clothes, and I was watching a movie, and he joined me and we fell asleep. We still hate each other," I say, with more conviction than I actually feel. Last night was...nice.

So was seeing him naked.

But I don't admit any of that, and when Madelyn starts fussing, Kennedy turns her attention to getting her a sippy cup. Ten minutes later, I'm sitting beside Beckett in his Jeep and shivering as I try to warm my hands in front of the heater.

I try for light conversation. "I think it feels extra cold out here because Kennedy keeps the house so warm."

He laughs. "When she's away, how about we turn the heat down, and tell no one?"

Laughing, I nod my head in agreement. It's crazy but I like conspiring with him. "It's a plan."

He drives carefully on the plowed, but still slippery streets, and while I'm done with winter, the snow is gorgeous as it clings to the trees. It won't be around long, not this time of year, but seeing it right now is kind of nice.

He maneuvers through the streets and while he's never been to my place, he knows where I live and pulls up in front of the house I share with Alysha Tiffany, a girl from the Hamptons who moved in with me for our winter semester. We've become good friends.

"Thanks for the lift." I snatch up my backpack and grab the door handle. "And, for letting me have your bed."

He grins. "I guess I didn't really, though, did I?"

I shrug in response. "You had good intentions."

*Unfortunately.*

Oh God.

"There's always a first for everything," he jokes, and I exit the car, and wave goodbye as I start for my driveway. That's when I notice Dryden coming down the street, his gaze going from me, to Beck, back to me. Great, I know exactly what he's thinking. He waves and I assume he's trying to get Beck's attention, maybe grab a lift to the rink to practice for Friday night's big game, but no, he steps up to me.

"Hey how's it going?"

Okay, Dryden has barely talked to me before. I'm roommates with his cousin Alysha, and when he stops by he barely says hello. Why is he doing it now? Does he think I slept with Beck and that means I'll sleep with every goalie on the team? I know the players sometimes share girls, but I'm not into that.

"Ah, good." I turn to find Beck still in my driveway a strange look on his face as he watches our exchange carefully, too carefully.

What the hell?

## 4

## BECKETT

With seconds left in our exhibition game, and the score one to nothing for the Storms, I move from side to side within my net as Sutherland, from the University of Cape Breton—we went to high school together—comes skating toward me, lightning fast. Keeping my eye on him and his moves, I prepare for the shot. It comes and bounces off my skate. Phillips comes in for the rebound, and I contort to save the puck, stopping it with my stick and falling over it as our defensive end fight off the opposing team as they close in on me, desperate for a goal.

The buzzer goes off and the crowd goes crazy, but what's really crazy is how I seek Piper out in the stands, and grin inwardly as she stands and starts clapping with the rest of our friends. My teammates jump on me, piling on until I can barely breathe, but I don't care. We just won, and after over thirty shots on net, I'm damn proud of my shutout.

By the time we all finish hugging, Dryden is the last one to come on to the ice and hug me, and my insides twist. It's strange. I never noticed his interest in Piper until I dropped her off the other morning. I mean, he can date her if he wants, and who she likes is her business. Heck, we're barely friends.

Why then, was it so damn nice falling asleep next to her, and more importantly finding her there in the morning when I opened my eyes?

*Fuck me twice.*

I hadn't set eyes on her since I drove her home, but I've found myself thinking of her more and more, maybe even looking forward to seeing her tonight at The Tap Room after the game. We all line up for the handshake—I give Sutherland a special fist bump—and my adrenaline is still pumping fast as we head to the locker room to get showered and changed.

The locker room is loud, everyone on a high after the game, and I strip off, and walk my soaked and tired body to the shower. I've turned on the spray and put my face underneath when I hear Dryden beside me.

"So, you and Piper. What's going on there?"

I groan inwardly. What the fuck am I supposed to say? Nothing is going on between us and most people know we avoid each other, so seeing us together would be all kinds of confusing. But the truth is, I don't want her dating Dryden. Why? Beats the fuck out of me. The only thing I can come up with is the guy is a man-whore, but hey who the hell on the team—other than those who are settled down—isn't?

*You're not.*

Okay, well that might be true now. I haven't been with a girl in a while, but I'm not about to parade a bunch of girls in and out of Matt and Kennedy's home. How fair would that be to Madelyn?

Is that the real reason, Beck?

Of course, it's the real reason. What other reason could there be? I grab my shampoo and glance to my left to see Dryden waiting for me to answer.

"I don't think she's your type," is all I say.

"Oh yeah." He snorts. "She has a pussy, doesn't she?"

An unfamiliar rage burns through my blood as I put my face under the spray. "Don't be so fucking crude."

"Don't tell me you all of a sudden like little miss pampered princess."

I want to tell him not to call her that, but how can I? I'm pretty sure I've used those exact same words. Unable to drown him out, I shrug, figuring I'm getting worked up about nothing. While Piper always comes out to support the team, I've never once seen her date a player. Come to think of it, I'm not sure she's been with any guy in the last couple years, and no I've not been keeping track. We just run in the same circles.

"No," I say between clenched teeth."

"I can hook up with her then?" Dryden asks.

I swallow down the unease punching into my throat. Why again, is he suddenly interested in her? "Why, do you want to?"

"Did you miss the part about her having a pussy?"

"Knock it off. Besides aren't you with Kylee right now?" I think I've seen them together a few times.

"Yeah, whatever."

Okay, so maybe he's just messing with me because he thinks I like Piper. I don't know Kylee well, but she's smart and driven, and probably isn't the kind of girl he should mess around on, not unless he wants to be neutered.

Matt takes the stall beside me. I turn to him and he frowns. "What's going on?"

"Nothing," I grumble, and with much more force than necessary, I turn off the tap, nearly tearing the lever from the wall.

I stomp back to my locker and try to smile as the guys all pat me on the back again, and goddammit, I should be in a good mood. Fuck, I should be in a great mood and I'm used to locker room talk. I just suddenly don't like it. Christ, maybe after living with Matt and Kennedy I'm getting soft. I don't know, but no girl, no matter who she is, should be talked about like that. I might have said Piper was pampered, but I've never disrespected her or anyone else.

I head outside and since today was warm, most of the snow is gone. At least April snow doesn't stick around long in Nova Scotia, but none of us are ready to shed our winter coats just yet. I hear my name and turn to find Kennedy running up to me. She throws her arms around me and gives me a kiss on the cheek. I hug her back.

"Great game tonight, Beck." She lets go, and jokingly I hold my arms out and glance at the girls surrounding us.

"Okay, who's next?"

Laughing, Sawyer throws her arms around me and gives me a hug. It was Chase who got the goal tonight, so he's going to get all the loving too.

"Hey, get your arms off him," Chase says as he comes out and Sawyer throws herself into his arms and he spins her around. My heart takes that moment to miss a beat. There's no denying that the two of them belong together, and I'm kind of envious at what they have. A girl I've seen around a time or two walks up to me and gives me a hug.

"Great game," she says.

"Do I know you?"

She laughs. "No, I'm Alysha. Piper's roommate." I gaze at the pretty girl. I remember Kennedy saying something about her being practically engaged. "I've heard a lot about you."

I glance at Piper and arch a curious brow. "Don't believe anything you hear."

Piper laughs. "It wasn't me. You do have a reputation, you know."

Alysha steps back and stands beside Piper. She nudges her and asks, "Aren't you going to hug him?"

"Ah, yeah, sure." She steps up to me, and her sweet scent fills my senses as she goes up on her toes and puts her arms around me. I breathe her in, much like I've been doing with my pillowcase for the last few days. Laundry is tomorrow and I've been debating on whether to wash my sheets or not, but in the end, I decide they needed a good clean, especially with the way I've been abusing myself lately.

"Great saves tonight," she compliments me when I let her go and she backs up a bit to put a measure of distance between us. I glance at her coat, hat and tight jeans. She was just at a game, but she always looks so put together. I have to say though, I liked her in her T-shirt and underwear.

"Thanks. Team effort."

"You don't have to say that to me."

"What's that supposed to mean?" I'm going on the defense, and I know it.

She steps a bit closer. "You could say, I kicked ass and saved all the shots."

I laugh at that. "It's not in my nature to do that." Maybe it's because I had a humble upbringing. My parents always praised me. It was the entitled ones in the community who looked down on me. I don't understand it, really. They loved when I helped win the game, but then they'd talk behind my back, saying I was keeping their kids from being goalie. I was damned if I did and damned if I didn't. That can mess with a guy in a lot of ways.

Once the guys are all out, Sawyer yells out. "Let's hit The Tap Room!"

I zip up my coat as I walk in silence, Piper falling back to walk with her roommate. Conversation is happening all around me, and I use that time to go over tonight's game in my head. What I did right and what I could have done differently. Everyone is in good spirits as we reach the campus pub and pile into our usual table.

Oddly enough I find myself sitting beside Piper and I'm not sure if the gods are conspiring with me or against me, because we suddenly seemed to be paired together a lot—and it started with us being seated together at Sawyer and Chase's wedding a couple months ago.

The server comes and I note that Piper is rather quiet, shifting almost uncomfortably beside me. I reach into my pocket when my phone buzzes and when I pull it out to glance at it, a bunch of broken animal crackers fall into my palm.

"Elephant's head," I explain and show the cookie to Piper, and a smile breaks out on her face. "Want a bite?"

"I think I'll pass." I toss it into my mouth and her jaw drops open. "You did not just eat that."

"Yeah, why?"

She inches back and stares at me. "My God, Beckett. That's disgusting."

"Kids," I laugh, like Madelyn is my own. "What can I say...life gets messy."

She toys with the drink coaster and her demeanor changes, goes soft and quiet. "You're really good with her."

My chest puffs up at the compliment. "Thanks. She's a good kid. She's the one who makes it easy."

She pulls a face, like she's terrified of children. "I don't know much about kids." She leans toward me. "I'm kind of scared of them."

"No way. Oh wait, you're an only child. I guess that makes sense. Didn't you babysit, though?" I babysat my siblings a shit ton growing up.

"Not kids that young." She puckers up her lips, confusion in her eyes. "I think Kennedy had a momentary lapse in judgement when she asked me to help out." She laughs but it holds no humor.

"You don't have to do it, you know."

She rolls one shoulder. "They're always there for me when I need them."

I take in the way she looks down, and while I've never gotten overly personal with her, I ask, "That's not the only reason though, is it?"

Her gaze jerks to mine, and her shoulders tighten. She stares at me for a second, and I can almost hear the wheels spinning. Her eyes narrow, almost angry, and then something happens, a change comes over her, like she can't fight the good fight any longer.

"No." Her voice is quiet and soft and I almost miss that one word.

"I'm sorry, Piper." I have no idea what's going on, or why I'm apologizing, but the vulnerability than cocoons her pierces something inside me.

She briefly closes her eyes. "You don't have anything to be sorry for." I reach for my beer, pretty sure that's the end of the conversation, and my hand stills when she speaks again.

"My parents hate each other."

What the hell. "Are you serious?"

"As serious as you were when stopping all those goals tonight."

"Shit, I didn't know that." I shift to face her, sensing she's telling me something deeply troubling, something she doesn't share with too many people and I'm not really sure why she's sharing with me. "They put on a hell of a show."

"Yeah, they deserve Oscars, I know." She forces a laugh, making light of it, but she can't hide the sadness radiating from her. Hell, maybe her life isn't perfect after all.

"You never said anything."

She looks at me like I might have a puck for a brain. "Why would I say anything to you?"

I take a swig of beer as her words hit me like a slap. The bottle slams on the table a little too hard when I respond with, "You're right. You wouldn't have."

She leans in. "I didn't mean that to be rude, Beck. Sometimes I just think we say the wrong things to each other."

"It's okay."

"No, it's not. The truth is, I haven't told anyone. Mom and Dad put on this happy image, the perfect little family, you know. It's not perfect and watching them at the resort pretending to like each other in public while they're seething inside, it's hard, and a little sad."

"Why do they do it?"

"I don't know. I guess maybe for the business. No one wants to be around people who argue all the time. It's uncomfortable, but I honestly think it's for the bottom line. The business has been in my dad's family for generations, and its success is really important to them."

I shake my head as she picks up her glass. "I'm not sure any business is worth being around someone you don't like."

She nods. "I agree."

I nudge her playfully. "Then again, are we any different?"

Her head rears back, and her brow narrows. "What do you mean?"

I glance around the table as my friends laugh and talk, and listen to the guy playing guitar on stage. "We hang out together, and for the sake of our friends, we pretend to like each other."

She frowns, and my stomach clenches. Dammit, why did I say something so stupid? "I'm just saying it's been a few years since we got along."

"That's true, but hey we're getting along now." She holds her glass out to me and as I clink it, I notice the way Kennedy is watching us. She's no doubt wondering what the hell is going on. We're always on our best behavior around our friends, but the tension is there. Jesus, at Sawyer's wedding when Piper thought I'd purposely smudged cake in her face, everyone thought she was going to murder me.

"Dryden's been asking about you." Shit, why did I say that? I guess a part of me still can't figure it out his sudden interest. And what were they talking about the other day when I dropped her off? It shouldn't be eating at me, but it is and maybe I brought it up because I really want to know.

"You don't like him, do you?" she asks quietly.

Okay, now that observation has taken me by surprise. "Why do you say that?"

"It looked like you were glaring at him the other day."

Glaring? Was I glaring?

"Yeah, no. I was just surprised. I didn't realize you two were friends." I really hope I don't sound like I'm fishing for information, even though I clearly am.

"We're not. Not really."

"Oh, okay, you just seemed like you were friends."

A slight grin tugs at her lips. "Did it?"

Fuck, is she on to me?

I shift in my seat and stretch out my legs, like I don't have a care in the world. "That's how it looked."

"We're not friends, but he's Alysha's, my roommate's, cousin. He comes around the house sometimes, and maybe he stopped because he was walking down the street when you dropped me off and didn't want to appear rude. He mentioned this new rollerblading rink that was opening in the city."

"I heard about it. Are you guys going?"

I am not jealous. I am not fucking jealous.

"I don't know." She laughs. "Remember that old rink back home? My God, the smell of the place."

"I remember. Parmesan and feet."

She burst out laughing. "Ohmigod, you're right. That's exactly what it smelled like. No wonder it shut down."

"To this day, I can't eat parmesan." I laugh. "Think that's where I learned to skate. I think I was three the first time my parents took me."

"Me too." She shifts, her leg settling against mine beneath the table. "The good old days," she laughs.

"When we were younger and full of hope," I joke, and give her leg a little nudge with mine. Yeah, okay sure, touching her is doing the most torturous things to my dick, but it's not going to stop me.

Ignoring everyone around us, we both laugh, and she looks off into the distance, clearly remembering something pleasant from her childhood.

"I loved having my birthday parties there when I was young, though," she murmurs quietly.

Well fuck. I sober quickly and tear my gaze away. Piper and her extravagant birthday parties which she stopped inviting me to in high school. We were getting along so well. Why the hell did she have to bring that up and remind me that no matter what I accomplish in life, deep inside I'll still be that unworthy boy from the wrong side of the tracks?

## PIPER

"Look if you want to cop a feel, all you have to do is ask."

Down on my knees on the kitchen floor, I glance up at Beck, and honest to God, I don't like this any more than he does. And why the hell does he have to be the right height for my mouth to line up with his...his...parts, as I rework the fabric around his muscular legs.

"I am not trying to cop a feel," I shoot back through gritted teeth.

"Well, I'm not sure you should be touching my junk like that." He turns to Kennedy as she feeds her daughter. "Did you let her touch Matt like this, before I was suckered into being Piper's model?"

Kennedy stifles a laugh. "It's for a good cause, and I don't think Matt was getting off on it."

Beck's jaw drops "Excuse me? Are you saying I'm getting off on it?"

Judging by the bulge in Beck's pants, I'd say yes, but I'm keeping my mouth shut for this one.

"Stay still," I order instead, as I pin the fabric.

"You owe me for this, big time," he announces.

Speaking of big time.

My God, Piper, stop thinking about that bulge.

"Fine, I'll buy you a drink when we go roller blading later," I tell him.

All indignant, he puffs his chest out and says, "I think I deserve more than a drink."

I exhale an exasperated sigh. "Fine, what do you want?"

"I'll think about it and let you know."

I eye him. I don't like that grin on his face. Not one little bit, but I'm not about to say another thing and risk him walking away. I need to get these pants made on the weekend, yet every time I come over, Matt has been busy, helping Kennedy's mom out with her house. Lately there always seems to be something wrong. Matt's not quite the handyman Beck is, but he is soon to be her son-in-law, and I suppose they don't want to take advantage of Beck, having him do all the work on Kennedy's mother's place.

But what it means for me, is I now have to use Beck as my model, and it's much harder than I ever thought it would be.

Speaking of hard...

"If you keep moving, I'm going to poke you, and you're not going to like it." I push a pin through the tight woven fabric. "Your legs are a little thicker than Matt's and I need to make these adjustments."

"Shit."

"What?" I glance up at him again.

"These aren't going to fit Matt."

"I know."

"But he's supposed to walk the runway."

I bite my lips and cringe a bit. "Yeah, I've been meaning to talk to you about that."

"Fuck no," he blurts out, and from the corner of my eye, I catch Kennedy's smirk.

She glares at me "Language!"

"Yeah, shit, sorry Madelyn."

I grin, and go back on my heels. "It won't be bad. The only people in the room will be other students, models and my teachers."

He shakes his head. "Nope, not going to do it."

Panic invades my stomach. What can I do or say to get him on board? This is important to me. "I'll do your chores around here for a week."

His brow shoots up. "Yeah?"

"When we stay here to watch Madelyn, I'll do all the cooking and cleaning and even make your bed."

"What about my laundry. Will you wash my boxers?" He grins like an asshole.

"If that's what it takes." The thought of handling his boxers doesn't bother me. I already know what they're packaging, having seen him naked and at full mast after his shower a couple of weeks ago.

"What else will you do?"

I go back on my ankles and my damn mouth is aligned with his cock again. "What do you want, Beck?"

He looks up and to the left as he makes a noise, to indicate he's thinking. "How about you do whatever I say."

My heart leaps, as my mind goes down a sexual path. Why oh why am I always thinking about sex when Beck is around? Okay, it's true. I think about sex with him even when I'm home alone, or in class...or at the mall. "What should I expect from that?" I ask.

"Okay, this is where Madelyn and I make our exit. This little one's ears aren't ready for this conversation."

Kennedy and Madelyn exit, and I don't look up at Beck. I don't want him to see the flush crawling up my neck. While my mind is on sex, I'm not sure his is. He's never tried anything with me, and while we've been spending a lot of time together, I'm convinced I'm the only one experiencing all this tension.

"So, you agree to it?" he asks.

"Tell me what I'm agreeing to."

"To do whatever I say."

"I don't think I can agree to that." I go back on my knees and work on the hem on the pants.

"Then I don't think I can walk your runway."

I lift my head and glare at him, all the while resisting the urge to purposely stick him with a pin. "Are you going to make me do things I don't want to do?"

"Nah, I'm not that big of an asshole." He grins. "I'd never make you do something you didn't want to do, Piper."

Since I need him, and would do just about anything—short of sleeping with him—I have no choice but to agree. "Okay, fine. I agree."

"Sweet."

Once I have the pants finished, I stand and work on the shirt, moving around his big body and rolling my eyes as he flinches and tells me I'm tickling him.

"Why are you so ticklish?" I ask.

"Everyone is."

"I don't think I'm that ticklish." I finish, and stand back to admire the clothes on his body. I think I'm nailing this outfit. He turns, puts his hands on my sides, and starts tickling me.

I yelp and run around the table, out of his reach. He's about to come after me, but I hold my hand up to stop him. "Don't. The pins might come loose and we'll have to start all over again."

He goes still. "How do I get out of this?"

"I'll help if you promise to keep your hands to yourself."

What the heck am I saying?

"Fine. One of these days I'll prove you're ticklish." I circle the table, and help him get the pants and shirt off, and try not to swallow my tongue as he stands there dressed only in his boxers. I try not to stare, but it's impossible. His body is magnificent.

"How did you get that?" I ask, and lightly run my finger over the scar on his lower right side. I've seen before, and always wondered about it.

"Knife fight," he informs me, dead serious. I stare at him. He can't be serious? "Walked into a bar, and this guy wouldn't leave a girl alone and I had to take care of it."

I do remember hearing about an incident where Matt protected Kennedy when she was singing. It's how they met. I notice a small quiver in his lips.

"You're lying."

He looks offended for a split second. "Had you going there for a second." He touches his side. "Appendicitis when I was fourteen. How about you? Missing any organs?"

Oh, God, now that's a loaded question.

"Nope, all intact."

I carefully fold the clothes, and put them in my bag. "Piper."

The seriousness in his voice hangs in the air as he says my name, and I lift my head, taking in his hard body as he tugs on his sweats, leaving his chest bare. "Yeah."

"How do you find time for a fashion design class with your heavy schedule at the academy?"

I shrug, and zip up my bag. "I really enjoy it, so I make time for it. I could ask the same thing about you. Hockey is a full-time job outside of schoolwork."

"Yeah, true, but I'm working toward something with it."

My chest clenches tight, and I try to breathe through it. "Not everything has to be about a career or an attainment."

Oh God, he's staring at me like he can see right through the lie I tell myself. That fashion is my hobby, a passion I can do while running a million-dollar resort. Who am I kidding? The resort will become my whole life, like it was for Mom and Dad, and probably the reason they're not a happy couple anymore. It's soul sucking and stressful and the thought of spending the rest of my life on Cape Breton Island depresses me. Don't get me wrong, it was a great place to grow up, and it's gorgeous and scenic.

I just want more. Guilt swamps me and steals the air from my lungs. Stupid tears prick my eyes and I dip my head and pretend to fuss with the zipper on my bag. Mom and Dad have given me so much, and I'm nothing but a selfish little girl, thinking only of herself...How fair is that?

His big warm palm closes over mine, and I pinch my eyes to clear them. I meet his gaze, and his eyes are softer than I've ever seen them before, with something that looks like understanding and compassion brimming in the depths.

"For what it's worth, I think you have incredible style and talent. It'd be a damn shame if Piper Thorne originals didn't have their own rack in the trendiest stores."

I smile, but it hurts my throat and my heart. "That's nice of you to say."

"That wedding dress you made for Sawyer. It was gorgeous."

"You knew I made that?"

"Yeah."

"I love that cut and design. It's what I'd make for myself if I..." I let my words fall off. What the hell am I doing. Feeling sorry for myself because I designed a dress for Sawyer, one I might have made for myself,

"...if you got married?" he asks, finishing my statement.

"I'm probably never getting married, Beck." I make a joke and add, "You remember me telling you about Mom and Dad, right?"

He doesn't find humor in my words. Instead of laughing, he says, "Yeah, but you're not your parents."

"That resort destroys marriages," I blurt out. "I'm not even sure my grandparents liked each other."

"Well then, there's an easy solution to that."

"You think?"

"Yeah, don't take over the resort and go into fashion instead."

I bite my tongue so I don't laugh hysterically at his insane—not to mention completely impossible—suggestion. While his intentions are good, and I honestly think he's trying to be helpful, he has no idea what he's talking about.

"I can't abandon my family, Beck." I mean for it to sound light, but it comes out heavy and his hand leaves mine.

"No, of course not. I understand that. I would never abandon mine either, Piper. I don't want you to think I would."

I fiddle with my bag. "I don't."

"I want to make something of myself, so I can give back to my family. They've all done so much for me, you know."

"I do know." This serious side of Beck is surprising, and sweet.

"So, I get that sense of obligation you have. It's just I get to give back by doing something that makes me happy." A beat of silence and then, "Do you really think your parents would want you taking over the resort if it makes you miserable?"

I glance down at my feet. It's a good question, and the answer is, "I don't know."

He cocks his head, waiting for more, so I add, "They've given me every opportunity in the world, but we've never had a conversation about what I wanted. It's just always been assumed that I would take over."

He glances at the pile of clothes in my bag, and gestures with a nod. "What do they think of your designs?"

I suck in air through closed teeth. "They don't know. This is just something I do for me."

"Fuck."

"Yeah." I throw my hands up. "I have no idea why I'm telling you any of this." I toss my backpack over my shoulder as he inches back, like I've physically wounded him with my words. Why the hell is it I can never say the right things around him? We were having an honest, intimate, trustworthy moment here, and I just made him feel like a guy I could never trust, a guy who wasn't worthy of hearing my feelings.

The doorbell rings and I jerk my thumb over my shoulder. "I just mean, that's Kennedy's sitter, and I need to get home and get changed before rollerblading and Alysha is giving me a ride to the rink."

"Oh, Alysha is coming?"

"Yeah, why?"

"She seems nice." He backs up, putting more than just a physical distance between us, and I remind myself that he's the guy who walked around high school like I was invisible. I'm not sure how he saw me—he clearly didn't want to attend my big seventeenth birthday party—but I'm guessing he thought I was a pampered princess who thought she was better than everyone else.

But we're not kids anymore and maybe he's not that guy who always hurt me when he went out of his way to avoid me. Wait, is it possible that he's being nice now because he likes my roommate, Alysha? He can forget about her; she's practically engaged.

"Beckett."

"Yeah?"

"Do you like squash?"

He angles his head, a small grin playing with the corners of his mouth. "The game or the vegetable?"

"Veggie."

"Yeah, why?"

Okay, now why do I suddenly feel stupid. "I had a little garden last year. The squash took over, and I froze a ton of it. I was thinking when I stay here, I could make us some squash pasta."

"It sounds amazing, but you don't have to cook for me."

"Maybe I want to," I say. "Besides, it's part of the agreement for you helping me out with my design class."

"Wait, is this about getting rid of all that frozen squash? Pawn it off on a guy who is making you do all the cooking, in exchange for a favor?"

I laugh, the air between us lighter. "Would I do that?"

His grin widens. "I don't know you well enough."

"After cohabitating for a few days, you'll probably be singing a different tune, and wishing you didn't know me well enough."

"Is that your way of telling me you're high maintenance?"

I laugh. "I guess you'll have to wait and see."

He leans against the counter and crosses his ankles one over the other, and honest to God, that sexy pose combined with his playful grin tease my body in the most torturous ways. How the hell am I going to spend days sleeping in the room across from him? "You remember I said you never had to do anything you didn't want to, right?"

"I know. Sometimes I like being in the kitchen. It relaxes me."

"Sometimes I like being in the kitchen too. It's great relaxation."

My eyes go wide. "You like to cook?"

"Nope."

I stare at him for a full five seconds before my brain registers what he's saying. I point to the kitchen table. "I am never eating on there again."

He laughs. "That's okay, that's not what I like to do on it anyway."

As I picture all the things he might have done on that table, all the things he could do to me, I turn and walk to the door before he can see the heat it arouses in me. Then again, Kennedy said he doesn't bring girls here, so I guess he's just messing with me, trying to get a rise, and dammit, I gave him one.

Wait, is he saying dirty things to feel me out, to see if I might like to be taken on the kitchen table when we play house?

Oh, God, I would...I really would.

# 6

## BECKETT

I shouldn't make crude jokes about having sex in the kitchen. Sure, it makes me sound like an asshole, but goddammit, I love the heat in her eyes and the flush on her cheeks when I say dirty things. I'm beginning to believe it's not just me who's affected whenever we're in the same room and where the hell is this attraction coming from? We don't even like each other, and when we were sharing something private, she was quick to point out that she had no idea why she was telling me that—like I was the kind of guy she couldn't confide in. It's crazy how she keeps reminding me we're from different worlds, even though we grew up in the same town.

But to seriously put out there that I like to have sex in the kitchen? I need to get my shit together—or maybe a brain scan. Maybe tonight, after rollerblading, I'll hook up with one of the puck bunnies and get Piper out of my head once and for all. With her soon staying here and offering to make me pasta, I don't know how I'll get through the days, or worse, the nights.

Voices from the other room reach my ear and I push off the counter and step into the room to find Kennedy going over things with Serena, the babysitter. "Hey Serena," I say and she twirls her finger in her hair as she glances at me, her gaze dropping to my chest. On that note, I dart upstairs and tug on a T-shirt and hoodie to get ready for tonight's roller skating rink's grand opening. Everyone I know is going, and I suppose Dryden will be there too. Christ, after the things he said in the locker room, I don't want him anywhere near Piper.

*She's not yours to protect, dude.*

I head back downstairs and tug on my shoes and coat. I told my buddy Ryan I'd pick him up, so I'm taking my own vehicle. "See you guys there."

"Bye Beck," Serena says and I catch Kennedy's gaze. Yeah, okay, it's not just me. Serena is flirting, or at least trying to, but I'm not about to play along with a seventeen-year-old. Christ, she's just a kid. Not only that, I think there's something wrong with me. I haven't been interested in hooking up with anyone for a while now. I just lectured myself on getting laid, and even though girls seem to be interested in me, I know it's not going to happen. I don't really want it to.

Yeah, maybe I do need a brain scan.

I drive the short distance to the Storm House, and Ryan comes barreling out the front door. I grin. The guy is a bull in a China shop. I guess that's the kind of build one gets with a background in potato farming, and that's what makes him a great defenseman. He doesn't talk about it much, but I'm not even sure his main goal in life is the NHL like the rest of us. He's just a happy go lucky guy who is loved by all.

"Beck, my man," he says, and he jumps in next to me.

"Hey bud." We pound fists and I'm about to circle the parking lot and hit the street when I notice Dryden walking toward me. "Ready for finals?" I ask my buddy as my gaze zeroes in on Dryden.

"Getting there." I make my way around the parking lot. "You?"

"Same." I gesture with a nod as Dryden flags us down. "What's Dryden want?"

Ryan rolls his window down and glances at me. "Shit, if you weren't with me, I would have thought Dryden was you."

It's true, Dryden and I have the same build and same color hair.

"What's up?" Ryan asks him.

"Can I get a lift to the rink. I was going with Kylee, but she's pissed at me about something now."

Probably because she likes him and now, he seems to have his sights set on Piper.

"Get in." He opens the back door and slides in and as I maneuver through the parking lot, I glance at Ryan and turn the conversation to Kennedy and Matt and their upcoming visit to Prince Edward Island. I hadn't been there in years myself, because when I have spare time, it's spent getting home to Cape Breton Island to see the family.

Ryan taps his fingers on the dash. "They told me you're watching Madelyn."

"Yeah, I am."

"How are you going to do that and work?"

I glance at Dryden in the rearview mirror and he's busy texting. "Piper is going to help out. We'll tag team."

"Tag teaming Piper," Dryden says, his tone vile and full of suggestion, and I'd really like to wipe it off his face. "Now that I can get behind."

I grip the steering wheel and consider my comeback. If I come too strongly to her defense, he'll know something is going on with us, but dammit, I'm not going to just let him talk about her like that. I used to think he was a good guy, now I'm not so sure. I'm also not sure if he'd go after a girl already taken, simply because he liked the challenge. I guess it's better to let him think there isn't anything between us, and let's face it—there isn't.

"She's just helping out," I explain.

"I bet she is."

He grins and wow, it takes all my effort not to pull over and punch the smirk off his face. As if sensing the sudden tension in me, Ryan turns the conversation to hockey and next year's season. Ten minutes later I circle the mall and park near the entrance to the new roller skating rink.

"This is going to be fun," Ryan grins as he opens his door and jumps out, Dryden follows him. We head inside and get our skates. By the time I have mine laced up, I hear Piper and Alysha laughing about something as they enter. I wave to them, and they wave back as Dryden steps onto the oval.

Ryan whacks my leg like fifteen times. "What?" I glance at him, but he's not looking my way.

"Who is she?" Ryan asks, his voice rushed and a bit breathless as I continue to stare at the back of his head. He keeps whacking my leg and I shift until I'm out of reach. I've never seen him act like this before.

"Who's who?" I try to see who he's staring at.

"The girl with Piper."

"Oh, her name is Alysha." Is he interested in Alysha? If so I'm a bit surprised. Ryan is a potato farmer, and she comes from a socialite family in the Hamptons. Talk about different backgrounds. Then again, Piper and I have different backgrounds too, but we at least came from the same town. "I think Piper said something about her nearly being engaged."

Ryan doesn't say anything. He just gives a curt nod, ties up his laces and hits the rink. I glance out and take in the array of colors lighting up the rink as a big disco ball spins from the ceiling. Old time music from the seventies and eighties blares from the speakers, and the smell of carnival fries reaches my nostrils.

I wait for Piper and Alysha and they both have big smiles on their faces as they walk toward me and sit on the bench. "This place is fantastic," Piper says.

"Unless you have epilepsy."

They both turn to me, and Piper's eyes widen. "Ohmigod, you're right."

I lean forward. "Hi Alysha," I say, and Piper stiffens.

"Hey Beck."

"Do you know how to rollerblade?" I ask.

"I can ice skate. Is that the same?"

"Sure, if you need help, let me know. I'll show you some moves."

She grins. "I didn't know you had moves."

As we joke, Piper's head goes left and right, keeping up with the fast conversation. "I've got moves," I say.

"In the net, sure. Fastest hands I've ever seen."

Piper snorts. "What?" I ask.

"Nothing." I stare at her and she adds, "Dryden is her cousin. I'm sure he'd be happy to help her skate if she's having any trouble."

"Yeah, sure." I glance into the rink and Dryden is chatting up cheerleaders. "He seems busy." As if sensing eyes on him, Dryden turns our way and a grin curls up his lips as he zeroes in on Piper. What the fuck is he up to?

"Anyway," Piper continues and stands after she finishes lacing up. A couple of girls I know come skating by and call out to me to join them. Piper practically huffs and says, "I'm sure you have moves to show lots of girls."

Alysha wobbles a bit when she stands. "I might take you up on that, Beck. I think Dryden has better things to do than hang out with his cousin."

"Yeah, absolutely."

Piper shoves her phone into her back pocket, and says, "Come on, Alysha. I can help you."

Jesus Christ, is she jealous of the way Alysha and I were playing? Alysha is practically engaged, and I'm not going anywhere near that. Besides it's Piper I like.

IT'S PIPER I LIKE!

Oh man, what the fuck am I saying?

I can't like her. No way. No how. Back home, she was the mean girl who purposedly left me out, to prove her family was better than mine. I would never—could never—like a girl like that.

I push to my feet and as Piper wobbles, I step onto the rink and mumble, "If you need any help, I'm here."

"Let me know when you want it," Piper says, and I turn back to her. Her words bounce around inside my head, and they're not making sense. The last we talked, I was joking about kitchen sex. Surely to God, we're not still on that subject, and if we are, I'm going to drag her out of here caveman style and show her just how much I want it.

*No, you're not doing that, dude.*

"Want what?"

"How quickly you forget." She grins and with a crook of her head, she gestures to the concession stand. "I owe you a drink. We just talked about that this afternoon, remember?"

"Right." We talked about a lot of things this afternoon. Happy things...sad things.

"What did you think I meant?" I stare at her, trying to see some telltale sign that she's purposely messing with me. I honestly think she is. Maybe it's payback for being an asshole in the kitchen.

Well done, Piper. Well done.

I grin at her and she grins back. It's spiteful and playful and fucks with my brain and my cock. Okay, getting a boner out here on the rink...not in my best interests. I reach out, and put my hand on her shoulder, playing a familiar kid's game.

"You're it."

With that I take off, and I laugh as her curses, trying to catch up to me. I weave in and out of the skaters, and wave to Matt and Kennedy as they enter. Soon enough Matt joins me and the girls all skate as a group.

I take a break and sit with a few of the guys from the team. The place is crowded, which makes it hard to keep an eye on Piper, not that I'm stalking her or anything, but she's not a girl to let me have the upper hand in the game I started. I spot her near the concession stand, talking with Dryden, and I try not to react. I don't know what his sudden deal is with her, and it's none of my business, but I have the worst feeling about it.

I stand and skate over as she places an order and the guy behind the counter hands her a soft drink. She grins at me, and hands it over. "I believe I owe you this." She pushes the drink into my hand, and taps me on the shoulder. "You're it." She grins, and steps back onto the oval, and I can't chase after her with a drink in my hand and I don't want to toss it because she just paid for it. But I can be patient when I want to be.

Dryden skates off, and I sip my drink, my eyes on Piper the whole time. I gulp the soda down fast, trying not to get a brain freeze as she chats with Alysha. I sneak up behind her, put my mouth close to her ear, and tap her.

"You..." she screeches as I take off.

For the next hour we play, and as the place grows more crowded, she yawns and skates off and I follow her. She's still *it* in our game when I reach her, and I hold my hand out. "Tag me."

She cocks her head. "Why?"

"I'm going to take you home, and we can't be slapping each other the whole way there."

She purses her lips in a stubborn manner. "Nope. I'm not going to do it."

"Why not?"

"That's too easy. When I tag you, you're not going to see it coming."

I laugh at that. "I think you just like chasing me."

"Maybe, or maybe I like to be the one in control, and I'm not ready for you to chase me."

Okay, that sounds interesting. "Wait, are we still talking about the children's game here?"

She nods. "I came with Alysha, so you don't need to drive me home." We both glance out to the rink and Alysha is laughing and having fun.

"I don't think she's ready."

She stifles a yawn, a new weariness about her. "I am tired. I do have to get up early tomorrow and finish sewing." She casts me a glance and frowns. "Are you busy tomorrow?"

"Studying."

"I might need you."

I resist the urge to tell her I might need her too, but I'm sure our thoughts aren't running along the same path and since I treasure my nuts, I shut my mouth.

"You know, for a fitting or any last-minute adjustments."

"Yeah, no problem." I gesture toward Alysha. "Want to let her know you're leaving?"

"Okay." She disappears as I get out of my roller skates and return them. I stand at the door, my hands in my pockets as I wait for her.

What the fuck are you doing, dude?

While I try to convince myself I'm just giving a girl a ride home, a girl from our circle, there's a part of me that knows that's a big fat lie. I shouldn't want to spend more time with her, but I do. I'm sure once we spend time together babysitting, we'll be sick of each other but right now, goddammit, I'm having a good time, and I can't remember the last time I enjoyed myself like this.

Fuck me.

She's a bit breathless by the time she reaches me, and I love it when her cheeks turn that pretty shade of pink. She tugs her coat on, leaving it unzipped. "Ready."

I nod and hold the door open for her. We step out into the dark night, the air much cooler now that the sun is down. Her breath turns to fog, and without thinking, I step in front of her. Her eyes go wide.

"What...what are you doing?"

I reach for her zipper. "Zipping you up."

"I can do that."

I pull the zipper to her chin. "Already done." I grin. "I have three younger siblings. I can't help myself."

"I think that's sweet. No wonder Kennedy and Matt have no problem leaving Madelyn with you." She touches my hand, runs her thumb over my palm and Jesus, I feel it all the way to my balls. "They know she's in good hands."

Christ, I'd love to show her how good my hands could be on her, but doors in the parking lot slam and jolt me into action. I turn and head toward my Jeep. She follows and we both climb in. We're mainly silent, the radio on low as we drive.

"Did you have fun tonight?" I ask, breaking the quiet.

"I did. You?"

"Yeah." I go quiet. We both do, lost in our own thoughts again, and I consider the studying I have to do tomorrow. Maybe I could crack the books at Piper's place. That way I'd be close if she needed me.

I reach her place and pull into the driveway. Before she can protest, I hop from my Jeep and meet her as she slips from the passenger seat. "Thanks for the lift."

I start walking with her, taking her to her door and she glances at me. I expect her to tell me she's got this, but she doesn't and she's extra quiet, almost nervous as she pulls her keys from her bag and slides one into the deadbolt.

She turns to me, our bodies close and unable to help myself, I dip my head, until my lips are close to hers. I touch a strand of her hair, running the silky lock through my fingers, and my dick twitches. Our breaths mingle as the world around me fades. I move an inch closer, and the chemistry between us generates enough electricity to light up the entire neighborhood.

Yeah, I'm not the only one feeling this...thing between us, whatever it might be. I'm not going to spend a lot of time putting a label on it. I'm sure it will pass as fast as it hit me.

I lean closer, our lips a hair's breadth away. "Do you think you're going to need me tomorrow?" I ask, my voice deep and hoarse even to my own ears.

Her cheeks are flushed, her breath coming fast. "Beck..."

"Yeah."

"I...I think I need you tonight."

My heart stops beating and I inch back, not at all sure I heard her right. "Piper?"

She touches my shoulder. "Tag, you're it."

## 7

## PIPER

I walk away from Beckett. Okay, more like run, and head straight for the stairs like the floor beneath my feet is on fire. The truth is, I'm the one who is on fire. I reach the first step and glance over my shoulder to find Beck still in the doorway, standing there like a deer in the headlights as his chest rises and falls erratically, his breath turning to fog in front of his face.

What am I doing?

I don't know, and at the moment, I don't care. As my body warms all over, I'm not going to try to figure out this momentary lapse in judgement, or why all common sense packed a bag and headed south. All I know is that I want him to kiss me, to put his arms around me and press his hard body to mine. I don't think I've ever wanted anything in my life so badly.

I tagged him, letting him know exactly what I wanted, and now the ball's in his court. What happens next is up to him, and it's better that way. If he stops this, which he very well might—and he probably should—then I can't ever wonder what if.

I turn back around and face the stairs, and a quake goes through my entire body as the door slams shut. I wait a moment. Is he inside or out? I don't turn around, and the second I hear his footsteps, I run the rest of the way up the stairs, my heart beating so fast, I'm sure it's going to jump from my chest.

I take a moment to recap. I'm in my house, and Beckett—the guy I've hated for years—is now following me up the stairs to my room after I told him I want more.

Does life get any better—or more complicated.

Those thoughts are for tomorrow. I stop outside my bedroom door, and he's right there, standing over me as I turn to face him. Without words, his big arm goes around my back, and an excited gasp catches in my throat as he pulls me to him. My body meshes against his and his cock is hard—for me—as it presses against my stomach.

Beckett Moore really does have more, and I'm not sure whether I'm excited or terrified.

He dips his head, his lips close to mine. "I never saw it coming."

"Does that mean I win?"

He bends more, his soft lips grazing mine. "I think it means you're no longer in control." A fine shiver goes through me. "I also think you like that."

Oh God, take me already.

He moves me until I'm pressed against the wall, and he puts his hands on either side of my head. Everything about the way he's caging me in and pressing against me is so damn sexy, it's possible I might combust. I stare up at him. Honest to God, I am losing my mind right now. This is what I wanted from him at my birthday party all those years ago, and something tells me the wait is going to be worth it.

"I never...said that."

He grins. "Not with words."

He takes my hands in his and puts them over my head as his lips find mine—finally—and he kisses me with a hunger and a need so fierce, I would think he's been going without for a very long time. Either that or he really likes me. But no, Kennedy told me he's not brought anyone home in ages.

*Okay, stop being stupid. This is about sex, not him liking you, Piper.*

Maybe this is just a hate fuck. I don't know. I'm not labeling it. All I'm going to do is enjoy.

My body melts against his, and when he lets my arms go, I put them around his back, dipping under his jacket to hold him to me. I spread my fingers, wanting to touch all his muscles as they bunch.

"Fuck, I need to take this off."

"We're back to that, are we?" I tease, and he groans as he inches back and hurries out of his coat, a new kind of urgency about him. He drops his coat on the floor and big deft hands go to my neck to release the zipper on my coat. He tugs it down and I shove off the wall so he can take the sweater off me. Urgent hands move to my shoulders, and he slides the cotton down, letting it join his coat on the floor.

"Is that your room?"

"Yes."

He pulls me to him and I yelp as he lifts me. My legs automatically go around his back as he steps into my room, flicks the light on, takes a fast glance around, and kicks my door shut. My God, does he practice those alpha moves or what? I don't know and I don't care. My hormones, however, they care and they're reacting like a teenage girl who just caught the eye of the quarterback. But I'm not a teenage girl, and he's a goalie.

Even better.

He turns me and presses my back to the door, his cock grinding against my center. A groan crawls out of my throat as we dry humps against my door, and I have to say, everything about this is already better than that messy night with Noah Blackmore on my seventeenth birthday.

My body ignites, and my panties grow damp and I swear if he doesn't touch me soon, I might lose my mind. "Beck," I murmur, and his name on my tongue does something to him.

He growls into my mouth, his kisses wet, hard, and fiercely hungry. He backs up, stumbles a bit, and the next thing I know, I'm on my desk, like the bed was simply too far away. He inches back, presses his mouth to my neck and breathes me in. He exhales and his breath tickles my flesh, and awakens a fiercely ferocious kind of need inside me.

He grips the hem on my shirt and tugs upward on it. His jaw muscles ripple as his teeth clench, and my God, being this man's sole focus is as disconcerting as it is exciting. I can totally see why so many women are infatuated with him. He's present with me, his concentration never wavering as he channels all his energy—into me. I'm not sure I ever met a guy who tuned everything out but the woman he was with.

He takes a breath, letting go of my shirt. "I'm trying to slow down," he murmurs. Is that what he thought I was thinking about just now.

"Did I say I wanted slow, Beck?"

He swallows and the sound reverberates through me. "You drifted. I was worried."

Is he for real?

I palm his face. "I was just thinking how nice it is to be the center of your attention," I say honestly.

He grins. "Oh, yeah?"

"Yeah."

"Let me give you a little bit more of that attention." His fingers curl in the hem of my T-shirt again and I lift my arms to assist him in peeling it over my head. "Fucking Nova Scotia, and all the layers we have to wear in April."

I laugh at that. Once he has my T-shirt gone and I'm sitting on my desk in my bra and jeans, I tug at his T-shirt, thankful that he burns hot and only has one layer. Maybe I won't hate how hot Kennedy keeps her place when I spend time there. I have to say it's been torturous but that's because I could only stare. No touching allowed. This time around, however, I can look and touch. At least I think I can. Unless, this is just a one-night thing. Something tells me one time isn't going to cut it—not when it comes to Beckett.

He peels his shirt off and his muscles bunch beneath my gaze. He growls and I glance up at him.

"Fuck," he growls. "When you look at me like that..."

"Like what?"

"Like you really like what you really see."

I grin. "I do."

"Then fucking touch me already." he groans like he's in total agony.

Am I—Piper Thorne—really driving this man wild? I never thought I'd see the day and who am I to talk? He drives me wild, too. But now we're channeling all that past anger into sex, and I don't care if this is a hate fuck. I want it.

I want him.

I put my hands on his body and spread my fingers. His muscles contract and a hard quiver goes through him as he curses in response. "Sorry, my hands are cold."

"They're not. I think I'm just that hot."

"Yeah, you are," I tease and he gives me a panty-soaking grin. Speaking of panties, I'm so ready to hand mine over. As if reading my thoughts, he easily picks me up and sets me on the floor. I'm about to walk to the bed, but his hands grip my hips and pin me in place as he sinks to his knees.

Oh, yes.

He presses his face to my stomach and breathes in the scent of my skin before pressing soft, hungry kisses to my quivering curves. I love the way he's treasuring my body, like he wants to touch every inch of me. I just wish I'd had the foresight to wear sexy panties. I wrack my brain, trying to remember the saying on my panties, but there's not enough blood circulating to form a coherent thought.

He pops the button on my jeans as I stand still, letting him do whatever the hell he wants with me. Wait, are his hands shaking? No, I have to be mistaken. This man is experienced

—a man with skilled moves, or so I've heard—and there is nothing about being with me that's going to turn him into a jittery mess of nerves.

He peels my pants down my legs and I put my hands on his shoulder to keep my balance as I lift my feet one at a time to aid him in undressing me. He tosses my pants toward the chair, and once I'm almost naked, he goes back on his heels and scrubs his face like he's in pure agony.

"Jesus, Piper."

Embarrassment floods me. Oh, God, he doesn't like what he sees. I get it, I might be blonde and have blue eyes, and I swim for fitness, but I'm no sex goddess like the women he usually undresses. I'm about to put my hands in front of my body to hide myself, but he captures my arms and holds them to my side.

"Beck..."

"I need to look, babe. I need to look a little longer." His head slowly lifts, and while I've known him for a very long time, he's never looked at me with such intensity. What is going on with him?

"You are fucking perfect," he says quietly, and my heart crashes so hard, I'm not even sure I heard him correctly.

"What?"

He touches my panties, which say, 'Bake cookies on Thursday', and I nearly die of mortification—until I realize the heat in his eyes went from hot to inferno.

"They were a gift," I tell him.

"Fuck me twice." He shakes his head, and runs his fingers over the words. "But it's Friday."

"I don't really pay much attention to the days. I just grab them from my drawer."

"Piper." His voice is thick and harsh and so full of arousal and agony, my clit swells with want.

"I want to bake cookies with you." He tugs my panties down, just enough to expose my clit.

"Okay," is all I can say.

He leans in and licks my clit, and a keening cry catches in my throat. He looks back up at me. "What do Friday's say?"

"I think...Friday, my day."

"You think?" he licks my clit again, and my panties grow wetter.

"I can't quite remember anything right now," I admit.

"I want to see them on you. I want to see every day of the week on you."

"I think Saturday's say—"

"Don't tell me," He blurts out, cutting me off. "I think I want to discover myself."

I take a breath. "I guess this means you'll have to get me naked every day of the week."

"Yeah, it does," he quickly agrees almost dreamily as he tugs my panties off, and leans in to bury his mouth between my legs. A noise I've never heard before crawls out of my throat as he parts me with his tongue and swipes from bottom to top, stopping to lap at my swollen clit.

Okay, this is nothing at all like that messy time when I was younger. I didn't expect it to be, but I also didn't expect every nerve ending in my body to come alive like this. I hold on to his shoulders, not wanting to fall as pleasure burns through my body and weakens my knees.

He eats at me, and the happy little noises coming from between my legs surprises and excites me. He likes this as much as I do. I rake my nails over his flesh, and he groans as I drag across his skin. My body goes completely still the second his finger slides into me, spreading pleasure to my core and beyond. I lightly clench around his finger, almost embarrassed that I'm so close, and air hisses from his lungs as he glances up at me.

"It's been a long time," I admit.

"That's okay," he responds, quietly, thoughtfully.

He moves his finger, and I blurt out. "A really long time."

"How long, Piper?"

God, do I admit it?

I don't answer as he moves his finger in and out of me. "You don't have to tell me. It's none of my business."

"High school," I confess.

His finger goes perfectly still. Dammit, should I not have told him? Will he think there's something wrong with me—that I'm a pampered princess no man wants to touch? While they might think that, I'm the one who chose to be celibate.

"Then you're really going to need all the attention," he responds quietly.

My heart skips a beat. I love that he's not judging me, that he's not concerned and simply wants to make up for lost time.

"I believe you're right."

He grins, and with his finger still inside me, he stands to his full height and uses his palm to press against my aching clit. His lips close over mine, and he devours my mouth as he slowly slides his fingers in and out of me. God, this is so much better than my vibrator.

"I want you on the bed, legs spread." I nod eagerly and it brings a smile to his face. "Now."

"Right. But..." I don't want to move, not with the way he's working his finger in and out of me. He's killing me in the most beautiful way.

"Now."

I slowly back up, and he follows along, never once stopping the action between my legs. I reach the bed and moan with disappointment as he pulls his finger from my sex and brings it to his mouth. I nearly orgasm as he licks. I drop to the bed, the strength in my legs completely gone, and he sinks to his knees again, grips my thighs and spreads them until I'm wide open and on display. I have never felt so exposed before, but when his gaze drops and his growl of hunger rolls through me, I suddenly love the way I'm bared to him.

He nudges my shoulder until I fall back and he takes my legs, putting them around his neck and dives back in. I let loose a happy sigh and he chuckles, the vibrations going through my body and raising my temperature even more. I cup my breasts and squeeze my nipples as he licks at me, putting his finger back in and I lightly clench around him.

"Babe, I love the way you squeeze me," he says, and I feel less self-conscious at how close I am. "I can't wait for you to come all over my fingers and mouth."

My stupid heart misses a beat at how sweet and encouraging he's being, especially knowing the girls he's been with are way more experienced than I am. But he's making me comfortable and secure with his supportive words. I lay back, and give in to the pleasure instead of trying to fight it.

I grow wetter, slicker between my legs and he runs his tongue all over my clit, sucking and licking and biting as he slides another finger in and I grip the bedsheets and tug, as my hips come off the bed, bumping his face as I gyrate, as every nerve in my sex sparks and dances beneath his deft ministrations. I can't believe that one messy experience turned me off sex, because holy hell, this is fantastic!

I move without inhibition, rock against his mouth and he murmurs encouraging words. I think he likes the way I'm coming undone. So do I. My throat grows dry as I pant, and chant his name and I glance at him, looking at the back of his head as he brings me pleasure like I've never before experienced. God, who would have known he'd be so sweet and giving and...easy to be with in the bedroom. My heart misses a beat as pleasure mounts and I close my eyes against the flood of emotions, needing to keep them at bay.

His fingers swipe the sensitive bundle of nerves inside me, and his name spills from my lips as my body lets go, giving in to the pleasure. He groans with need and something that sounds like pride as I come all over him, my hot release burning my thighs as it pours out of me.

"Fuck yeah," he murmurs. "Just like that. It's perfect."

My heart thuds and the world closes around me as pleasure overtakes my entire body. I call his name over and over and he continues to give attention to my pussy, drawing out my orgasm with slow easy strokes of his finger. The spasms finally stop, and I lift my head, spent, exhausted...sated.

His head lifts, his face wet from my release as he grins up at me. "Did I give you enough attention?" he asks playfully.

"Not quite." I grin back as I crook my finger, wanting him inside my body.

He stands, his hot gaze on my body as he rips into his pants, freeing his gorgeous cock. He takes it into his hands and I practically salivate as he strokes himself. Will I be any good at this? The last time was a disaster, but I suspect under Beck's guidance, not only am I going to know what to do, I'm going to like it.

I sit up, and open my mouth, desperately wanting to taste the pre-cum dripping from his crown. I almost laugh to myself as he steps closer, because if this is a hate fuck—and he hasn't even been inside me yet—I can't even imagine what love-making might be like. Nor do I want to because that...well, that might bring emotions into this, and I'd be a damn fool to let that happen.

# 8

## BECKETT

My heart beats double time as Piper opens her sweet mouth, urging me to put my cock inside as I stroke myself. Is this really fucking happening? Yeah, it is, and despite everything, I don't regret it at all. I step close and as my pre-cum spills and lands on her tongue my cock throbs. Christ, she was close the second I touched her. I'm close too. The only difference is, she's not been touched in years, and I tugged one out the other day. I'm about to have a goddamn premature ejaculation without a good excuse.

"Piper," I murmur as she shifts even closer and moans as she licks her lips. "Fuck, girl. Keep that up and I'll lose it even before I get my cock between your lips." I don't want to lose it. Nope, I want to draw this out, and wring out every ounce of pleasure in her body.

I can't believe she hasn't been with anyone since high school, and I can't believe that she actually admitted it to me. I'm not sure why or what might have happened, I only know I want tonight to be special.

I drop my hand, my cock ramrod straight as she wraps her small palm around my girth and widens her mouth to accommodate my thickness. Her hot pink tongue snakes out to lick my crown again, and I groan and throw back my head, staring at her ceiling as I fight to hang on. While I'd love to shoot down her throat and just let pleasure take over, I really, really want my cock inside her pussy. She wants that too, which means I need to get my shit together and stop acting like a boy about to get laid for the very first time.

Why the hell does it feel like that?

I don't know and it's crazy. I've been with plenty of women. None were Piper and really, does that matter? Shit, maybe it does.

She leans forward and my cock slides to the back of her hot mouth, and all thought evaporates as pleasure grips my balls and takes over. I rock my hips, and moan as I pull her hair from her shoulders and grip it in my fist. Barely able to control myself, I piston forward and she chokes when I hit the back of her throat.

She glances up at me, and I go still. Is that worry in her eyes —vulnerability?

"So good, Piper," I tell her and totally mean it. "I love the way you're letting me in your mouth." I force myself to move my hips slower, not wanting her to gag again, or worry that she's not rocking my world, because she sure fucking is.

She works her hand over me, mimicking the motion of her mouth, and I close my eyes and bite down on the inside of my cheek until it hurts—but everything hurts in the best fucking way. I suck in a lungful of air when she tries to take me a bit deeper, I tug on her hair to stop her. She doesn't need to do that for me.

My entire body tightens, a good sign that I'm about to lose it, and I inch my cock from her mouth. She wipes the back of her hand over her wet lips and the innocence of the gesture makes it the sexiest thing I've ever seen. My dick jumps.

"I want to fuck you." She nods and her breathing is harsh as she lays back down, shifting to the center of the bed. I pull a condom from my pocket and kick off my pants and boxers until I'm completely naked too. "There's only one problem."

She goes up on her elbows, worry filling her eyes as I climb onto the bed and nestle between her legs. I lower myself over her, my mouth inches from her gorgeous tits. I grin up at her. "I need to spend some time here first." I lick her nipple and I'm rewarded with a moan of pleasure. I lift my head. "That's okay with you, isn't it?"

"Yes," she murmurs, and grips the back of my head, bringing my mouth back to her puckered nipple. I laugh as I take her bud into my mouth, but it's replaced by a moan of pleasure as I suck her nipple and her feet dig into my ass, pushing my body against her wet pussy and grinding against me. Fuck, I love how much she wants me.

*It's your dick she wants, dude, not you.*

At that reminder, I switch my mouth to her other nipple, eating at her as I massage her other breast with my palm. She keeps her hands in my hair, holding me to her as her whimpers fill the room. My cock throbs, needing to fuck, and I pull back. Her hands fall from my head as I go up on my knees. She watches intently, her gaze completely focused on my cock as I rip into the condom and sheath myself. Her chest rises and falls erratically as I roll the rubber on, then dip my finger between her legs and lightly stroke her clit.

"Beck...please."

Jesus, I can hardly wrap my brain around the fact that Piper is begging me for it. Me. The guy she's hated since we were teens.

I fall over her, and position my cock at her entrance. "You want my cock inside you, Piper?"

"Yes," she answers without hesitation and it's absolutely mind-boggling how excited I am to hear that one word. "Do you want to put your cock inside me, Beck?"

"Absolutely." With that I power forward and completely fill her. Her nails scratch against my back as I hit her cervix and it brings on a full body shudder from her—and me. I go completely still as I seat myself high inside her, my body on edge, ready to erupt with the slightest movement. I take a few deep breaths. So does she. It's like we're both trying to get a fucking grip. Once I have a modicum of control, I move my hips and she groans, loudly.

"Beck, that is sooo good."

I lift my head, and our eyes lock. I rock into her, and her body opens for me, accepting every inch as I feed it to her. Her lids fall, her eyes half closed as I push deep and use my pelvic bone to stimulate her clit. She wets her lips and I kiss her, a new kind of desperation taking hold as I taste her sweetness.

I break the kiss, and our bodies are damp as I bury my face into the crook of her neck and her gorgeous tits press against my chest, arousing me more as we rock together. She's so goddam slick as I spear her with my cock, I move in easily, and her muscles tremble around me, teasing my mounting orgasm.

I lower my hands and grip her hips as I angle my body for deeper, harder thrusts. Why is it I can't seem to get deep enough inside her?

"You like my cock inside you, Piper?" I ask, even though her moans tell me she does.

"Yes. It's so good. Nothing at all like the last time," she murmurs. My chest puffs as she strokes my ego, and it's incredibly satisfying to know how much she likes this. "Is it... good for you?"

Once again, I hear that hint of vulnerability. I lift my head, and glance into her glossy eyes. "If you want honesty, I'll give it to you. I don't remember the last time it was this good." A growl of pleasure erupts from my throat. "Fuck, Piper, I'm not sure it's ever been this good."

She smiles like I'm providing lip service, but I'm not lying. I don't know what it is about being with her. I'm not going to lie to myself and say I've not thought about it over the years. There's no denying I crushed on her in the past, but she gutted me when we were seventeen. I don't know, maybe the fact that she wants me is some kind of sweet reparation in my mind, which makes it all that much more satisfying.

Whatever it is, it's fucking amazing.

"Beck," she moans, her body tightening, her sex gripping my dick harder. I shift and reach between her body to give her clit the attention it needs and as soon as I touch her, she comes apart beneath me and we both groan as her muscles hug me harder. I breathe through the pleasure as her hot heat sears me, and I rock into her, doing math in my head so I can hang on a bit longer.

She cups my face, and looks deep into my eyes as she rides out her pleasure, and I'm not sure I've ever seen anything so real or honest before. My heart stops beating and air evacuates my lungs as she completely opens to me, showing me the depths of her soul as she lets her body go.

I lightly brush my lips over hers, and my heart starts beating again, a different kind of beat. I know that sounds odd, but I think something might be happening to me. I don't know what to call it, but it's strange and unfamiliar, and it's messing with my head and my heart.

Our lips barely touch as I let go, a foreign kind of warmth and heat flooding every vein, saturating every bone as I let go high inside her. What the hell is going on with me? I come and come some more as she runs her fingers down my back, moaning in bliss with each hard pulse of my cock. When my body stops spasming, I press my forehead to hers and we breathe together, as I come down from some sort of strange spiritual experience.

After a long while, her fingers rake through my hair and I lift my head. Her eyes seek out mine, and a smile curves her lips. "I...I...just..." She swallows and it sounds pained. "Thirsty."

I grin. "Need something to drink?" She nods, and I roll to the side and she turns to face me. I revel at the dazed, sated look on her face as I tuck her hair behind her ears. "Was it enough?" She arches a brow, confusion in her eyes, and I smile and add, "...attention."

"For now," she says as she stretches her arms over her head, like the cat that ate the canary and has zero regrets. While she looks relaxed and sounds like she's completely in charge here, like she just totally whipped me—and let's face it, there's a good chance she has—there's still something unsure about her.

Then again, why wouldn't she be unsure, especially about us, considering our history, but I'd like to think we've come to some sort of truce here, and the best we can do is hope it holds while we're cohabitating. After that, things can go back to the way they were.

"Be right back." I drop a soft kiss onto her swollen lips and I don't miss the flinch, or the look of surprise in her eyes that she's trying to hide. I have no idea what happened after sex in her past, but I'm not about to just up and leave. She nods and I stand to tug on my jeans. Since her roommate isn't back yet, I don't bother with my shirt, as I head downstairs to her kitchen. In the fridge I find bottles of water, and I grab a couple. I open mine and take a big drink as I head back upstairs, taking my time to glance into the rooms.

Her place is nicely decorated, and books and stacks of cotton and other material are piled on the coffee table in her living room. In another room, one that's probably called a den, she has a sewing machine, and shelving units with tons of material. On a mannequin, I spot the shirt she pinned on me earlier today. I still don't love the idea of modeling it, but I like what I'm getting in exchange: her having to do what I want, and dammit, I want a lot. That might make me sound like a total prick, but the reality is, she never has to do anything she doesn't want to do.

Know what's really weird? I get the sense that there are a lot of things she wants to do, and this tit for tat agreement gives her the freedom to do them, without guilt, responsibility, self-blame, or regret. But what do I know? I study business not psychology.

I step back into her room and she's scrolling through her phone. She drops it, and her gaze is sexy as she focuses on me. I slide back in beside her, uncap her bottle and hand it to her. She takes a big drink.

"Thank you."

I take another drink of my own, and recap it when she cautiously asks, "Beck?"

"Yeah."

"That was...it was...I just didn't know sex could be like that."

*Neither did I.*

"It hasn't been great for you, huh?" I ask.

"No."

"Was the last time really high school?" I slide down, and drag her with me. We face each other and I rest my hand on the lush curve of her hip.

"It's embarrassing."

"Hey, no need to be embarrassed with me."

She covers her face with her hands. "It was the night of my seventeenth birthday party. It was kind of my first and last time."

My heart literally stops beating. Her first time and last time was the night of her party? My mind instantly rewinds to that night, and my stomach cramps. I'd thought I'd be invited to her birthday. I'd even bought a gift, which is still in my dresser drawer back home. I have no idea why I haven't tossed the stupid thing. How fucked up is that?

"Really?" I ask, trying not to sound like I was just gut punched as memories bombard me. Now is not the time to be thinking of past hurts.

"Yeah, I uh...I just haven't wanted to. Been busy and stuff."

She gives a gesture with her hands, like it's no big deal, but her eyes say it certainly was. "So, it was with someone I knew?" I ask, my pulse jumping because I don't think I'm going to like what I'm about to hear.

"Uh, yeah. Noah."

Before I can catch myself, I slam my fist into the mattress, and murmur, "Fuck, I knew it," as the pieces of a long-ago puzzle fall into place.

Her brow furrows as she questions, "What?"

"Nothing."

Shit, did I say that out loud? She doesn't need to know what I know about Noah fucking Blackmore. Now I get it, though. It all makes perfect sense. The day after her birthday, I was out walking with my buddy David, who had boycotted the party because I wasn't invited, and we caught Noah spray painting the word slut on Piper's car.

I never liked the guy to begin with. His father is the town's longtime mayor and Noah always thought he was better than me. He walked around fucking any woman with two legs, and then bragged about it to the guys and shamed the girls. Since Daddy was mayor, he pretty much felt like he was untouchable, and maybe he was, but when we caught him shaming Piper with a bottle of spray paint, and I told him to stop, he asked me what I was going to do about it. I showed him with my fist, giving him one hell of a shiner.

Afterward, I warned him never to go near Piper again, or the next beating would be worse. He didn't go to his daddy. Then he'd have to admit what he did. I took care of his retribution myself, and left him with a black eye and a warning, so when I was accused of doing it, I didn't bother outing him. David wanted to tell Piper and the cops, but what was the point? Piper's parents were never going to believe me anyway. But Christ, I can't tell her the guy she gave her virginity to did something like that afterward. That would really hurt her, and I don't want that.

"It was bad, huh?" I say, working to keep my voice even as a storm brews inside me. I should have given the bastard two black eyes.

"How did you know?"

"Because if it had been good, you'd probably still be doing it."

"Maybe I'm defective," she jokes, but beneath the words there's real pain.

I put my hand on her arm, and run it up and down. "A lot of times, the first-time sucks, Piper. Practice makes perfect."

"No one's really been interested in...there's just never been anyone I wanted to be with..." She grins and adds, "Except maybe Bob."

"Who the fuck is Bob?"

*I'm not jealous. Nope, not even a little bit. But who the fuck is Bob?*

She laughs and taking me by surprise, she rolls, reaches into her nightstand and takes out her vibrator. "Battery Operated Boyfriend."

"Holy shit." I laugh and take the purple device from her, turning it around to take it in from all angles. "I kind of love that you showed me this." Truthfully, I'm shocked, but also really super pleased that she feels comfortable enough with me to show me something so personal. No girl has ever showed me her vibrator before.

"Okay, well since you showed me this, I'm going to tell you something personal," I say.

"Ooh, do tell." She takes Bob from me and places it back on the nightstand.

"The night you slept in my bed, I had this wicked sex dream about us."

She grins from ear to ear, pleasure dancing in her eyes. "No way."

"Yeah," I say and blow out a breath.

"Desperate times, huh?"

She's joking, so I pat her mussed bed and ask, "For you too, huh?"

She laughs, and as it dies we both go quiet. After a few beats, she quietly asks, "How come you haven't been with anyone lately?"

"How do you know that?"

Her eyes go wide. "I haven't been keeping tabs or anything. I mean, my world does not revolve around you."

I grin. "Good to know."

"It's just Kennedy said something, and you told me your bed was a virgin, remember? Are you not bringing girls around because they have a child?"

"Yeah." It's a lie. I can't tell her that it's her I've been thinking about, and sex with a puck bunny has lost its appeal. Ever since the wedding, I haven't been able to get her out of my head. Okay, let's be honest here, she's been in my head long before the wedding. Christ, she lives there rent free and I was sort of hoping if we had sex, she'd move out of my brain, but no, that didn't work. She's entrenched in there now, and let's not forget I told her I wanted to see her 'days of the week panties'.

She stifles a yawn, and I snuggle in closer. With finals coming and her needing to finish her design project, I say, "I was thinking..."

"About."

"If you need me in the morning, you know for another fitting..." I pause briefly, giving her a chance to say she might need me for another reason. When she doesn't, I continue. "Maybe I should just spend the night. It will save commute time."

She shrugs, looking nonchalant, and I think she's going to kick me out, until she says, "Since we're saving commute time on the other end, maybe on this end we can talk about that thing you said."

I eye her, taking in the heat staring back. "What thing did I say?"

"Something about practice makes perfect."

# 9

# PIPER

y body hurts in the most glorious ways as I turn to my side and open my eyes. As the reality of last night seeps into my brain, I smile, unable to help myself. I slept with Beckett Moore, and it was fan—frigging—tastic. My body warms all over as I glance at him lying beside me, eyes closed, his arm over his head. With the blankets hovering around his waist, and with nothing on underneath, I let my gaze rake over his hardness. My God, he's a beautiful creature.

I stifle a yawn and check the clock. I usually swim first thing in the morning before the pool is even open, and while the exercise helps invigorate my mind and body, I'm a little reluctant to leave the bed.

Do I wake him, or do I let him sleep?

As I debate that, I slip from the bed, tug on my fluffy pink robe and step into the hall, leaving my door open a crack. Alysha's bedroom door is closed as I walk past it. I didn't even hear her come in last night. She must have been out late.

Either that or I was too lost in Beckett to notice. My heart misses a beat as I recall the ways he touched me, and that kiss after sex. Wow, I felt that deep in my soul.

*Careful, Piper, don't think this is anything more than it really is.*

I hurry to the bathroom, and by the time I make it back to my room, Beckett is wide awake and staring at me.

"Sorry," I begin quietly and close the door behind me. "I didn't mean to wake you."

"You want me to close my eyes so you can go back to sneaking away?"

I chuckle at that. "I wasn't trying to sneak away."

"Good, then get over here." He holds his hand out, and as I look at his fingers, my body shivers, loving the way the rough pads of his hands felt on my flesh. I walk up to him, and he tugs on my robe. "You're overdressed."

"I wasn't going to go to the bathroom naked."

"Now I'm not so sorry I was asleep." I arch a brow and he continues with, "You look as good going as you do coming."

Is there a double meaning in there...

"Well, you're awake now."

"Yeah, I am," he agrees and I try not to squeal and wake Alysha as he pulls me to him, and in a swift move that I don't see coming, he has my robe open and me beneath him. I grin up at him. A girl could get used to waking up like this.

Before I can say that, and I'm not sure I should—I don't want to give him the wrong idea—his mouth closes over mine, for a deep mind-numbing wake up kiss. While there's hunger in his kisses, there's something else, something soft and tender...

intimate, and those are the things a girl needs to watch for. If she doesn't, she could mistake them for something else.

He breaks the kiss, and I'm breathless. "Good morning," he whispers with a grin.

"Great morning." He kisses my exposed shoulder and angles his head to see the clock. "Why are you up? Oh God, you're one of those morning people, aren't you?"

"You say that like it's a bad thing?"

"Piper, morning people do not get along with night owls. I'm not even sure we can be friends anymore."

"Friends," I echo and put my palms on the side of his face. "Is that what we are?" I really like the idea of that.

"No, did you not hear the part where I said we couldn't be friends."

"I did stay up very late last night, didn't I?"

He narrows his eyes. "I guess. Okay, we can go back to being friends?"

I laugh at that, and unable to help myself, I lift up to kiss him. "I'm up early because I usually swim in the morning."

He groans. "Are you kidding me? What is wrong with you?" He shakes his head, like he can't wrap his brain around that.

"You're one to talk. Growing up, you were at the rink at the crack of dawn every morning."

He huffs and groans, "Do you have to be right about everything today?"

My God, I love this easy, fun banter far too much.

"Want to come?"

"The pool isn't open this early. We'd have to break in."

I look down, a bit sheepish. "I have my own key."

He doesn't call me on it, instead he taps his chin, pretending to be in deep thought. "Let me see. Stay in this bed, and sleep a few more hours or jump into an ice-cold pool and swim with you. It's a no brainer."

"You're coming?"

"Hell yeah." I laugh and he kisses me again. "First this," he growls and grabs a condom from the nightstand.

I don't remember it being there when I went to the bathroom. He tears into it and sheathes himself. "What makes me think you had this planned...oh, wow, yes," I murmur as he positions between my legs and slides into my body, stealing my words.

"What was that, Piper?" His eyes fall shut for a brief second as my muscles clench around him. "You were asking me something? Had a complaint?"

"Nope, no complaints here."

He goes perfectly still, his eyes now open, a frown on his face. "You're not too sore, are you?"

An invisible hand squeezes my heart. "No." I put my arms around him, grip his perfect ass and start moving my body.

"Fuck..." he curses, and moves with me, letting me set the pace and rhythm, which is slow and soft this morning—the perfect wake-up morning hate fuck. Even though everything about this feels like it's the opposite of hate. Not love. Wait, no, that's not what I mean. I just mean it feels so damn good, that it certainly doesn't feel like hate.

I close my eyes and he buries his face in the crook of my neck, his breath hot on my flesh as we rock together, no fancy moves or drawn out foreplay. No, this morning is about two people wanting to feel a surge of pleasure before beginning a long, hard day.

I hold him to me, run my fingers along his back, reveling in the way his muscles tense and relax again beneath my fingertips.

"You feel so good," he murmurs into my throat, and presses soft kisses to my skin. He reaches between our bodies, pressing his finger to my slick clit, and a keening cry catches in my throat as the pressure sends me over the edge. I tumble into an orgasm, my entire body tightening around his cock as he sinks in deeper, throwing his head back to orgasm with me.

I close my eyes and concentrate on the glorious pleasure between my legs and the way his cock swells and pulses inside me. I breathe through each powerful clench, and ride the wave as we soar together. We both stop spasming, and he stays inside me as he puts his hands on either side of my face and smiles at me.

"Do you wear a bikini or one piece?"

I laugh at his question. "We just had sex and now you're thinking about my bathing suit."

"Do the bottoms have days of the week with cute little sayings?"

"No, they don't. I wear a one piece." He shifts to the side and we both groan as he pulls out of me. He removes the condom and wraps it in tissue to dispose of later. He turns back to me, lays on his side and goes up on his elbow.

"Do you have a bathing suit?" I question.

"What, no." He taps the bed three times. "Okay that's it, I'm out. I thought we were going skinny dipping."

I whack him. "No, you didn't. You just asked about my bathing suit."

"If it's just the two of us, why can't we go in our birthday suits?"

"Uh, what if someone comes." His grin is wicked and mischievous. "That's not what I mean."

He runs his finger along my arm and I shiver when he asks, "Are there cameras in there?"

"No, but you can't go naked."

He rolls to his back and huffs like a child who didn't get their own way and honestly, it's kind of adorable. "Fine, I'll wear my boxers." He turns to see me. "They'll do, won't they?"

"We could run back to your place first."

"Nah. That's in the opposite direction and we don't want to wake Madelyn. I'm good." He rolls into me again. "Or we could have sex again, and get all the exercise we need right here in this bed."

"While that does sound like a great idea, I still want to go to the pool. My parents...uh..." How do I say my parents paid for it without sounding spoiled and privileged?

"They sponsored it. I know."

I nod. "Yeah, so I like to make sure I use it. I don't want them to think I don't appreciate it, you know."

"I know." He stares at me for a moment. "You worry a lot about your parents, don't you?" I nod. "You want to make them happy." I nod again. "I hope they worry about you as much, Piper, and want you as happy as you want them."

I swallow. Hard. Wow, he sort of hit the nail on the head with that statement. I walk the straight and narrow all the time, never wanting to rock the boat or upset them. I'm expected to take over the resort, but the thought of it doesn't make me happy. They never asked me what makes me happy, or what I wanted to do, and every time I think about that, guilt swamps me. They've given me so much, and it's my duty to carry on their legacy.

"I'm sorry. I didn't mean to say anything to upset you."

I lift my head. "No, it's okay. It's just...our relationship...it's complicated."

"You know what's not complicated," he says and sits up. "Swimming. Come on. Let's do this."

I stand and snatch up my robe. "I need a fast shower."

"Me too." He tugs on his boxers. "Let's shower together to conserve water."

"I didn't know there was a shortage."

"Oh yeah, it's been all over the news. I can't believe you haven't heard about it. I mean even Santa has resorted to watering his reindeer vegetable garden with a ho-ho-hose."

"Ohmigod, really?"

He arches a brow. "So, you really haven't heard. Oh, then I guess you never heard the police arrested a water bottle. It was wanted in three different states."

"Okay, which three states?" I put my hands on my hips and stare at him.

He continues with, "Liquid, solid, and gas."

"One more bad joke and you're showering alone." He grins and I press my finger to my lips and open the door.

"What, am I your dirty little secret or something?"

"Or something," I respond. We step into the bathroom and I close the door, wincing as it clicks shut. "Maybe you should have parked your Jeep down the street. Everyone knows everyone's business in this city."

"That they do."

"We should keep it a secret, though."

Looking confused and maybe even a bit offended, he asks, "Why?"

I reach into the shower and turn it on as he tugs off his boxers and stands before me buck naked like it's the most natural thing in the world and I'm used to hanging out with naked men. I'm not. Seeing him like this does affect me. A lot.

"Kennedy told me she asked me to help out with Madelyn because she knew we didn't get along, and we wouldn't be distractions for one another."

"Really?"

"She thinks a girl other than me might distract you from taking care of Madelyn."

"I can't believe she thinks I'm distracted that easily. I'll have you know I have a lot more control than that. It takes a lot to distract me."

"She didn't mean anything by that. She loves you. She was just basically saying we don't get along and..." I wave a finger back and forth between the two of us as I slip off my robe, and his head drops to take in my body. My nipples harden beneath his widening eyes, and I can't help but chuckle. "Nope, not distracted easily at all."

His head lifts. "What?"

I shake my head and grin. "Exactly."

"Come on. How could I not get distracted?"

"I'm a lot, am I?"

"What?" he asks, his voice distant again as his gaze moves over my curves.

I laugh again, and really, it's kind of flattering that I can distract him. "You said it takes a lot to distract you. Am I a lot?"

He looks at his hard cock. "Damn thing has a mind of its own. Can't keep any secrets."

I step into the shower and crook my finger. He follows me in and puts his arms around me as he positions us beneath the spray. "If Kennedy knew, it could get you out of babysitting."

"No, I owe them a lot."

"And if you're not babysitting, you'd have to go home."

I nod, and stick my face under the water. Beck grabs the soap and lathers me up, which probably shouldn't be turning me on as much as it does. Once we're both washed, we dry, and he tugs his boxers back on to hurry to my bedroom. Twenty minutes later, after a fast bowl of cereal, we reach the sport-splex. I tug my key from my bag and put it in the lock. It sticks a bit, which is odd. Was someone messing with this lock? I glance over my shoulder.

"What's wrong?" Beck asks his body close to mine as he cranes his neck to see what's going on.

"Nothing. I'm just having a hard time with the key."

"It really is nice to have your own key to the sportsplex," he says without judgement, which I appreciate, as I struggle to get the key in. He takes it from me, unlocks the back door to the pool, lets us in, and locks it back up behind us.

I step up to a bench, kick off my boots and coat, and shrug out of my clothes. I hear a big splash and turn to see Beckett already in the water. How did he strip so fast? I walk to the deep end, and dive in, and when I come up, he's right there, a big grin on his face. He drags me to him, and his cock rubs against my body.

"Beckett, where are your boxers!"

"Marco," he says and dives under the water.

# 10

# BECKETT

"You keep that up and I'll end up walking down that runway with a mega boner," I groan as Piper brushes her hands over my crotch in an attempt to get the khaki pants to sit just right over my dick, which is growing thicker by the second—all thanks to her fussing with me.

She shakes her head but it's easy to tell she likes it when I get aroused by her touch. "Do math in your head or something." She inches back to look at me and puts her hands on her hips, scrunching that sexy little dress around her hips. All I can think about is what she's wearing underneath it. Has she gone commando, hoping I'll touch her, or is she wearing her sexy 'days of the week' panties? I groan and my cock grows even more.

"Math, Beckett. Now."

"No, I hate math."

"That's the point."

"Fine, six plus five equals...Jesus stop touching me like that."

She chuckles. "If you hate mat so much, why are you doing a business degree?"

"I'm doing it because it's something good to fall back on. But I'm more into the marketing than accounting. Why are you doing it?" I counter and she glares at me. Sure, I know she's planning to take over the family business, even though I think it's a horrible idea. But now is not the time or place for a discussion on her degree choice, but she seriously loves this design stuff. She's glowing, completely in her glory as she readies me to walk the runway for her teachers. "Hey," I murmur quietly, leaning down to her. "You nailed this. I look amazing."

That makes her laugh. "Your ego knows no boundaries."

"Right now, the only thing bigger than my ego is my co—"

"Stop!" she stands up straight, and I put my hand around her waist and tug her to me, messing up all her work. She opens her mouth, and I kiss away her protest until she melts into me. I too love the way she gets aroused by me. "You're getting all wrinkled." She groans.

"No worries, the wrinkles are smoothing themselves out, thanks to that dress you're wearing." I lean in. "Hey, what are you wearing underneath?"

"Ohmigod, you have such a one-track mind."

"When you keep touching me like that, what do you expect?" I let her go, and I straighten my clothes out again. "Good?"

"Yeah." She smiles at me, and I swear I'd wear a dress down the runway if it meant seeing her this happy.

"You got this." I cock my head and take in the way she keeps tugging on my clothes. "You know that, right? I'm not going to do anything to fuck this up for you."

She leans in and gives me a fast kiss. "Thank you." Her name is called from the other side of the curtain, and her eyes go big as she claps her hands together. "They're ready for you," she practically squeals, her voice quivering with excitement and nervousness.

"Yeah, but they're not ready for you, babe. When you start to take fashion seriously, and get your designs in stores, you're going to knock everyone on their asses."

For one brief second, elation fills her eyes, but then her brow furrows and she says quietly, "Thank you, Beck. But it's just a hobby." Not wanting to dig into this right now, I nod, and she opens the curtain, and holds it for me. I step out and she says, "Just like we practiced."

"I got you, babe."

As the lights zero in on me, making it hard to see who's watching, I put one hand in my pocket and walk to the end of the runway. Once there, I turn giving her teachers a good look at the fit of my pants. Murmurs reach my ears, along with a few giggles from her fellow classmates when I wink at them as I walk to the left, and then to the right. I stand there for a few moments and the next thing I know, I'm back behind the curtain, Piper jumping into my arms as one the guy modeling her classmate's designs replaces us on the stage.

"You did so great."

With her legs still wrapped around me, I carry us from behind the curtain, down the stairs, into the change rooms.

"I totally nailed it." I grin at her as she slides off my body.

"Speaking of nailed…"

I laugh and ask, "Now who's the one with the one-track mind?"

"Clearly, I've been hanging out with you too long," she responds. "You're rubbing off on me."

"I love it when you talk dirty like that." I laugh as I start unbuttoning the shirt. "What are you going to do with the clothes now?"

"They're yours if you want them."

"Of course, I want them. How many guys get to say they're wearing a Piper Thorne original?"

She taps my nose. "Only you."

I shrug and the shirt falls from my shoulders. Piper folds it and neatly puts it in a box. "That was far less painful than I thought it would be," I tell her.

She drops to her knees, and tugs my pants down, and her damn mouth is aligned perfectly with my cock.

"Does that mean the tit for tat is over and I don't have to do everything you say?" She arches a hopeful brow, but I'm on to her. There's a hint of mischief in her eyes. She likes our agreement, wants to see where it's going to lead as much as I do.

"No."

"What do you want me to do, Beck?"

"Right now, I want your mouth wrapped around my cock." Her eyes go wide, and I cup her chin.

"We can't. My classmates. The teachers."

"Afraid of a little risk?" I ask and take delight in the flush crawling up her neck. She likes the idea of risk, but no way am I going to do anything to mess with her grades, or get her kicked out of school.

"Tomorrow," I begin, before she can answer. "When you move into the house, there'll be nothing to stop you from saying, *we can't*."

I lift my legs as she removes my pants, and she stands, her body vibrating with excitement as I slide my hand around her back and pull her to me, my boxers doing very little to contain my arousal.

Something in her gaze changes, from uncertainty to boldness and before I even realize what's happening, she's taking hold of my hand and ushering me down a long hall. She fishes her keys from her pocket, and glances around before opening a door. I enter the dark room, lit only by the moonlight shining in and find mannequins and desks and sewing machines. Near the window there's a long sofa, but goddammit, it's just too far way.

"What is this place?"

She doesn't answer. Instead, she locks the door behind us and drops to her knees. With hurried movements, like she can't touch me quickly enough, she frees my raging cock and takes it to the back of her throat. Fuck, I was sort of only kidding earlier when I asked if she was afraid of a little risk. The truth is, I know she's afraid of risk and she walks the straight and narrow, wanting to make the world a little better for everyone around her. She's a peacekeeper by nature, a total rule follower, and what we're doing here goes against every fiber of her being, and as good as this feels, no fucking way am I going to let her take unnecessary risks and fuck up her future.

"Piper," I say quietly and try to push her back, but she puts her hands around my body and hugs my ass. I can break away if I wanted to, but I don't, and while standing here letting her blow me in some classroom is inappropriate and risky, something tells me this is what she wants. Little miss pampered princess is cracking the mold framing her life—and this is more about her than me.

"I never knew you were so bad ass," I murmur, and she sucks harder. I grin, totally understanding what she wants. "Sucking me off like this when we could get caught."

She moans and cups my balls, and my body tightens as I try to hold on, but her mouth is so hot and wet, and ravenous I have no choice but to do math and calculate just how much trouble I might be getting into with Piper, because dammit, I can't stop thinking about her. When we're not together, I'd move mountains just to get to her, and it's not all about the sex. I like being with her. I like talking and laughing, and simply just being together.

"Fuck me twice."

Her eyes lift as I speak, and the heat in her baby blues, the sheer pleasure she's taking from this shatters all my control and I begin to spurt before I can get my dick out of her mouth. Her eyes go wide as she swallows me, drinking me in as fast as I fill her mouth. It's a beautiful sight that feeds the parts of my heart I closed off to her years ago.

My spasms die, and I grip her shoulders and pull her to me. I lift her, and set her on one of the tables, and spread her legs so I can get closer. I run my fingers through her hair and grip it tightly, tugging her head back until her lips open for me.

"Is there something else you want me to do, Beck?" Her voice is low, breathless and full of arousal, and I might have just climaxed, but my cock is growing again. "Oh, what do we have there?" she asks as she wiggles her hot core against my dick.

I inch back and slide my hand under her dress, my fingers meeting with damp panties and that just fucking thrills me. Sucking me off got her wet and that's a huge turn on. I push her panties to the side, and run my finger over her soaking pussy, stopping to tease her opening before applying pressure to her swollen clit.

She moans, and puts her hands on the desk behind her, and rocks against me. "You have a thing for desks, huh?" she teases.

"No, I have a thing for you, and twice now a desk was closer than anything else." I hear the need and urgency in my voice every bit as much as she does, and I'm okay with that. I couldn't hide it even if I wanted to, and yeah, carrying her to the sofa by the window, or to her bed when we were at her place, was simply too far away.

I slide my finger into her and she moans with pleasure. She lifts her hips more, encouraging me to give her more, so I do. I slide a second finger in, and her muscles squeeze my fingers deeper as her body quakes, keening little noises catching in her throat.

"You needed this?" I ask.

"Yes, we've both been so busy, it's been too long."

"Once you're under the same roof as me, I'm going to fuck you every night." Her pussy clenches, her body telling me without words that she likes that idea.

"What am I going to do when I leave for the summer?" she asks. "I don't think Bob is going to cut it."

I chuckle at that. I want her to use her toy and get herself off, but I also like that she'd prefer for me to do it. "Maybe I'll come see you. Maybe when I drive back to see my family we can hook up."

She moans. "That would be so nice."

Another idea hits and I whisper, "We could sneak into one of the empty rooms at the resort and fuck all night long."

"Oh God, wouldn't that be crazy...and fun."

I think there's a part of her that wants to rebel, needs it even. Damn if I don't want to help her find another side of herself, where she does what she wants, not what she's expected to do. I know. I'm one to talk. I want to succeed to help my brothers and sisters, and put them through college. I realize a huge chunk of our household income went to further my hockey, and I do feel a sense of responsibility. But hockey is what I've always wanted and Piper isn't living the life she wants, and what can a little harmless rebellion hurt? I guess it could hurt if her family caught her with me. It's possible they'd disown her. But unlike Matt's grandfather, who cut him off, they wouldn't cut Piper off completely, would they? Nah, it's the twenty-first century and what we're doing is hooking up. Her parents don't have to worry about it becoming anything more. Nope, the good girl will return home and marry a man good enough for her family.

As she stares at me, her face flushed, her eyes dazed like she's imagining what it would be like for us to sneak into a room and have sex, I add, "No one would ever have to know." I don't think I have to sweeten the deal for her, but maybe knowing it will be our little secret and she has no worries of her family disowning her would help ease her apprehension.

"No one can ever know," she agrees, and I get a twinge in my chest, right around the vicinity of my heart. Her words remind me of who I am and where I came from and that no matter what, her parents would never allow their daughter to be with a guy like me. "Our little secret," she whispers. "I like having secrets with you, Beck."

"Yeah?" I ask, knowing the real reason why she likes that. But I'm currently finger-fucking her in some back room at her college, and now is probably not the time to be thinking about my lack of worth to her family, and how we need secrets to be together.

She pulls her hands off the desk and puts them around my neck as I rub my palm on her clit and work my fingers inside her. She begins to breathe deeply, bursts of air hot on my face, and I give her just what she needs to topple over the edge.

"Beck," she moans a little too loudly. I press my lips to hers to stifle the sound, and I have to say, sneaking around like this, is kind of fun. She floods around my slick fingers, and I stay inside her to wring out every last ounce of her pleasure. Once her body relaxes and grows limp and sated, I pull my fingers from her, and bring them to my mouth. I inhale her sweet scent and lick my fingers clean as she watches in sheer fascination.

I wink at her. "So much better than cookies."

She laughs as I reference the panties she was in the first time we got naked together. Someone moves in the hall, shuffles by, and she puts her fingers to her lips, and tries to quiet her laugh.

I lift her from the desk, and she fixes her panties, which are soaked and no doubt uncomfortable. I tuck my dick into my boxers, and because my clothes are in the other room, I have nothing to put on. But it's not the lack of clothes that's going to give us away. One look at our flushed faces and it'll be easy to tell what we've been doing.

She smooths her hand over her hair and gestures to the door. "Maybe you should go out first and I'll follow."

I nod. I get it. She doesn't want to get into any kind of trouble here at the school, but the little boy from my past, the one who still resides inside of me and was always left out of things, knows the real truth. I'm good for a fuck, but that's it.

"We could just tell them we had to duck in here because of a clothing emergency," I tease, not wanting to dampen the mood with those dark thoughts.

"A clothing emergency?"

"Sure." I touch her dress, lightly run my finger over the fabric covering her pert nipple. "The emergency was that you had on too many clothes and they were preventing me from touching you."

She laughs and whacks my chest. "But you're only in boxers."

"I'm in boxers because you dragged me in here before I could get dressed."

She grins. "Yeah, I did, didn't I?"

"So now I have to run back down the hall naked."

She blinks dark lashes over innocent eyes and feigns worry. "Should I not have done this?"

"Oh, yeah, babe." I chuckle. "You should have done this. And when I get you alone again, I'm going to show you how much I like it when you forget you're a rule follower."

"I can't wait."

## 11

# PIPER

My body is still tingling from last night, and while I can't wait to have Beck's hands on me again, I can't wait to see him and tell him my news. It's crazy, really. Who would have thought that at the beginning of the semester I'd be going out of my mind anxious to tell him something—anything—about fashion school. More importantly, who would have thought he'd actually care?

He does care, though. My heart warms as my mind returns to yesterday, and the way he walked the runway for me. If he didn't care, he wouldn't have done that.

*Maybe he did it just to play with you. He did say you'd have to do whatever he asked, right?*

Okay, sure that was part of the bargain, but he was playing, and I can't deny that we're both having fun. I just have to remember that what's going on here is about having fun, and I am a part of the same friendship circle, and I see the way he cares about Kennedy and the others, so why wouldn't he extend that friendship to me?

*Because we became enemies in high school.*

Not wanting that thought to darken my mood—we have to cohabitate for the next week—I push it back and drive around the corner, pulling into Kennedy and Matt's driveway when I see their vehicle is already gone. Have they left already? I thought she was going to go over Madelyn's schedule with me. A bout of nerves grip my stomach and for a second I fear I might throw up.

*I know nothing about kids.*

I tentatively open my door and Beck comes outside, Madelyn in his arms like it's the most natural thing in the world. The man was born to be a father, of that I have no doubt. It's a good thing we're not serious about each other. Kids and marriage are not on my bucket list.

"Well?" he asks, his eyes big, and full of hope.

I grin. "I got an A plus."

"No way," he says and comes running to me in his bare feet. He leans in, and is about to kiss me, but I back up a bit, not wanting to make a spectacle of ourselves on the street, and this hook-up is supposed to be private, just between the two of us.

He nods. "Yeah, right."

"But we got an A plus," I say. He holds his fist out and I bump it as Madelyn leans into me and tugs on my hair.

"Ouch," I wince, and Beck helps pull her wet fingers from my strands.

He leans in and puts his mouth near my ear, his words meant for me alone. "You never complain when I pull your hair."

"Not funny."

"Why are you laughing then?" He walks to the trunk with me, and as soon as I pop it he grabs my bag.

"I can do that. Your hands are full."

"I'm a great multi-tasker. Now come on. I was about to get Madelyn's lunch ready."

I glance around and shade the early morning sun from my eyes. "Are Kennedy and Matt gone already?"

"Yeah, I told them to take off, and that I'd fill you in."

I nod, and follow him up the pathway to the cute little house. I grew up in such a big place, and I have to say there's something so cozy and warm about their tiny home. In the kitchen, he sets Madelyn into her booster seat and pushes her in to the table.

"Did you eat?" he asks me.

"I was so excited to tell you about my grade, and getting packed I completely forgot."

This time he does lean in and give me a kiss. "I'm proud of you. You worked hard and earned that A."

My heart trembles as warmth bursts through me, and it's not because Kennedy keeps her place hot. "Thank you."

"Have you told your folks?"

I brace myself. At some point I figured he'd bring this up, knowing my passion lies with fashion, yet I'm doing a business degree to take over the resort. "No, they don't know I'm taking design classes."

"How could they not know?"

"Don't you have to work tonight?"

"Nice change of subject," he mutters and places a sandwich in front of me, and a tray with meats, cheeses, vegetables and crackers in front of Madelyn.

"Yum, yum," she says, and I laugh as she digs in.

"I don't even know what to feed a two-year-old. I probably would have made her a sandwich."

"And she would have been fine with that," he tells me.

He sits down across from me, a sandwich in front of him. I look at mine, and my appetite dwindles. He stares at me—like he's a great interrogator—and with my need to fill the silence I say, "It's just different in our family."

"I'm sorry."

I shake my head. "No, don't be sorry. It just is what it is." I take a bite of my sandwich and moan. "This is delicious, Beck."

He smiles. "Good."

I'm grateful he leaves our conversation at that, and grabs a puppet and starts playing with Madelyn. I watch in sheer fascination.

"She loves it."

"We sometimes visit the children's hospital, and we bring these puppets."

"You do?" I don't know why that surprises me so much. The team does great things around the city, and I guess I just never pictured the rough and tough Beck playing with puppets before. Although back home, I've seen him with his younger siblings, and it always warmed the depths of my soul.

"I was always a little jealous of you and your family," I admit without thinking. His head lifts slowly, and he cocks it to the side, looking at me like I was an alien who didn't grow up in the same town as him. Yeah, I get it. My parents are snobs. I'll be the first to admit it, and how dare they act like they're better than anyone else. God, they're living a lie. Pretending to be this big happy family when behind the curtain, they're miserable. "I was always miserable."

What the hell. Why on earth did I just say that?

His hand snakes across the table and he takes hold of mine. "Hey."

That one word, that one simple word has me saying, "Your parents and family have always been supportive of you. They were always at the rink early in the mornings, until late at night, and as a child—as crazy as this might sound—I used to wish we had less of everything. Less money, less guests, less popularity with tourists…just less. Maybe then we'd have things like the Moore family." I grin as I think…the Moore family had more.

He swallows. "I had no idea, Piper."

"And the Oscar goes to the Thorne family." I laugh and it comes out sounding tortured and that's when I realize I probably sound like the poor little rich girl. God, I don't want his pity. I don't want anyone's pity. I keep my head down, afraid to even look at him. He's a guy who grew up with nothing, and I'm afraid that it won't be pity I see on his face—it'll be disgust. Why would he feel sorry for the rich girl who had everything? I'm sure he's staring at me with pure disdain. If he's not, he should be. I hate myself for even feeling sorry for myself.

*Is it really so bad to want something different, Piper?*

"I think you're pretty genuine," he says softly.

My head jerks up. "You do?"

He has a strange look on his face when he continues, "You care about your friends." He looks at Madelyn. "You wouldn't be here if you didn't. You care about school, and family, and you've been pretty open with me since...you know."

I chuckle. "Yeah, I know." I like how he tries to keep things PG in front of Madelyn.

"You know what you want and what you don't want." A beat of silence as Madelyn flings a slice of meat onto the floor. "But you carry this huge obligation on your shoulders which makes you bury what you want." I stare at him. "Am I wrong?"

"No."

He bends down to pick up the meat, giving me a reprieve from his probing gaze. How can he read me so well? He stands and opens the compost bin to toss in the slice of meat and then sits down, leaving me to my own thoughts as he goes back to playing with Madelyn, and ensuring she eats her food instead of dropping it on the floor.

"I should..." I gesture to my suitcase.

"You're in the master suite," he says.

I nod, and the disappointment curling in my belly is insane. I guess I thought we might be sharing a room. But with Madelyn in the house, that's probably not a good idea. Although she is only two and wouldn't understand.

"But don't get used to having that big king-sized bed to yourself."

Excitement pushes back the disappointment, and a smile lights my face. "Oh, will Madelyn be sharing with me?"

At the sound of her name, she holds out a piece of turkey. "Pee-prrrr," she mutters, and I grin.

"I don't think she's ever said my name before."

"Now you have to eat it."

I make a face, and look at the meat all squished in her tiny fingers. "Really?" I ask, and pull a face that displays just how horrible that sounds to me.

He laughs. "You don't have to do anything you don't want to do, remember?"

I wipe my brow. "Whew."

He laughs and I turn to leave. "Do you want me to carry your bag up for you?"

I swallow. That would mean I'd be left alone with Madelyn, and I'd rather get a hernia carrying my heavy bag. God, I am so pathetic.

"No, it's okay, I got it."

He starts making chicken noises, and flapping his arms like wings. Madelyn laughs and what can I say, I am a chickenshit.

"Hey," I warn, as Madelyn tries to mimic him and looking at the two of them makes me laugh.

"Don't worry, Piper. By the end of the week, you'll be wanting your own little family." He pulls Madelyn's chair from the table and releases her belt.

My heart squeezes tight. "Doubtful," I say, my voice lacking the conviction it once would have had as I watch the easy way he pulls her into his arms. He tosses me a grin. My God, could the two be any sweeter together.

"Your parents must be so proud of you, Beck," I say, almost under my breath.

He makes a sound, while he's cocky on the ice, and around town, deep inside he's humble. "Yeah, and yours must be proud of you too."

I nod, and turn to get my luggage. I carry it upstairs and step into Kennedy's room. the scent of freshly laundered sheets fill my senses, as I set my luggage on the chair, and unzip it. I have no idea why I packed so much. My own place isn't far, and I can go there in a heartbeat if I need something.

My phone rings and I snatch it from my purse. I see that it's Kennedy, so I slide my finger across the screen. "Hey," I say. "Everything okay?"

"Everything is great. I just wanted to check in and say sorry that we left before you got there. Beck said he had everything under control and Matt wanted to catch the earlier ferry."

"Everything is great. I'm just getting settled in your room now."

"I cleared the top two drawers in my dresser for you."

"Thanks, I could have worked out of a suitcase though."

"No, I want you to be comfortable, and treat the place like it's yours. Don't be afraid to touch anything."

Does that include Beck?

As if reading my thoughts, she asks, "You and Beck are okay? You're getting along?"

"We're adults. We'll be fine."

"He knows Madelyn's schedule, and Matt and I really appreciate this. It's been forever since we've had a night, let alone a days alone."

I grin. "You get it, gurl."

She laughs. "Yeah, you too."

"What?"

"Yeah, ah, I don't know why I said that. You and Beck have your hands full this week, so there'll be no 'getting it, gurl' for you."

Oh, if she only knew, and I can't tell her. She might not trust us to be responsible around her daughter if she knew we were drooling over one another and having sex every chance we can get. But no matter what, she can trust us. Or rather, she can trust Beck. He's amazing with Madelyn. I'm still afraid to be left alone in the same room with her and tonight Beck works. Oh God!

"Oh, I don't know if Beck told you or not, but we were given tickets to a romantic evening boat tour on the harbor for Saturday night. There will be wine, and hors d'oeuvres, and I'm sad I'm going to miss it. But we don't get back until Sunday."

Wow that sounds romantic, and definitely not something for Beck and me. We are not romantic partners by any stretch of the imagination. "Can you reschedule? It sounds amazing. Wait, it's the long weekend, why aren't you staying until Monday?"

"The harbor tour tickets were and engagement gift and I can't reschedule. I think you and Beck should use them and we're coming back Sunday because traffic will be crazy Monday."

She's right about traffic on Monday, which is the day I plan to head back to Cape Breton Island. But I'm about to protest over using the tickets when she laughs and adds, "I know it's for couples, and you two are anything but, but you should go and enjoy the wine and apps, if nothing else. Just try not to throw him overboard if he annoys you, which he seems so good at."

I laugh with her. "How can we go? We have Madelyn."

"Beck has Serena's number. She's our sitter. I'd honestly hate for those tickets to go to waste."

"Oh okay. I guess I didn't realize the sitters could get a sitter."

"I don't want it to be all work. I want you guys to have fun too." She covers the phone and her voice is muffled as she says something to Matt. Honestly, if I didn't know better, I'd say the two were matchmaking. They're not, of course. She explained the reason she paired us and really, I'm not looking for anything serious and she knows that. Right? "We're just pulling up to the ferry now. Call if you need anything, and I know you'll do fine with Madelyn."

At least one of us has faith in me.

"Have a great time," she says her voice rushed.

"You too." The line goes dead and I stare at my phone for a second. Why, all of a sudden, do I have an anxious knot in my gut? Their trip isn't about being away so they can hook me up with Beck and the waterfront boat tour just happened to be the night before they return home from their vacation. Music blares from downstairs and pulls me from my reverie, and I shake off the unease cruising through my veins.

I walk to the stairs, and take a few steps. Beck and Madelyn's voices reach my ears, and my knees go so weak when I see them, I drop down, and sit on one of the steps as he holds her tightly, the two of them singing—okay Beck is singing and what's coming out of Madelyn's mouth is gibberish—as he dances them around the floor, holding one of Madelyn's arms out as he spins her. I grip the handrail, my heart somewhere in my throat as the mean boy from my childhood is having the time of his life with little Madelyn.

Okay, one of two things is going on with me. I either have indigestion, or I'm jealous of a two-year-old, which is insane. It's just that the last time someone held me, danced with me and looked into my eyes with pure adoration was…never.

But I don't want that from Beck… We can't have that, right?

He spots me on the stairs, no doubt noticing the ridiculously jealous look on my face, and turns the volume down. "Hey."

"Hey," I respond, and in an instant, I know…I want more from Beck than I can ever have.

# 12

# BECKETT

After doing an oil change on Mr. Beazley's Honda, I close the hood, wipe my hands on a rag and glance at the clock hanging on the back wall of the repair bay. I've probably looked at the clock fifty times since I first arrived a few hours ago. I'm perfectly confident that Piper and Madelyn are making out just fine, but, and as much as she tried to hide it and assure me they'd be fine, I saw the worried look in Piper's eyes. I hated leaving her worried, but it was too late to call and ask for the night off.

I gave her a complete rundown on Madelyn's bedtime rituals, and she has my number if she needs to call. Hell, I'm only three blocks away, but I don't think she'd call unless it was a real emergency. She wouldn't want me to think less of her if things went south. Not that I would, and not that I think anything will go wrong, but she'd worry about how it looked, nonetheless. I guess I can understand that. Her parents are big on image, and they likely spent their entire life ingraining it into Piper.

She has to walk a fine line, and being seen with me—me going in for a kiss on the sidewalk earlier today—that's not something she can risk. I'm not upset about it. Much. Okay, I might have been for a second, but then I took another second to see things through her eyes, and I get it. I really do. It's a lot harder to be Piper than I ever knew.

My phone pings and I snatch it from my greasy coveralls. My heart lurches when I see it's from Piper, but the second I open the message and see Piper giving me a thumbs up, Madelyn on her lap watching her favorite show, a bowl of popcorn beside them, my heart swells, and a smile I can't control tugs at my lips.

"Do I even want to know?" my boss Ross asks. I laugh. He's a good guy. Married with children. He thinks all the young guys like me are having sex with a different girl every weekend and that I'm currently smiling because chances are some girl sent me a shot of her boobs or something. I admit, it's not out of the realm of possibility and I have received sexy selfies before.... well before I stopped going out all the time, and partying at Storm House.

I hold the phone out to him, and he quickly covers his eyes. "Dude, I'm married."

I laugh. "It's Madelyn."

"Oh, okay." He takes the phone and shakes his head. Madelyn has been by a few times, and she totally loves Ross. It might have something to do with the jar of jellybeans he keeps behind the counter. "She's getting so big." He smiles and adds, "What a cutie."

"Yeah, she is."

I take my phone back and he gives me a playful wink like he's on to me—or on to something—as he nudges me with his elbow. "I'm talking about the girl holding her."

"That's Piper." My gaze moves over her smiling face in the photo, and for a second I almost forget how to breathe. I'm so happy that my girls are doing well. Okay, well they're not my girls. Madelyn isn't even my daughter. But I do take care of her and that accounts for something. I take care of Piper too—in a much different way. Does that account for something? "She's helping me take care of Madelyn this week." I chuckle. "She's a bit nervous, though."

"About time you got yourself the girl you've been pining after. When you first started here, you used to tell me all about your parties, and then nothing. In fact, you've been moping around for months. Glad you finally hooked up with the love of your life. You're in a much better mood now."

I square my shoulders. I've been moping for months? "It's not—"

"You're with her, aren't you?"

"No...I mean yes." I shake my head to get it on right. "I haven't been moping and Piper is just a friend." Friend? That's what we're calling each other now, and that's a surprise considering our past. "She's not the love of my life. We go way back, to kindergarten, actually and I've been busy with school and helping with Madelyn and work. That's why I've not been out partying."

"Yeah, okay," he says, his voice full of disbelief.

"She's a student at the academy. We shared some classes and she's also doing fashion design at the community college." I laugh. "I just modeled the clothes she made for her final assignment." Ross doesn't say anything, instead he stands there and stares at me. "What?"

"Maybe you should make her your girlfriend. You can't seem to stop talking about her."

"Hey, you're the one who brought her up."

"And you're the one who can't shut up." He laughs and adjusts his ballcap and I open my mouth and close it again, not sure how to respond, because he's right, I couldn't shut up. "Just messing with you, bud."

I laugh with him, but it's forced, because the truth is I like thinking about her, and talking about her. I better work on reining that in because this is a hook-up, nothing more.

"If you want to clock out, go ahead. I don't think we'll have any emergencies in the next hour."

While I need the hours, I also want to get home, simply because I want to see Madelyn—and Piper—before they go to bed.

I try to be super casual as I say, "If you're sure."

He gives me a knowing grin, and I just shake my head in response. Clearly, he's on to me. I unzip my coveralls, and shrug out of them, hanging them on the hook before I head to the sink and wash the night's grime off me. I always smell like oil and gas when I get home and tonight, I want to smell nice.

I clock out, and head outside. The sky is dark, and it looks like it might rain, as I hurry down the sidewalk. I left my car at home since the shop is within walking distance. The car seat is also in my vehicle, and not that I thought there'd be an emergency, I figured it was best to leave it behind with Piper just in case.

I open the front door quietly, and when I round the corner and Madelyn comes rushing into my arms. "Beck," she squeals and I take in the mortified look on Piper's face when I spot a whole bowl of popcorn on the floor, and Madelyn's juice cup upside down, the juice spilling everywhere.

"You're early," Piper gasps. The look of failure on her face wraps around my heart.

"Things were quiet." I step closer. "Hey, it's only popcorn and juice."

She digs her front teeth into her bottom lip and crinkles her nose. "Things were going good..."

"Until they weren't." I grin, wanting to lighten her mood and let her know no harm has been done. "Kids," I mutter and scoop up Madelyn. "You know how they are."

"Actually no. I mean, yes. I guess I do now."

"They can take you buy surprise, that's for sure. Remember the time she fell off Kennedy's lap, and ended up in the hospital."

"Yeah, I do. Kennedy was so upset, but it definitely wasn't her fault."

"Agreed." I kick off my shoes. "What happened?"

She laughs and shakes her head. "We were sitting here watching her show, and then a commercial came on with singing and dancing and loud music. She got excited and... things went flying."

"Did I forget to tell you she uses a sippy cup still?"

She points to the end table, where the sippy cup is sitting then points to the glass on the floor. "That was mine. She scared me so much, I jumped and I knocked it over." I try to stifle a laugh, and I pretty much fail. She puts one hand on her hip. "Hey, it's not funny."

"It's a little funny." As she glares at me, pretending to be mad —yes, I see the twinkle in her eyes—I add, "Yes, no, maybe?"

"Beck!"

Madelyn squirms and I check the time. "Leave it, I'll clean it."

She sighs and glances at the soda getting into the cracks on the wood floor. "No, I can do it."

"How about I get this little chicken nugget into her bed, and then we'll clean it together."

Her shoulders sag. "Did you come back early because you didn't think I could hack it?"

I step up to her. "No, I came home because Ross let me go. I could have stayed, but I wanted to be here more."

A smile touches her mouth. "You should have gone into politics. That was totally believable."

I take her hand. "It's the truth."

"It's a good thing I'm not having kids. I'd be a terrible mom."

"Nah, by the end of this stint, you'll be a pro."

"I'm not sure I want to be a pro. Honestly, the kids that stay at the resort...total, privileged monsters."

I laugh. "It's different when you have your own. You'll see."

"Madelyn isn't your own and look at you two. Besides, I'm not sure I want to see, you know."

"Yeah, sure. Parenthood isn't for everyone."

"No offence, Madelyn," she apologizes to the little girl in my arms. Just then, Madelyn squirms to reach Piper. She cups Piper's face and plants a big sloppy kiss onto her cheek. I laugh as Piper's eyes go big.

"I think she likes you."

Piper smiles, all the spills and accidents no longer mattering as she lets out a breath, expelling the stress with it. "Yeah?"

"Yeah,"

*I like you too.*

"I'll be back in a few minutes." I resist the urge to cup her face and plant a big sloppy kiss onto her as well. Later though, I definitely plan to do it later, and it might not be so sloppy. I tap Madelyn on the nose. "Say goodnight to Piper and thank her for watching you."

Madelyn kisses her palm and throws it at Piper. "Night, Pee-prrrr. Tank you."

We laugh at her pronunciation. "You're welcome," Piper responds and throws a kiss back. "Thanks for keeping me company."

We both give her a wave and I carry Madelyn upstairs and wash her face and hands in the bathroom. Teeth brushing is never fun, so that's where my puppet, Gus the Goalie comes in. We have numerous versions of Gus hanging around the place since Madelyn loves him so much and it's great for making her smile.

I pull open the cabinet drawer and grab Gus. Knowing Piper can hear and probably thinks I'm a big goof, I dance and count as she brushes her teeth. When she's finally done, she rubs her eyes, and I scoop her up. She lays her head against my chest and my heart melts. It's moments like these when it cements home that I want a family of my own someday. Piper and I are so different that way, and I can totally see why we have different views.

Piper is quiet downstairs, as I cross the hall, change Madelyn into pajamas, and settle her into her bed. I rub her back and whisper quietly for a moment, and as soon as she settles, I check the monitor, tip toe from her room and close the door. My steps are quiet on the stairs and I peer into the living room as I descend.

I momentarily go still at the sight of Piper kneeling on the floor, working her phone as mounds of paper towel covers the spill. Her head is forward, her hair covering her face, but I don't need to see her expression. Unease and panic radiate from her.

I start to walk again and the bottom step creaks under my weight. Her head lifts and her eyes soften when they meet mine. I crouch down next to her, and wipe up the rest of the spill. "You okay?"

She expels air and waves her phone. "My mother."

"Ah."

"I guess I don't need to say any more, huh?"

"Only if you want to." She stares at me for a second. "What?"

I drop the damp paper towel into the plastic bowl that once held all the popcorn. Her fingers lightly brush mine, and there's a warmth about her when she says quietly, "How did I not know..."

"How did you not know what?"

She frowns and opens her mouth, and when her phone pings again, whatever it was she was going to say to me dies an abrupt death. "She's not happy," she says almost to herself.

"I'm sorry, Piper. It kind of sucks that you're not excited to return home."

"I don't want to sound like I'm complaining. It's just...as much as I'm worried about doing the right thing with Madelyn, this is probably the first time in my life I actually had a vacation. No school, no work, no one expecting anything from me...I mean, Madelyn is my responsibility, but—"

"I understand."

She eyes me, her look conveying doubt, and why wouldn't they? She knows how I feel—felt—about her. That she was simply a pampered princess, living her best life.

"Yeah," she whispers, leaving it at that.

I inch backward until I'm pressed against the sofa, and tap the floor beside me. She moves in next to me, and I grab my phone and turn on some tunes, keeping the volume low so we don't disturb Madelyn.

We fall quiet, lost in our thoughts for a moment and I break it with, "On snow days, when I was sound asleep in bed, you worked, didn't you?"

Her brow is furrowed, when she turns to me. "Yeah, why?"

I shrug. "Summer vacations, when I was fucking around at the lake, and jumping off bridges into the river, you were working, weren't you?"

"Yes, but—"

"Family dinners. Did you just scoff some food down from the resort's restaurant?"

She makes a sound, a snort of sorts. "It's not as bad—"

"I know it's not. I'm not saying it is. I worked too, but it was when I was older. I helped my brother out at his garage."

"Your dad worked in the coal mines, didn't he?"

"Yup, just like his dad and his grandfather before him. They wanted something better for all of us. Coal mining." I shake my head. "Nasty business. My older brother is a mechanic, and I'm the hockey player. They all helped out to get me here, so I do understand obligation."

She nods. "I know you do."

"But for these next few days, why don't we just have some fun, do the things you missed out on growing up? You can sleep in, do fun things..." I nudge her. "Do risky things." She smiles at that.

"I'm not leaving all the babysitting responsibilities to you. You're holding down two jobs as it is."

He shrugs. "Things slow at the campus cafeteria in summer, and taking care of Madelyn, that's no hardship at all. It's fun and as far as you doing all the things you missed out on, the three of us can all eat as a little family." An idea hits. "Hey, after you go back home, maybe you can come to Sunday dinner at my mom's place. It's noisy and chaotic, and—"

"Wonderful?"

"Yeah, wonderful," I say, missing everyone. It's a little sad that she resents going home when I can't wait to get there. She frowns, like Sunday dinner at my place is a really bad idea. While she's probably right, I don't give a shit. Surely to God, she can sneak away for one night without her parents knowing, and enjoy a good old fashioned, loud and rambunctious Moore family Sunday dinner.

I stand and pull her to her feet when a slow song comes on. I wrap my arms around her and dance, holding her one arm out the way I did with Madelyn. She seemed to like that so much, why not do it with Piper?

She laughs quietly. "Are you going to sing to me too?"

"Sure, I could. But I'd prefer to take you upstairs, put my cock in you, and listen to you sing out instead."

"I think I might love that idea." I pull her onto my hips and she wraps her legs around me.

*I think I might love you...*

Wait, what?

# 13

# PIPER

I wake to the sound of Madelyn chattering quietly to herself in her bedroom, and I turn to find Beck fast asleep. He carried me to his bed last night, and after we made love—I mean had incredible sex—I fell asleep next to him, our bodies entwined all night.

My heart beats a little faster as I take in his mussed hair, his hard gorgeous body, but he's so much more than something pretty to look at. Last night, when we sat on the floor together, it occurred to me that there was so much more to him than I knew. Don't get me wrong, I liked him back in high school for a reason. I'd seen the way he was with his family and friends. When he cares about someone, he really goes out of his way to show it. I don't think I've ever met anyone like him.

But I guess I just never knew how incredible he really was. God, that night of my seventeenth birthday party. If only he'd shown up. Maybe things could have gone down so differently. Maybe we'd be a couple today. Up until that night, he'd talk to me in the hall, or in class, but afterward...nothing.

What did I ever do to him?

Honestly, I'm not sure I'll ever know. I don't want to bring it up, and relive old painful memories. I'm sure he doesn't either and from the looks of his naked body next to mine, we've moved past our teenage years.

I slide from the bed, not wanting to wake him, and pull on my metaphorical big girl panties. If he was good enough to come home early last night and get Madelyn off to bed, the least I can do is get her up and make us all breakfast. That what I'm good at. From laundry to the kitchen, I've pretty much worked in every position at the resort, helping out where I was needed, which has given me valuable life skills. Beck is sort of a jack of all trades himself. I guess maybe we're a little more alike than I ever thought.

I tug on the clothes I wore yesterday and sneak to the door as I think about last night, and Beck's invitation to have a family dinner at his place. I'd love to do that. Just once I'd love to sit around a big table, and listen to a happy family talk about their day. At least that's what it's like on television. I really don't know what they talk about. Seriously though, while it was a nice offer, I probably won't be able to get away from the resort, and my parents...well, they wouldn't like it one little bit.

*What would you like, Piper?*

I open Madelyn's door, and the big smile she gives me curls around my heart and hugs tight. For the briefest of seconds, I was worried, thinking she might not remember me, or maybe even be frightened that it's not her mother or father, or Beck collecting her.

"Good morning, Madelyn."

She kicks her blankets off and shows me her hockey puppet. I put it on, and try to be as goofy as Beck, but she stares at me like I'm an idiot, and I probably am.

"How about some pancakes?" I ask.

"Pan-sakes!" she belts out loudly and I put my finger to my lips.

"Shh."

She does the same and it makes me laugh. I quickly cover my mouth, and giggle. She does the same. Who knew children liked to parrot everything?

"Come on, kiddo." She holds her arms out and I pick her up. She's heavier than she looks. I take her to the bathroom to clean her up. I show her the toothbrush and she frowns.

"Okay, maybe I'll leave that to Beck," I murmur to myself. I don't want her to hate me. Downstairs, I set her down and she tugs on the fridge door. I help her with it, and she reaches in to pull out the apple juice. Before she drops it, I help her with that too. Who knew two-year-olds were so damn independent. I grab a clean sippy cup, and fill it. "Want to help with the batter?"

She nods and I pull a chair up to the counter, and she climbs onto it. I give her instructions, and she helps stir as I pour water into the mix.

"Madelyn, you are doing a great job."

She blows me a kiss, and I laugh as I catch it. "Okay, now I'm going to use the stove, so you'll have to sit at the table, okay?" I'm about to glance around. I'd seen some blocks around here last night, and hopefully they'll occupy her while I cook. I turn, and find a very sexy, barefoot man leaning against the doorjamb watching us, an adorable, yet sexy smile on his handsome face.

"How long were you standing there?"

"Beck!" Madelyn shouts and he crosses the room and scoops her up. She cups his face and kisses him.

"Did you make the batter?" he asks her. She nods and he spins her. "You are the best cook in the whole world."

My heart lodges in my throat as I watch him, and while I like Madelyn, it doesn't mean I want kids of my own, and even if I did want a life with Beck, and he wanted one with me, it could never happen. I'd never keep him from having children of his own. He would come to resent me for it.

"What are you doing up so early?" he asks me, leaning in to kiss me on the mouth, like couples do. We're not a couple, though, but after what we did last night in bed, I like the early morning greeting.

"I heard Madelyn and thought I'd make us breakfast."

"You're supposed to be on vacation."

I laugh and glance at the clock. "This is much later than I'd get up at the resort and it's...fun."

He smiles at me. "Good."

I point the spatula at him and say, "I was thinking maybe the three of us could go to the pool. Do you think Madelyn would like that?"

"Ask her."

"Oh, okay. Madelyn, would you like to go for a swim at the pool?"

"Wimmm," she blurts out and Beck laughs.

"I think that's a yes."

I smile, happy that I got something right. "Okay, pancakes up in five." I give him a pleading look. "Can you start on the coffee?"

"I'm on it."

He sets Madelyn in her booster seat, gives her some toys to play with and makes the coffee. Every few seconds he brushes against me, and a jolt of pleasure goes through my body. I grin at him and when his phone pings, he frowns.

"Everything okay?"

"Yeah, it's Dryden, asking if I want to hang out today." His frown deepens. "That's weird."

"Why is it weird?"

"Didn't Alysha go back home to the Hamptons after finals?"

"Yeah, she did."

"I wonder why Dryden is still here and why he wants to hang out with me. We don't really do much outside of hockey."

"Maybe he's lonely and looking for a friend. Should we ask him if he wants to join us at the pool?"

"No, I don't think that's quite his speed." He grabs two mugs from the cupboard. "Most of the guys moved out of the dorm already."

A lightbulb goes off in my head. "I think I remember Alysha mentioning that he was moving out of the dorm and staying in her room at our apartment."

He stiffens. "Are you serious? Did she clear that with you?"

"I think I said yes. Oh, God, I completely forgot about it until now. I was busy with studying and getting my clothing assignment finished for design class." I suck air in between my teeth. "I should text Alysha." I snatch my phone off the counter and send off a message. She quickly replies that he's only going to be at the house for a few days, while I'm staying at Kennedy's. I breathe out a sigh of relief as I show Beck the text. "I guess I had nothing to worry about, and really, I'm not even going to be there while he is. That could have been awkward. We're not really friends."

"Yeah, but it's all your furnishings and things in the place, and you don't want him throwing parties."

"You're right, I don't. Let me send Alysha another text." I fire off another text and she responds that he's going to be on his best behavior.

I show the text to Beck and he narrows his eyes as I go back to tending to the pancakes. "Has he...been in contact with you?" He shrugs. "I mean, have you two been hanging out or anything like that?"

I flip the pancakes and grin at him. "Wow, if I didn't know better, I'd think you were jealous."

His head lifts an inch, the muscles along his jaw tightening as he says through clenched teeth. "So what if I was?"

Okay, I didn't expect that answer, and why does that excite me so much. For clarification, I ask, "Are you?"

He takes a fast glance at Madelyn, who isn't paying us any attention and drags me to him. His mouth is near my ear, his breath hot on my neck and he says quietly, "While you're here with me, and we're fucking, I don't want to share you, okay?"

I nod, and swallow as my throat tightens at his possessiveness. I've never been into possessive guys before—I don't condone behavior that can lead to dangerous aggression—but there's something nice about him not wanting to share me, and I don't think that he's an insecure or a vengeful kind of guy.

"I don't want to share you either," I tell him, honestly.

"Good. Now flip."

Heat rushes through my body, and I croak out, "Flip?"

His grin is wild and wicked, and I'm guessing I gave him the reaction he was hoping for. "The pancakes, they're burning."

I laugh and flip the pancakes as he grins, knowing my mind went back to last night to when he suggested I flip so he could take me deeply from behind. My knees weaken just thinking about it, but now is definitely not the time to be thinking about that.

"Are we breaking into the pool, or is there a family swim?" Beck asks as he grabs the plates.

"It's not breaking in when you have your own key, remember?" I don't know why, but I feel less ashamed about having my own key. Maybe I think Beck knows me a little better now, and hopefully has a different opinion of me. "Are you going to spend any time with Dryden today?"

"No, I messaged him back that I was busy. I thought we'd just hang out." He looks out the window, as rain begins to pelt against the windowpane. "A good day to nap and read, and really, we don't even have to go to the pool if we want to get soaked. We just have to stand outside."

"Madelyn will like it, though." I plate Madelyn's pancake, and Beck pours syrup on it, and lets it cool a bit as he cuts it into bite-sized pieces. I never even would have thought of that. God, I would have given it to her whole and she probably would have choked half to death on it. I have so much to learn, but I know I'm in good hands with Beck.

I plate the rest of the pancakes and we all sit at the table and eat. I smile. This is so nice. Nowhere to rush off to, no resort client needing this or that. I could get used to this and as nice as it would be to spend the summer here with Beck, it's impossible.

"Yum, yum," Madelyn shrieks, and I laugh before taking a big sip of coffee.

I wave my mug at Beck before I set it down. "I'm going to need about eight more of these."

"Didn't get enough sleep?"

I grin at Beck. "I'm not complaining."

"It's a rainy day, later we can read and nap."

"You were serious about that?"

"Yeah, Madelyn loves to read, and we can build a fort, and even nap in it." I smile as my mind drifts. "Have you ever built a fort, Piper?" He must know by the look in my eyes that I'm not one hundred percent sure what defines a fort. "You know, pile blankets and pillows over furniture."

I look down, sheepishly. "Do making beds in a resort room count?"

He laughs but there's a measure of sadness in there for me too. "Madelyn, do you want to show Piper how to build a fort later?" She giggles and nods. "I'll show her how to nap in it, since that's the area where I excel."

I laugh this time and take another big drink of coffee. I take a glance at my watch. "We should get a move on before the pool opens to the general public."

Beck gathers up the dishes. "We can do these later. Lazy Sundays are for letting dishes pile up."

My palms itch to do them. At home I was never allowed to leave dirty dishes in the sink. Everything had to be white glove clean, even in our own house, which was right beside the resort, in case a guest needed something and came over.

"I'll get Madelyn ready, and grab her life jacket from the garage."

I poke him in the chest as he sets Madelyn on the floor and tells her to go to her room to find her bathing suit. "Don't forget your bathing suit. You have to wear one this time."

A boyish grin flirts with the corners of his mouth as he says, "Yes, Mom."

I shake my head and he gives my ass a slap as I walk past him. I yelp and dart up the stairs laughing as he follows behind me. In the master suite, the bed is still untouched—I might have to muss it up before Kennedy and Matt return home—I go through my things.

"Oh no."

"What?" I hear from the doorway.

I shake my head, prepared for some smart-ass comment, especially after telling Beck he had to wear a suit. "I forgot my bathing suit at home."

He simply laughs. "We can stop by your place and grab it. No big deal."

I smile at him. I love his easy-going nature. Once we're all packed with towels, water toys, and lifejacket, we buckle Madelyn into her car seat. Correction: little miss independent works to shove our hands away and buckle herself in. Was I that independent at two?

Rain pelts on the window, and thunder rumbles in the sky as we drive the short distance to my place. I glance at Beck, and while I never loved rain, it's so darn cozy in the car with him and Madelyn, it wraps around me like a warm blanket and I smile. He casts me a glance and instead of asking what I'm smiling about, he reaches for my hand and gives it a little squeeze. Need zings through me and settles on the left side of my chest like he's actually cocooning my pounding heart in his strong palm.

He pulls into my driveway. "I'll just be a second."

"I could go." His voice is raspy, his frown deep.

I grin at him. "I'm not sending you to my room to look through my underwear drawer."

He doesn't laugh. "What if Dryden is in there?"

"I'm sure he is, but I'm also sure he's probably still asleep in Alysha's room."

"He texted me this morning, so he's not sleeping."

"I'll be in and out in a second. Even if he is in there, it's no big deal."

"What if he sees me out here waiting for you?"

"He knows we're babysitting." I glance at Madelyn and choose my words carefully. "He doesn't know we're...you know."

"Yeah, I know." He scrubs his face, and I'm getting the sense he's not too sure about Dryden. Maybe there's some competition there since they're both goalies.

"Be right back." I tug up the hood on my rain jacket and dart to the steps. I slide my key into the lock and the second I enter. My steps slow as a strange sensation overcomes me. I don't want to call out and wake Dryden if he's sleeping, but from the way the hairs on my neck are standing up, it's clear someone doesn't feel right to me.

I set my keys in the bowl by the door. It's a habit I'd gotten into after losing my keys so many times and walk quietly through the foyer to the stairs. I ascend quietly, avoiding all the creaking steps and go to my room. I glance at my bedroom door, which is cracked open. I stand still for a second. I'm sure I closed it tight when I left, some part of my subconscious remembering Alysha's cousin was going to be staying here.

I step inside and while nothing is out of place, everything feels...disturbed. Surely to God, Dryden didn't go through my things. I glance over my shoulder. Okay, I'm just being silly here. I need to get my suit and get back to the Jeep.

I step up to my drawer and pull it open. I root through my things, searching for one specific bathing suit, and when I find it, I pull it out. I turn, ready to head back to the car, and nearly jump ten feet in the air, when I spot Dryden standing at my door, blocking my path.

"Dryden," I say, my voice breathless. For a second I thought it was Beck. They have the same build and same color hair, and while others might think they look alike, to me they really don't. "You scared me."

He grins, and leans against the doorjamb. His body language showcases confidence, a man who won't be easy to move.

"I was just leaving. I'm heading to the pool."

"Sounds like fun."

I take a step toward him, but he doesn't budge. "If you'll excuse me."

"How's the babysitting going?" he asks, keeping the conversation going, like he's not ready for me to leave.

"Good," I say and take another small step but he's either not reading the room or choosing to ignore it. This time he takes a step toward me and glances at the suit in my hand. "I messaged Beck this morning. I guess he's going swimming with you, huh?"

"We're taking Madelyn."

He glances down, his shoulders sagging slightly. "So, are you two a thing now?"

"We're friends."

A big smile lights up his face. "Oh, great. If you two are just friends, I was thinking maybe you and I can catch a movie sometime. The drive-in in the valley is opening next weekend."

I find it so strange that he's all of a sudden showing interest in me, even staying at my place. He barely looked at me before...well, before Beck and I started hanging out. Is this one of those situations where I'm worthy of his attention now because one of the guys on the hockey team likes me.

Not in a girlfriend sense, but I've been Scotia Storm hockey player approved?

"I probably won't be here next weekend. I'm heading back to Cape Breton Island for the summer."

"Oh, I didn't realize. Alysha said you'd be going back some-time after finals. I didn't know it would be so soon."

Something niggles at me, and I remember Alysha told me he'd only be here for a few days. "When do you go back?"

"I haven't decided yet." He smiles at me. "I'll stay here for a bit and see what Halifax has to offer this summer." I nod and he continues with, "Maybe we can do something through the week. Alysha told me you liked art and that Van Gogh exhibit is in town right now."

"I really do want to see that. I just don't have time."

I take in the sad look on his face and my heart squeezes. Maybe he really is lonely, now that school is over for the summer, and his cousin went back home—as did most of the guys on the team.

"Think about it?"

A sound catches my attention and I look past his shoulders, and spot a very possessive Beck standing in the hall, his big body tense. "Ready?" Beck asks.

Dryden head spins so fast, I'm sure it's going to pop off his shoulders. "Hey Beck," he says and holds his fist out for a bump and Beck half-heartedly gives him one. "Are you ready?" Beck asks again his eyes on me. I step around Dryden, and Beck turns sideways to let me pass.

"Catch up with you later, Piper," Dryden calls out.

Beck goes still, his body hard, like he's ready for a fight. "Head out to the car," he tells me as he hands the keys. "Madelyn is inside, and it's locked."

I hesitate for a second. What is going on with the two of them? I'm not sure, but I didn't like the way Dryden made me feel like a trapped animal.

I take the keys and head outside, climb into the passenger's seat and wait. A few minutes later, Beck comes out, his features hard, his eyes dark and ferocious. He slides in next to me, and says nothing as he backs out of the driveway. He puts the car into drive and casts me a glance.

"What happened?"

## 14

## BECKETT

I take a deep breath and let it out slowly, working to calm the twitching nerves in my body. Honestly, if Dryden likes Piper and she likes him there isn't a damn thing I can do about it.

"I told him you weren't his type," I admit. God, I'm a fucking asshole. Right after I told him to forget about Piper, he stood there staring at me, a challenge in his eyes. I don't know what the fuck his problem is—or what's suddenly gotten into him —but now he seems all that much more interested in Piper and quickly pointed out that she'd just told him we were nothing but friends. He's right, and that's the label we put on this, which is a far cry from the enemies we've been since high school.

Her eyes are wide, and not only does she look mortified, she looks hurt. She swallows, and clasps her hands tightly. "Why would you tell him that?" she asks, her voice an octave higher. "Actually, what do you mean? Why aren't I his type?"

"I just meant that you two...that you were..."

"I was what, a pampered princess?" Her eyes grow watery, and I could punch myself in the face right now.

"No, that's not what I meant." Desperate for her to understand that this is about me, and not her, I have no choice but to be completely honest here, even if it makes me look like a possessive asshole. "I overstepped, I'm sorry. It's just that we said for the next week while we're living under the same roof and babysitting—"

"We wouldn't see other people," she says, her voice a little softer, understanding brimming in her eyes as she finishes the sentence for me.

I scrub my chin and flick on my signal. "It wasn't fair of me. If you want to see Dryden..." Fuck, what am I saying? I hate the thoughts of them together. Dryden has always been nice to me, and a good team player, but lately, I don't know, I haven't been getting good vibes, and that could simply be because he's interested in Piper and I don't like it.

"Remember when you said I never had to do anything I didn't want to do?" I nod, and she continues. "I didn't have to agree to it, Beck. I wanted to."

My heart thumps a little harder. "Yeah?"

"Yeah, I don't want to be with anyone else while we're sharing a house. Honestly, I don't even know Dryden, and I'm not interested in him." I grip the steering wheel, and try not to smile like the village idiot. "Now can we enjoy this rainy day with a swim, a blanket fort and..." she stretches her arms as she stifles a yawn. "...a nap."

I laugh, the heaviness leaving my shoulders as I take a sharp left and pull into the empty lot at the pool. "You got it," I say and without thinking, I lean over and give her a kiss.

"Kiss," Madelyn says from the back seat and starts kissing her hand and throwing it our way. "Kiss...kiss...kiss."

I adjust the rearview mirror and glance at Madelyn. "We might be keeping this a secret, but someone back there is going to out us," I laugh quietly.

"I guess we need to be careful around her." Piper turns in her seat. "Are you ready to go swimming?"

She throws her arms up. "Wimmm!"

I shake off the unease in my body and grab our bags from the back as Piper unbuckles herself and helps Madelyn. With the rain still coming down, Madelyn reaches for Piper's hand and Piper looks at me with a mixture of surprise and delight. As I look at the two, I could actually imagine Piper with kids someday, doing all the things with her child that she never got to do herself.

"Do you have your phone?" Piper asks as she tugs on her hood and adjusts Madelyn's to keep the cold rain off their faces. Not that it matters, we're going to be soaked in a few minutes.

"Yeah, why?"

"We need to get some pics of Madelyn swimming to send to Kennedy and Matt. They would love it."

"They would." I smile. That's just like Piper, always thinking of others happiness, and forgoing her own. This week though, it's all about her, too. I plan to make it that way. She searches her bag and frowns. "What?"

"My keys, I think they're lost in the bottom of my bag." She digs around. "I'll find them later. I do have a spare, right here." She unzips a small punch and there's a key attached to a clip inside. She unlocks the door and we slip inside the empty pool and I have to say I do like the perks she comes with.

Piper goes into the change room to put her suit on, and I get an excited Madelyn ready and put on her tiny life jacket. She's squirming so hard, it's near impossible to get the thing buckled, and I can't help but laugh at her cuteness. Piper comes out in a one-piece suit that hugs her sweet curves, and I'm not laughing anymore.

"You look great," I murmur.

She points at my jeans and sweater. "You look overdressed."

"That's because I couldn't take my hands off this chicken nugget, or she'd jump in head first. She has no fear."

"Grab your phone, I'll take her in."

I fish my phone from my pocket as she walks Madelyn to the shallow end. They use the stairs to climb in, Piper going first and holding her hand out to Madelyn, who practically throws herself into Piper's arms. Once Madelyn's body is fully submerged, she shrieks and shivers, but it soon passes as Piper lets her go and she begins to kick her legs to get herself in motion. After recording the entire thing, I strip down to my bathing suit, and scream "Cannon ball!" as I jump in, creating a huge splash that leaves Madelyn and Piper's hair and face dripping.

For a second I think that might not have been my best move but as I swim toward them and find them laughing and wiping their faces, I breathe a sigh of relief.

"Are you twelve?" Piper yells.

"On a good day. Come on, Madelyn, let's race Piper to the other end." I grab hold of Madelyn, put her in front of me and push her through the water as I kick my legs hard.

She giggles and laughs and when we make it to the middle of the pool, she screams, "Faster," as Piper yells and tries to catch up to us.

"You guys are cheating," Piper complains, a few feet behind us, even though she could easily catch up. But she's having fun and letting Madelyn win. She'll have this parenting thing down in no time at all.

We spend the next hour swimming and playing until Madelyn grows tired and she's not the only one who's slowing down.

"Who's hungry?" I ask.

"Me!" Madelyn screams.

I gesture toward the locker rooms. "Let's get dried off and get something to eat."

We all climb from the pool, and by the time we dry off and dress, we're all starving. Our movements are slow, lethargic as we head back to my Jeep, and Madelyn fights sleep in her car seat as I drive.

"We wore her out," Piper says quietly.

I grin at her. "Watch this."

I pull into the driveway and kill the ignition and Madelyn perks right up. Piper laughs.

"When I moved in and she fought sleep, I'd give Kennedy and Matt a break and drive her around for hours."

"You're so good to her, Beck."

"I want pizzzzzza," Madelyn yells from the back seat.

Piper frowns. "I don't think that's on the approved food list."

I grin. "I won't tell if you don't."

"It's eleven in the morning. We can't feed a two-year-old pizza at eleven, can we?"

"Oh, Piper. You have so much to learn." I laugh and climb from the car and Madelyn starts clapping, because she knows I'm going to order a pizza, and we're going to eat it in the blanket fort.

I grab our bags with the wet towels as Piper opens Madelyn's door and unbuckles her. On the sidewalk, I glance around, and spot an elderly lady walking her dog. Odd, it feels like someone is watching me.

I shake it off and we head inside. "Do you like Alexandria's pizza?"

"Does it have carbs?" she asks.

"Yeah."

"Then I love it."

I laugh, toss the towels and suits into the washer, and order the pizza as Madelyn takes Piper to the closet where we keep all the fort blankets and pillows, and we head to the living room to make a tent. I put on Madelyn's favorite shark song and Piper looks like she's going to lose her mind after the tenth time it plays.

She puts her hands over her ears, and Madelyn pulls them away and laughs. "I am never going to get this song out of my head."

I wink at her and drop down to tuck the blanket around the arm of the sofa, anchoring it with pillows. "Every time you hear it, you'll think of me."

"No doubt." Piper fixes the blankets over the side chair, and goes down on her hands and knees to spread it out a bit.

"Hey, you say that like it's a bad thing." Madelyn crawls into the tent, and still down on her hands and knees, Piper crawls to me and gives me a sweet kiss.

"No, it's not a bad thing."

"You'll play it back in Cape Breton, when you're missing me."

She arches a brow and I love it when she's playful. "How do you know I'll be missing you?"

"Hey, it's me." I pat my chest. "What's not to miss?" I tease, pretending to be another cocky hockey player.

She whacks me. "That's some ego."

"Piper," Madelyn calls out, and Piper crawls into the tent just as our pizza arrives.

"Be right back."

"I can go splits with you," Piper says, sticking her head out, and I stare at her for a second. She cringes, realizing what she said and how it might make me feel. "I will, after all, be eating half."

"Half?" I cock my head and eye her. "You think you can eat half of an Alexandria pizza?"

"Sure, I'm starving."

"I bet you can't."

She folds her arms and lifts her chin in defiance. God, she's so adorable. "Bet I can."

"It's on," I tell her, pretty sure she'll be full from one slice.

"Wait." She uncrosses her arms, and fluffs up a pillow. "What are we betting on?"

"Indigestion," I say, and she laughs. Madelyn starts laughing too even though she has no idea what we're talking about, which makes her giggles that much funnier. I pull my wallet from my back pocket, and head to the front door.

I pay for the pizza and grab a few of Madelyn's plastic plates from the cupboard. I walk up to the tent and hear the girls whispering and giggling. "Knock knock."

"Who's there?" Piper calls out.

"Pete."

"Pete who?"

"Pete-za-delivery!"

Piper groans and pulls the tent open so I can climb inside. We all sit cross-legged and I hand out the plates. The delicious smell of pepperoni fills the small space as I open the box, and hand out the slices.

"Hey Piper, do you want to hear a pizza joke?"

She arches a brow. "I don't think so."

"Good, because it's too cheesy."

"I do, I do," Madelyn says as she takes a bite, getting sauce all over her cute little face.

"Okay," I begin. "What's a dog's favorite kind of pizza?"

"Do no," Madelyn answers.

"Pupperoni."

Both girls laugh, and the sweet look Piper gives me curls around my heart and squeezes. "You're the corniest guy I know."

"Hey, I resent that comment."

She laughs again and takes a big bite. "Fine, tell me another one."

"More," Madelyn screams.

"Okay, okay. What song does a pizza maker sing?" Madelyn shrugs. "Slice, slice, baby."

Madelyn laughs, even though she has no idea who Vanilla Ice is, and Piper rolls her eyes at me.

"No more!"

"If I don't stop, are you going to give me a pizza your mind?"

"Madelyn, what do you think? Should we vote him out of the tent?"

Madelyn giggles, and picks a big slice of pepperoni off her slice and chomps on it. Her eyes are a bit heavy and it's easy to tell she's fighting sleep. I'll get her down for a nap once we're done here. I wouldn't mind a nap myself.

We finish our slices, and I make a quick trip to the kitchen for drinks and paper towel. I clean Madelyn's face, and she lays on the pillow.

"Time for a nap, kiddo."

"Pee-prrr," she jabbers and pats one side of her. "Beck here."

"I'm game if you are," I say to Piper as she puts her hand over her mouth and yawns.

"You don't have to convince me."

I take all the plates and drink cups and set them outside the tent, and we all snuggle down. Madelyn squirms between us, and I smile at Piper as Madelyn's eyes close. But before she falls asleep, she takes my hand in hers, and then reaches for Piper's with the other. For a girl who claims she doesn't want kids, or a family of her own, she sure does look content and happy as we fall asleep next to Madelyn.

I've always wanted a family, and as I close my eyes, I take a moment to imagine what that family might look like. My eyes fly open as I picture Piper in that scenario. Goddammit, what am I doing? I'm really starting to feel things here, with a girl who's been my enemy for years—a girl whose family hates me, would never let her be with me. A girl who would never stand up to her family and fight for what she really wants.

Which begs the question, what does she really want?

## 15

## PIPER

Where did the days go?

If I had to guess, I'd say it went by in a flurry of fun, daytime activities with Madelyn, and sexy nighttime activities with Beck. It's honestly been the best week of my life, and while I'm excited to go on the wine cruise tonight, I don't want to go, because that means Kennedy and Matt will soon be home, and I'll be on my way back to Cape Breton Island.

My mother has been calling nonstop, telling me how swamped they are now that college is out and summer travel has begun. At one point, I almost suggested hiring on more staff, but kept my mouth shut. Tourism is a hard business; I know that firsthand. I just wish the lion's share of the responsibility didn't fall on my shoulders because Mom and Dad hate working together, and I know the resort, and every department within it, inside out.

"Are you okay?" Beck asks, as he comes into his bedroom, and steps up to me. His arms go around my body, and I meet his gaze in the mirror.

I set my brush down. There's no denying that we've grown closer over the last week, and he's been honest with me, so I say, "Just thinking about the resort." He nods, and goes quiet. "Say it," I push.

He takes a deep breath and lets it out slowly, hugging me a little bit tighter. "Babe, you already know what I'm going to say."

It's crazy how much I like it when he calls me babe. I turn to face him. His arms stay around me, holding me to him. I absorb his warmth and strength as I put my hand on his chest and count the beats of his strong heart. "It's complicated."

"I know."

I blink up at him. "I owe them."

"I know that, too."

I glance at his chest and toy with the button on his shirt, loving the way it hugs his torso and arms. Of course, I also love him in his work coveralls. I took Madelyn to visit him at the service station, and she loved it. No doubt because Ross keeps treats behind the counter. I have to say it's been nice playing house, and it's really started me thinking more about my future. In fact, the more time I spend with Beck, the less accepting I am of following the path that's been laid out for me since birth.

"I don't want to spend the rest of my life working the resort," I blurt out, not telling him something he doesn't already know. "I want to travel, see new things, and someday, open my own clothing store." There's more that I want but that's all I say for now, as I lift my head to see him, not at all surprised at the adoration in his eyes. This man believes in me, believes with all the confidence in his body that I can achieve all those things if I put my mind to it. "I mean, my business degree wouldn't be going to waste. If I ran my own business, I'd want a business background. I think it meshes nicely with fashion design, actually."

He takes a strand of my hair between his fingers. "Is it me you're trying to convince, or yourself?"

"Maybe me."

"Anyone else?" I go quiet and he adds, "Like your parents?" He glances around. "As far as I can tell, they're not here to hear you. Maybe you need to say all this to them when you go home."

"Home...this is home," I say quietly. "Here in the city, this is my home now. It's where I want to be. I don't think I could ever tell them that and let them down."

He lightly runs the back of his knuckles over my face, and a shiver goes through me. I love the way this man touches me, listens to my foolishness, and most importantly, supports that foolishness.

*But is it really foolishness, Piper?*

"You'd rather let yourself down then, huh?"

"Beck..." I lightly hit his chest, and he grabs my hand, brings it to his mouth and kisses it.

"Just think about it, okay? When you're back at the resort, I want you to really think about what you want to do with your life. You have the whole world in your palm, Piper."

"No, I don't."

"Yeah, you do." He runs his finger over my palm. "You just have to open your hands and your mind to it."

Just then the doorbell rings. "That's Serena." He leans in and gives me a kiss. "We can talk about this more later. Let's go have some fun tonight."

I go up on my toes and kiss him before he turns. "I don't want to talk about it later. It's our last night together, and there are other things I want to do."

"Me too, but it's not our last night together, Piper."

"No?" My heart leaps. Is he asking for more? Even if he is, how could we possibly make that happen. Our situation has Romeo and Juliette undertones and look at how that turned out.

"I'm coming to Cape Breton next weekend. I plan to see you then."

"You're really coming?" My heart does a happy dance, although I can't imagine how my parents would react if they saw him at the resort. In their hearts, they believe he's the one who vandalized my car. I don't know why, but I never believed it. Even when he gave me the cold shoulder, didn't come to my party, and acted like I didn't exist—although I can't blame him after my parents accused him of vandalism—I still didn't believe it. Am I naïve? I don't think so, but maybe I am. I have been sheltered at the resort most of my life. I always thought of him as a nice boy who was raised in a nice family, and like me, he wouldn't do anything to disappoint his family. Because of that, somewhere deep inside him, he must understand why I have to take over the family business.

"Yeah, I'm coming," he responds, breaking my thoughts.

"Your family..."

A smile full of warmth and love moves over his face and my heart clenches. "I miss them."

I nod. I miss mine too, I just don't want to take over the business. I wish a trip home was about spending time together, not getting all caught up in the guests, and their needs. And truly, I know Beck is heading home, but I'm smart enough to realize that tonight is probably our last night together. Chances are he'll be busy with his family and catching up with old friends, and that's okay. I don't want to take him away from that and I'll be too busy to see him anyway.

The doorbell rings again, and he breaks from my arms. I turn back to the mirror and take one last look at the coward staring back. I sigh as Beck heads downstairs and opens the door to greet the babysitter. I leave the bedroom, glance in on Madelyn, asleep in her bed, and turn to see the master bedroom. I'll have to put the sheets in the wash just to make it look like I've been sleeping in there.

I stand back a moment and smile, noting the way Serena stares at Beck with pure fascination. I can understand her crush. He has that effect on all the girls. While he might be coming to Cape Breton, I can't let myself get carried away, believing he's coming because of me. No, he's not, and sure, we might be able to have a couple secret hookups. If I was smart, I'd put a stop to it here and now before I get in too deep. Our lives converged in our childhood and in college, but when we're done, he's going one way and I'm going back home.

"Hi Serena," I say, and she turns to me. Her gaze moves over my jeans and little black top.

"I love what you're wearing."

"Thanks."

She lightly touches Beck's forearm. "You look nice too."

He smiles and responds with, "We should be back around midnight."

Serena hugs her hands to her chest. "A wine cruise sounds so nice. I'm jealous." Her nose crinkles. "It's a bit chilly tonight, so be sure to bring a coat."

"Yes, Mom," Beck teases, and she laughs. I laugh to. He's funny and corny and so sweet, and thoughtful, not to mention how good he is with Madelyn. The guy is a real catch and any girl would be lucky to have him.

I grab my light coat from the closet and hand Beck his. We step out into the night, and our two vehicles are in the driveway. "Do you want to walk or drive?"

"It's not that cold, maybe we can walk. If we drove, we'd have to take your car. I can't find my keys. I think Madelyn hid them somewhere."

"She's been having fun. I think she wants to keep you."

*Do you want to keep me?*

"I'll have to find them before I go back to my place on Sunday, and I leave for Cape Breton on Monday."

"We'll search tomorrow." Despite our hook-up being a secret, he takes my hand in his as we walk down the street. I cast him a glance, but he doesn't look back at me.

"I have a spare set at home. I have to go pack up anyway. Let's just hope Dryden is still there to let me in, otherwise, we'll have to break in somehow."

"Not a problem," he says.

"Oh, is that because of your misguided youth?"

He grins at me. "How'd you know?"

"Oh please. You might have a reputation here at the academy as a player, but you were the poster boy for a well-mannered son and a stand-up citizen back home. All the parents loved you."

"Yours didn't." His words come out fast, and without thought, which leads me to believe it's been on his mind, something that has hurt him for a very long time.

"I'm sorry."

He shrugs it off, and as we pass by the service station where he works, there's a dark figure crouched down by a chain link fence. His steps slow, and nervousness grips my stomach.

He must sense my unease because he says, "It's okay. It's Gerald. He's harmless."

"Okay."

"Just stay right here." I nod and he crouches down next to Gerald. I can't hear what he's saying or what Gerald is mumbling. After a moment, Beck picks up some scattered litter and comes back and takes my hand. We walk a few feet and he tosses the litter into a garbage can bolted to a post.

"Is he okay?"

"Yeah, on the way back, I'm going to get him something to eat. Is it okay if we stop at the burger place on Prince Street on our way home?"

Is it okay? Why would he ask that? Oh, maybe because if my parents saw a guy in need they'd go the other way. "Yes, it's fine, but only if I can buy."

He smiles at me. "You want to buy?"

"Yup."

"Okay. If that's what you want."

He puts his arm around me and drags me to him. It's dark out, and while lots of people are milling about, most of those who know us have left the city, gone home or away for work. Chances of anyone discovering we're having a fling is slim, and I'm glad. I don't want to have to explain why we're not together come next semester.

The smell of fresh donuts and Beaver Tails, a Canadian pastry treat, reaches my nose as we hurry along the boardwalk. Waves lap against the docks, and sailboats and speedboats dot the harbor. We reach our destination, and Beck pulls two tickets from his pocket. Twenty minutes later, we're aboard the Murphy Tour Boat. The bottom level has seats with wine and hor d'oeuvres spread out on a board in the shape of Nova Scotia.

I pick up a napkin and small plate. "What a gorgeous charcuterie board."

Beck leans into me. "Back home we call that cheese and crackers."

I shake my head at his joke, and we both fill our plates with the delicious offerings and head to the upper-level viewing deck.

We move to the side of the boat, and look out over the waterfront as we nibble and get ready for the two-hour tour. The captain goes over the safety rules and we set out into the harbor as the tour guide points out all the wonderful sites. We pass George's Island, a small parcel of land located in the middle of the harbor, apparently, it's full of tunnels, and...

snakes. So, I'm super glad we're not stopping there. We look at all the landmarks and the gorgeous mansions along the water. It's interesting to hear the history as we sip our wine and watch the sun dip lower in the sky, touching the horizon. Maybe we can incorporate a cruise like this at the resort.

Stop!

I take a deep breath, not wanting to think about the resort, and let all my worries leave my body as I exhale and lean against the rail to look into the water.

"Careful," Beck warns quietly and puts a stabilizing hand on my back.

I chuckle, loving the way he touches me, and the way he makes me feel safe and secure, like I can handle anything with him by my side.

"When Kennedy first told me about the tickets, she was worried one of us might throw the other overboard," I tell him.

He laughs and takes my empty wine glass from me, setting it on the table. "If only she knew."

"You don't think she knows, do you?"

"What do you mean?"

I shrug. "I don't know. I had this weird feeling she was trying to set us up."

"I'm pretty sure she knows better than that, and Matt would veto the idea if she even suggested it."

I nod, a little less convinced than I was a week ago. "Yeah, you're probably right. Wait," I say and look up at him. "Is that because he knows our history?"

"He doesn't know much."

"You're a private guy, aren't you?" He cocks his head. "I mean, you're kind of like this introvert extrovert."

"I think those mean the opposite things."

A server comes with a tray of wine and we both accept a glass. "I mean, when you're out you're loud and fun, but when you're home—"

Feigning offense, he squares his shoulders and says, "Are you saying when I'm home I'm not fun?"

"No, you're fun, but you keep things to yourself, don't you?"

"Yeah, I guess so. How about you. Did you tell Kennedy about our past?"

"No." I don't like to talk about how he made me feel when we were younger, it's upsetting. "Although..."

He angles his head. "Although what?"

"There was this one night, when Alysha and I were having wine at our place, and maybe I told her some things." I shake my head. "I'm such a lightweight."

"So, you talk about me when you're drinking, huh? Wait, do you talk about me when you're not? Are you unable to stop thinking about me, Piper?"

I laugh, and whack him. "Ohmigod, Beck. That ego." He laughs with me, because we both know he doesn't have an inflated ego at all. He's hardworking, modest, and the sweetest guy I know.

I go quiet and explain, "I sort of told her about my seventeenth birthday party..." I glance at him, waiting for a reaction, and when he braces his arms on the rail, and stares out into the wide-open mouth of the harbor, I add, "And what happened to my car." Again, he remains silent, but I notice the slight tensing of his shoulders, the way he turns his head so I can't see his face, and it's so odd. For the first time in... ever, I think he might know something about my car. But there is no way he did that, right? I didn't believe it before, and now, after getting to know him better, I'm even more convinced he didn't do it. But that doesn't mean he doesn't know something.

"Beck..."

He takes a moment, like he's trying to pull himself together, and then turns his body until our hips are aligned. "Yeah."

A woman behind me laughs and bumps into me, and I smash against Beck, spilling a bit of my wine on him. "Shoot."

"It's okay."

"Oh, dear, I'm so sorry," the woman says, and Beck gives her a nod.

"No harm done," he says, and tips his fingers toward his mouth, gesturing that she might have had too much of the free wine. I stifle a chuckle, and he puts his hand on my waist, turning me to face the water. I take in the lights glistening on the waves as the boat tours around the harbor. Soft music pours from the speaker system, and whatever it was I was going to ask has passed. This is not the moment to bring up old memories and hurts. No, this is the moment to enjoy the here and now.

"My God, this is so romantic." I breathe in the fresh ocean air. "Kennedy would have loved it."

I smile at Beck, take in his body silhouetted in the moonlight. He's close to me, close enough that our bodies are touching, our breaths mingling. "Yeah, she would have. I know I do."

He touches my face, his knuckles rough on my cheeks. "I know what we're doing here is a secret, but I really want to kiss you."

I wet my lips, and his head dips. "That's kind of risky, isn't it?"

He nods, and is about to inch back when I reach for him, and put my hand on his chest. "I'm not a risk taker, Beck."

He nods again and I love that he never pressures me. "I know. It's okay, Piper. Just know, that when I get you alone tonight, I plan on kissing the hell out of you."

"You didn't let me finish."

His brow bunches together. "I'm sorry."

I chuckle. "What I was going to say is I'm not a risk taker, but I like taking them with you." He goes serious, his eyes roaming over my face, a million questions dancing in his eyes, and I answer the one I think he's about to ask. "It's because I feel safe with you."

I hear him swallow over the soft music, and the waves splashing against the side of the boat as the captain cuts through the water.

Without words, he tugs me to him, and his thickening cock presses against my stomach as his lips lightly brush mine, a soft caress that travels through my body and wraps around my heart.

I'm losing myself to this man.

I need to be careful. Jesus, the last thing I need to do is fall for a guy I can't have. A guy who wants different things than I do. But I'll worry about that tomorrow. Tonight could very well be our last night together, and I want to enjoy every second of it.

"You should know. Just because you're kissing me now doesn't mean you still can't kiss the hell out of me when we get home." I go up onto my toes and put my mouth near his ear, my words for him and him alone. "Everywhere..."

He pulls back from me so abruptly, my body stiffens. What the heck? He glances around, his eyes searching, seeking, an almost desperation about him. "What are you doing?"

"Searching for the captain. He needs to dock this boat...now." He winks at me, "I need to get off," he adds, his teasing words reminding me how I used those exact words when I slipped in the snowstorm and landed on his face—and again when I was trying to get my pants off in the bathroom and he stormed in.

God, I'm in real trouble here, aren't I?

# 16

# BECKETT

Piper remains close, a little lost in her thoughts as we all file off the boat and scatter in different directions. Our steps are hurried as we make our way to the sidewalk and head for home. Voices and music from nearby pubs, and outside patios fill the downtown with a lively atmosphere, and in the past I would have been on one of those patios but tonight, I just want to be alone with Piper.

"We still have to get Gerald something to eat," she says as she loops her arm through mine and hugs me tight.

"You remembered."

"Of course." Her eyes are a little glossy beneath the street-lights, and her smile is soft as she gazes up at me, and while we're both anxious to get home, I love that she hadn't forgotten about Gerald. "Do you think he'll still be there?"

"Yeah, but if he's not, I know where to find him."

"Do you...buy food for him a lot?"

"Whenever I can. He's a guy down on his luck. But he's a human being like the rest of us."

She squeezes my arm tighter and I get it. Where she grew up, at an elite resort, she's used to being surrounded by wealthy people. But just because she hasn't seen a lot of poverty or people struggling doesn't mean she's not sympathetic toward them.

We make our way to the burger joint on Prince Street, and it's not too busy. Later though, when everyone comes from the bars, the fast-food places will be packed. Inside the restaurant, Piper glances at me for guidance.

"How many should we get?"

"I usually grab about four. He shares if others are around, or he'll have them tomorrow."

She steps up to the counter, and I check my phone as she orders. I find a message from Matt and let him know we just finished the boat tour and we're on our way home. He messages back, teasing about Piper not throwing me overboard, and I stare at it. Could Piper be right? Are our friend's matchmaking?

"That was Matt checking in," I inform Piper as I slide my phone into my pocket. She nods and holds up the bag.

"Four burgers and some fries."

"Ooh, fries." I try to open the bag, but she hits my hands away.

"They are not for you. Besides we just had wine, cheese and delicatessen meats. You can't be hungry."

"I'm always hungry."

"Okay, fine," she says and holds the bag out to me as we step outside. "You can have fries, but then you probably won't have any room for dessert when we get home."

I instantly get the gist and hold my hands up. "Fries are overrated. In fact, I hate fries and hope I never see one again."

She laughs and nudges me. "Come on, let's go find Gerald." We walk through the dimly lit streets, the sky clear and speckled with stars and find Gerald around the corner from the service station from where I work.

"Wait here."

She shakes her head and keeps hold of the bag. "Can I say hello?"

"Sure, if you want."

I call out to Gerald as we approach, not wanting to startle him. "Hey Gerald, I hope you're hungry. We ordered too many burgers and thought you might like a couple."

A smile lights up his face as he pushes his hood from his head and glances up at me. "Beck," he says. "You're back."

"Yeah, this is my friend, Piper."

He turns to Piper and she squats down and hands him the burgers.

"Bless you," Gerald whispers and when she stands back up, I pull her to me. Gerald opens the bag. "These are my favorite."

"Mine too," I respond.

Gerald pats the ground. "Come sit, have one with me."

I rub my stomach. "No, those are for you. We already ate, and we have to get home. I'm watching Madelyn tonight."

"Be sure to bring her by to say hello soon."

Piper glances at me, surprised that Gerald knows Madelyn. "Okay, Gerald you have a good night." I search for Piper's hand and Gerald grins at me as I capture it.

"You got yourself a good one there, Piper," Gerald tells her, as he unwraps a burger and takes a generous bite.

"I know," she answers quietly, and I give her hand a tug, leading her down the sidewalk. She falls quiet. We both do, and when we reach my place, I use my key to let us in, and find Serena on the sofa, scrolling through her phone.

"How was it?" Serena asks and jumps up.

"It was great," I tell her and Piper nods in response, still quiet, and while I'd like to ask what's on her mind, it will have to wait.

"Ready?" I ask Serena as I open the door to walk her home.

"All set?"

"Back in a sec," I say to Piper and she nods. I tug the door shut and lock it, even though I'm only going a few doors down. "How was Madelyn?"

"Sound asleep. I checked on her a few times, but not a peep."

We walk the few doors down to her house, and I stay on the sidewalk until she's safely inside. Once her door closes, I hurry back to Piper, an odd sensation in my chest. Piper was quiet a few times tonight. When she talked about her seventeenth birthday party and after we left Gerald. Are those things on her mind, or maybe she's thinking this is our last night together? Kennedy and Matt are home tomorrow and yes, I said I was going to Cape Breton, but I'm not even sure if she'll want to see me. I teased about taking risks, and while I really fucking loved how she said she felt safe with me, once she gets home, under her parents' influence, what's going on here will surely be over.

Is tonight our last night?

I step inside the house, lock the door, and listen for sound. When I hear none, I search the main level, but Piper is nowhere to be found. I tiptoe upstairs, peeking in on a sleeping Madelyn and walk by the master suite, and breathe a sigh of relief when I find it empty. I'm not sure why I thought she'd be in there. I just sense a change going on in Piper and I think it's because she's leaving for home after the weekend.

I walk into the bedroom and find her standing at my dresser, combing out her hair. I take in a fast breath as she turns to me, wearing my absolute favorite panties. I read the message on them and let my gaze leisurely stroll back to her face, taking in her full breasts and gorgeous puckered nipples, which are beckoning to my hungry mouth.

"It's not Thursday," I whisper, shutting the door tight.

"I know, but I also know you like cookies." She sets the brush down and her hair falls over her breasts, blocking my view and that just won't do.

"Babe, you taste better than any cookie I've ever put in my mouth."

She smiles and crooks her finger and I shake my head no. She narrows her eyes, which are brimming with curiosity, and cocks her head, waiting for me to continue. "On the bed. Now."

"Oh, I see," she teases playfully. "Tonight is about making me do what you say, payback because I made you walk the runway."

I bite back a grin. I get it. She's reminding me of that exchange because this is what she wants. Okay, if she wants to play, I'll play. "Do you have a problem with that?" Her grin is mischievous, and sexy as she shakes her head, and I start unbuttoning my shirt as she crosses the room and just as she reaches the bed, I order, "Stop." She listens to my command and goes still. "Turn and face me."

Her cheeks are flushed, her chest rising and falling rapidly as she turns around and I toss my shirt on the floor. I take three big steps to cross the room. I stand before her, and move her hair to expose her pert nipples. She stares at me, waiting for my next command, and I know what I want, what I've always wanted, since we were teenagers.

"Touch me."

She puts her hands on my chest and I suck in a fast breath as the heat in her palms curls through my blood and wraps around my cock. "Fuck," I say under my breath, and tilt my head back as she explores my body. Her fingers reach my pants, and she unbuttons them and slides her small hand inside my boxers. She strokes me and I groan as pleasure grips every nerve in my aching body.

She uses the pre-cum to lubricate her hand and when I look at her, she's staring at me, pleasure on her face. "Is this what you wanted?" she asks, her voice thick with arousal.

"Yes."

She rubs the long length of me, and I move my hips and fuck her small palm. But I want her so much that if she keeps it up I'm going to shoot my load off with my pants still on, and there are so many things I need to do to her, that I need her to do to herself.

"Take your hand out of my pants and put it in your panties." Her eyes go wide and her hand stills on my cock. "Do it, Piper." Her chest rises and falls quickly, and from the gleam in her eye, it's easy to tell she's excited by my command.

She swallows and her hand slowly slides from my pants. I stand back a bit as she puts her hand on her stomach, and slowly starts to lower it into the cookie jar. "Touch yourself, babe. Show me what you like."

"You know what I like," she murmurs.

"You're saying you like the way I touch you."

"Yes." Her breath is coming faster now, and while I want to see her fingers on her pussy, watching her hand work inside her panties comes with its own pleasure.

"God, yes," she murmurs, and I put my hand over hers, the thin fabric the only thing separating skin from skin. I find her finger and push it lower, encouraging her to put her finger inside herself, and she catches on quickly.

"Is this what you want?" she asks.

"Babe, it's exactly what I want." I let my gaze move back to her face, and my heart thumps at the sheer pleasure living there. Fuck, I have never wanted anyone more than I want this woman. Her lids fall closed and a murmur catches her throat. I grip her hips and slowly sink to my knees, putting my mouth on her sweet panties to breathe in her aroused scent. My mouth waters for a taste, and I tease the panties down, just enough to see her work her finger in her hot pussy.

I take her small wrist in my hand and tug it and she groans as the movement leaves her body empty, but I plan to rectify that very shortly. I let her hand go and lean in and lick her, savoring the flavor of her juices on my tongue.

"God, you taste good," I moan, and grip her hips again for leverage and bury my face in her. She grips my hair, and her hips rock against my face, soaking me from my nose to my chin and I fucking love how wet she is. I scrape my teeth over her engorged clit, and her entire body trembles, and I'm pretty sure she's seconds from toppling over. Her nails rake my scalp as I push her onto the bed, and as she falls back, I follow the movement, keeping my face buried between her legs.

I slide a finger in, and her moan is deep and guttural, and the second I brush her nerve endings, her body gives way to the pleasure and her muscles clench hard around me.

"Just like that," I murmur, and my dick twitches, aching to be inside, but I am not done having fun with her yet. I stay between her legs until her body calms down, and once she stops trembling, I stand and push my pants to my thighs. She licks her lips and sits up, her eyes on me, like she's waiting for her next command.

"Is there something you'd like me to do?" she asks.

"Down on your knees," I command and her chest rises as she takes in a fast, excited breath. "Keep your legs spread. I want to see your juices drip down your legs."

"Oh my God," she groans under her breath as she drops before me and widens her knees. I bend, and put my hand between her legs, running it along her inner thighs as her juices drip. "So, fucking sweet." She blinks rapidly. "Open your mouth." Her gorgeous lips part, and I push my finger inside. Instinctively, she sucks and my dick throbs and jumps, bouncing off my forearm.

She inches her head back until my finger sits on her bottom lip. "If you want, you can put your cock in my mouth."

Jesus. I nearly shoot off at the innocent way she's on her knees staring up at me. "You want my cock in your mouth, Piper?" I take my dick into my hand and stroke it, and her breath rushes out of her mouth. I reach down and lightly rub her breasts. Those are definitely going to need my attention tonight.

She parts her lips to let me know what she wants, and I step up to her. "Stick your tongue out, and don't do anything else."

Her pretty pink tongue snakes out and she balances on her knees, waiting for me to do whatever the hell I want to. I inch closer, and lay the tip of my cock on her hot wet tongue as I stroke myself, until pre-cum spills from the tip. Jesus, I have never seen anything sexier, and the way she's wide open for me, trusting me with her body, and knowing I'd never do anything she didn't want me to do, fills my heart with so many unnamed emotions.

Her eyes are glossy, so much arousal and pleasure there as my cum sits on her tongue. I pull my dick back. "Swallow," I whisper, and she runs the cum on her tongue over her top and bottom lip before pulling her tongue back into her mouth to drink me in.

Lips wet with my cum, she holds her tongue out again, and this time I put my cock into her mouth. She does nothing but sit there waiting for my command, and I really love this game we're playing.

"Suck my cock, babe. Take me as deep as you can." She leans forward and relaxes her throat and my God, I go deeper than I ever have been before, but it doesn't matter when it comes to her, I can't get deep enough.

I simply can't get enough, and that's fucking insane.

She puts her hand on my hips and rocks into me, and my dick throbs as she sucks and licks and does the most magical things with her mouth. I'm so close, so fucking close, and I'm not ready to lose it. I lightly tug on her hair, and my dick pops from her mouth.

"On the bed."

She sits on the bed, and keeps her legs wide open, and the sheen of her arousal on her legs totally turns me on. I step up to her, take her hands and put them on the sides of her breasts until they form a nice tight channel.

Her breath comes fast when she glances up at me. "I've never done this."

I touch her cheek, run my thumb over her flushed face. "Do you want to?"

She nods and I pump my cock until my pre-cum drips onto her gorgeous tits and provides lubricant. "Mouth open," I command. I slide my dick between her tits and watch intently. Each upward thrust ends with her hot wet tongue on the tip of my crown, and while I want to fill her throat with my cum, if this truly is our last night together, I want my cock inside her.

I fuck her like this for a few more minutes, wanting her to experience so much, and then I step back, grab a condom, and quickly sheathe myself.

She moves to the middle of the bed, and I climb over her. I don't know what the rest of the summer brings, or if she wants to end things when she leaves, but tonight...she's all mine.

# 17

# PIPER

A noise downstairs, the sound of a door opening, I think, pulls me from my very deep sleep. My heart starts racing as I sit up, and glance around. I swipe the fog from my eyes and see that it's far too early in the morning for Kennedy and Matt to be home. Is someone breaking in?

I nudge Beck and he stirs. "Come back to sleep," he murmurs.

"Beck, I think someone is downstairs."

He goes perfectly still for a second, and then when his brain registers what I'm saying he throws his blankets off, jumps up and tugs on his jeans. "Wait here."

I nod and scramble for my clothes, tugging on last night's pants, top and underwear, in case I have to grab Madelyn and get somewhere safe. He tiptoes from the bedroom, and the mumbled voices from downstairs reach my ear as the steps creak. A moment later, I hear Beck, and he's telling whoever it is downstairs, he was about to get a hockey stick across the head. That's when I realize it's Matt down there.

I hurry to the door, peek out, and when the coast is clear I dart into the master suite, climb into the bed and muss the sheets up as best I can.

"We didn't mean to wake you guys," Kennedy says. "We decided to get an early start home and we took the bridge instead of the boat and the roads were quiet. Go on up back to bed."

"Nah, I'm up now."

"Did we wake Piper?"

I stop breathing, waiting to see how he responds. Is he going to tell them I was the one who woke him, because I was sleeping next to him? A beat of silence and then he speaks.

"I don't think so. Hey, let me help you with the luggage." I hear a handle being extended and the wheels rolling on the floor. Kennedy asks about Madelyn, and how our week went, and then their voices fade as they head into the kitchen. I tug the blankets up to my chin, and try to regulate my breathing, as I try to decide how long I should pretend to be asleep.

Fortunately, Madelyn wakes up, and I jump up, and head into her room to get her. I meet Kennedy in the hall, who seems surprised to see me. Or maybe she's surprised to see me coming from her room. No. No. No. She was not matchmaking. She's just surprised I'm awake is all—and fully dressed.

"Hey," I say and put my arms around her for a hug. "You look so well rested. The vacation did you good."

"It was amazing. I owe you big time for helping Beck with Madelyn."

I bite my tongue before I tell her I probably owe her, since I've had the best sex of my life for the last week. "No, you don't. Madelyn is a sweetheart, and I loved taking care of her."

"Oh, really. You're not still terrified of her?"

I chuckle. "If you thought I was terrified of her, why did you ask me to watch her?"

"Like I said, I needed someone Beck wasn't interested in, so he wouldn't get distracted."

"You know, even if it was someone he was interested in, it still wouldn't have distracted him." My God, look at me coming to his defense. "He's very responsible and he loves Madelyn like she's his own."

Kennedy smiles, and I'm not sure if it's because she loves the relationship Beck and her daughter have, or if it's because I jumped to his defense. Madelyn cries out again and I'm grateful for the distraction.

"Matt put on coffee. Go on down and have a cup. I'll get Madelyn. I'm dying to surprise her."

"Okay."

She puts her hand on Madelyn's door and I head down the steps, a huge smile tugging at my lips when I hear Madelyn screech at seeing her mother, and Kennedy nearly crying as she gets her arms around her daughter. I absolutely love it, and yes, I am a little envious at what they have. I'll get a hug when I get home tomorrow, but then it's straight to work. What would it be like to have my own child who I could love, and hug daily, and raise and encourage them to do whatever they wanted to do in life?

I reach the kitchen and the guys turn and smile. Matt jumps up and throws his arms around me. "Thanks, Piper. Beck says you did so much for Madelyn, especially when he had to go off to work."

"It was my pleasure. Madelyn is a dream." I'm about to go grab a coffee when Beck stands, pours me a mug and slides it in front of the empty chair. I smile at him and try to keep my mind off all the wonderful things we did in his bed last night.

"Do you hear your daddy?"

Kennedy's voice fills the hallway as she carries a squealing Madelyn into the kitchen and the smile of Matt's face fills my heart with want. I turn to see Beck, and we stare at one another for just an extra second as Matt scoops his daughter up and spins her around. After everything Matt and Kennedy had gone through, it's nice to see them so happy. I sip my coffee and join in the conversation as it turns to our boat tour last night, and soon the morning is slipping by, and I have laundry and a ton of things to do before I hit the road tomorrow.

I lift my arms up and stretch. "I should get going. I head back tomorrow and still have a lot to do to get ready."

"Oh, you don't want to stay for lunch?" Kennedy asks.

"No, thanks though."

"But you're still coming back the beginning of July for your birthday party, right?"

"You don't have to—"

Kennedy exchanges a look with me that says I'll need the break from the resort by the end of June, and she's not wrong. "It breaks up the summer, and gives us all reason to get together before we're swamped in our last year at the academy."

"What's going on?" Beck asks, clearly in the dark.

My eyes meet his. "Kennedy is having a birthday party for me."

His entire body stiffens. "Oh, I had no idea." His head rears back a bit, like someone might have actually slapped him. I still—ridiculously—feel the sting of his hurt when he shunned me all those years ago.

"Sorry. I thought I mentioned it to you," Kennedy says. "We're going to do a Hawaiian luau party."

Beck snorts to himself. "What?" I ask.

"Nothing, just you always wanted to go to Hawaii."

I blink up at him. Honestly, I didn't even know he knew that.

"I invited everyone...Daisy, Brandon, Sawyer, Chase and..."

I'm happy to hear she's invited all our friends. Goodness when was the last time I'd seen Daisy, Brandon, or Sawyer and Chase? Daisy has been spending all her spare time studying to take her medical college admissions test. With the way she cares about others, she'll be a great doctor. She loves hockey, but her heart is in medicine. I smile as Kennedy finishes listing off the people, and turns to Beck.

"You're coming of course, Beck," Kennedy says breezily. "I mean if you're still in the city and aren't working that night."

He shrugs. "If I'm invited."

Okay, what a strange thing to say. Kennedy whacks him. "Why wouldn't you be invited?" He doesn't answer, he just shrugs again.

"I guess I should get going," I pipe in to break the sudden, awkward silence, or maybe it's not awkward to anyone but me.

"What about your keys?" Beck asks.

"Shoot, right. I haven't been able to find them." I snatch my purse up off the counter and check it. "I have a spare set at home." I turn to Kennedy and explain how Dryden has been staying there in Alysha's room, and he should be able to let me in. She has the strangest look on her face, like she too thinks that's odd.

Beck stands up. "I'll walk you."

"No," I blurt out quickly, my protest too fast and too loud judging by the three sets of eyes staring at me. "I'm just around the corner. You stay and enjoy the rest of your morning. I'll get my things together and I'll be back down to give Madelyn a hug before I go." Feeling a little raked out and hollow inside, I rush up the stairs and start packing my bag. I stuff everything inside, and stop when a noise reaches my ears. I turn to find Beck standing in the doorway, dressed only in his jeans.

"Are you okay?"

"Yeah, just a lot to do."

He takes a step toward me, his eyes roaming over my face, full of concern. "You sure you don't want me to walk with you and help you look for your keys?"

"I'm good." He extends his arm and his fingers brush mine. Warm sensations trickle through my body and curl around my heart. God, what am I doing with Beck? What have I gotten myself into? This was just a game, right? Sex. He's not asking for more and even if he was, how could we possibly survive when my life is in Baddeck, Cape Breton, and his will be on the road? Don't even get me started on how much my parents hate his family, and I have no doubt his hate me, too.

"I'm asking." I smirk, needing desperately to lighten things.

He angles his head. "Asking what?"

I grin. "You once told me if I wanted to cop a feel, all I had to do was ask, so I'm asking."

He laughs out loud. "Permission granted."

I reach around him and pinch his ass and he shakes his head. He looks like he's about to pull me to him, but his hands remain at his side as the staircase creaks.

"I'll be back to get my car after I find my keys."

"Okay," he says and leaves the master suite, his footsteps loud as he heads downstairs, taking the steps two at a time. I go to the bathroom and gather my things, and leave my luggage at the front door. I give Madelyn a hug. "Back in a few minutes."

I head outside, and the days are growing warmer and warmer. I breathe in the fresh air, and note the gorgeous blossoms on an apple tree on someone's front lawn. I get closer to my place, and worry gnaws at me. How will I get inside if Dryden isn't there, and while I really hate the idea of him being in my place, I also hope he's not gone yet.

I walk up my steps and try the door, happy to find it locked. I peer into the window, and the place is quiet. At least he hasn't been having parties. I spot my keys on the side table by the door, right where I tossed them the day I stopped to get a bathing suit. I knock, and wait, and glance around the neighborhood wishing I'd left a spare key with a neighbor. The door opens and I spin back around, coming face to face with Dryden, dressed only in his boxer shorts.

"Hey." He yawns and rubs his hand over his chest, his eyes glazed like I'd just woken him.

"I'm glad you're here."

His grin is cocky. "Yeah?"

I get it, a lot of girls love him. Heck, they throw themselves at him, at all the hockey players, and he's used to being adored. I guess he must think I'm one of his groupies, and honestly, I still can't understand his sudden interest in me when he can have anyone. I'm not really his type.

I nod toward the table where my keys are sitting, feeling like a stranger in my own house. "I left my keys here and had no way to get in."

He backs up and makes room for me to enter, but not enough that I don't have to brush against his near naked body. I snatch my keys up and give them a shake. "I need to go get my car."

He leans against the doorframe, like he has all the time in the world. "You're coming back to stay here?"

"I'll be here tonight, doing laundry and packing. Um...how long are you staying in Alysha's room?"

"I'm here until tomorrow."

I breathe a sigh of relief, knowing he's not going to be in my place much longer, but that relief is short-lived when I realize we'll both be here tonight. I'll be busy though and going to bed early so maybe we won't even cross each other's path.

"I uh...have to grab something in my room." I dart upstairs, and enter my room and the hairs on my nape rise. I turn quickly expecting to find Dryden there, but he's not. I grab the bag sitting on my desk and my body warms, remembering the things Beck and I did on that very smooth surface, and hurry downstairs. I find Dryden waiting at the front door. "I'll be back in a bit." He shifts his body, and once again I have to brush up against him to step outside. I can almost feel his eyes drilling into my back as I hurry down the steps and practically run back to Kennedy's house and find Beck standing at his front door, like he was watching for me. His eyes are narrowed, full of concern. I shake my keys at him, and he nods and opens the screen door to bring out my suitcase out.

"Dryden is still there?"

"Yeah." I don't bother telling him he was barely dressed. It doesn't really matter. It's not like Beck is my boyfriend and is going to get upset about such things. "He's leaving tomorrow."

"You want me to come stay with you tonight?"

Actually, I do, but I also think the less time we spend together going forward the better it will be for my head and heart. "No, I'm good, thanks." I hand the bag over.

His eyes narrow. "What's this?" He opens the bag and grins as he pulls out the pants and shirt I made for my final design exam. "You want me to have these?"

"I know they're not really your style—"

"You don't think I clean up good?" he teases.

I wink at him. "You do, but you don't need these clothes to look good. Besides they were made for you, and I'd like you to have them."

"I would love to have them. Thank you." My heart flutters as he picks up my suitcase and follows me to my trunk. He tosses the suitcase into the trunk and his smile is long gone by the time he closes it. "Text me later, okay? Just let me know how things are going."

"You mean with Dryden?"

"He likes you."

"He doesn't know me, and I don't know him, and come tomorrow morning, that won't have changed." He nods like he approves of that, and we both stand there for one awkward moment, before I glance at the door. "I need to go say goodbye." He nods, and I dart into the house to give everyone a hug. I step back outside and my heart skips a beat when I find Beck still at my car. He opens the driver's door and gestures for me to get in.

I slide in, and glance at him. "I'll see you later, Beck."

"Later, Piper."

My stomach clenches as he shuts the door. Everything about this feels so final and honestly, I have no idea if I'll even see him over the summer, and come fall, when classes start again...I have no idea what that will look like.

I drive back home and tentatively open the door to my house, expecting to find Dryden standing right there, ready to jump and scare me. I have no idea why my mind went there. I walk through the main level and it's empty. Upstairs, the room to his bedroom door is ajar and I peek in. It too is empty. I guess he must have left and without realizing it, I breathe a sigh of relief. I simply need some space and time to myself after a week with Beck and Madelyn and of course I have to mentally prepare for my trip home. I wish I was looking forward to it, as much as Beck is.

I spend the rest of my afternoon doing laundry, packing, cleaning out the fridge, and basically getting the place cleaned up for my return in early July, for my birthday party. For dinner I fix myself a peanut butter sandwich, debating on whether to make one for Dryden or not, but I've not heard from him all day. I freeze the rest of the bread, and I'm about to go upstairs for a shower, and do a little reading before getting a good night's sleep, when the front door inches open and the sound of keys hitting the side table jingle in the air.

I walk into the hall, and jerk my thumb toward the stairs to let him know I'm about to call it a night, but stop at the strange look on his face.

"Is everything okay?"

He nods toward the door. "Have you seen your car?"

"No, why?" I walk toward him, and he turns to the side. I glance out and my car is in the driveway. As far as I can tell it looks fine. "What's wrong?"

"The back two tires are flat."

"You're kidding me?" I push the screen door open and dart down the steps, my jaw falling open as I glance at the two 'flat' back tires. "What the hell?" I glance up and down the street, looking to see if any mischievous kids are nearby, but all is quiet, save for an elderly couple walking their dog.

"I'm sorry, Piper. I just noticed it coming home."

I shake my head, an uncomfortable feeling closing in on me as he comes closer and puts his hand on my shoulder. "I'm not sure you can get it fixed tonight. All the service stations are closed by now."

He's not wrong. "I leave tomorrow."

"I don't think that's happening now."

While one part of me is a little thrilled that I can delay going home there is another part—the part of me that carries a huge amount of guilt and responsibility—that knows I have to get this fixed, and fixed now. But Dryden is right, no service stations will be open.

"We can look into it tomorrow. Hey, did you eat? I was going to order in."

*We* can look into it?

I eye him. "Aren't you leaving tomorrow, too?"

"Change of plans. I don't leave until Tuesday."

I nod and head back inside, and go straight for my phone. Dryden follows me, talking about Thai or Chinese food. I shake my head no, and punch in Beck's number.

"Hey," he says quietly, answering on the first ring, even though he sounds like I woke him, and it's absolutely insane how my heart starts thumping at the softness and warmth in his voice.

I find Dryden standing in the archway of the kitchen watching me, and I turn from him. "I hate to bother you..."

"What's wrong?" His voice changes, and I can almost picture him siting up in his bed, going into protective mode.

"I have two flat tires, and it's late and nothing—"

"I'll be right there."

"Beck." He's gone, the connection dead, before I can even get his name out, and while I wasn't asking him to come and help, I was simply looking for advice, I can't deny that I like that he's on his way, and that he would come to help me without question.

I set my phone down and glance at Dryden. "Beck is coming to have a look at it." He frowns. "He works at the auto repair shop, remember?" From the surprised look on his face, I really don't think he remembered.

"That's great. I'm sure it's closed this time of night, though."

"He's coming anyway."

He nods and pushes off the wall. "Great. I'll hang around and see if he needs my help." He walks down the hall and heads outside, and I stay back and wait for Beck. A few minutes later, he pulls into the driveway behind my car, and I burst from the door like a child about to meet Santa for the first time. He glances at me, and I give a stupid awkward wave as the features of his face soften when our eyes meet.

"Any idea what happened?" he asks, turning his attention to Dryden as he makes his way toward Beck.

Dryden shrugs. "Came back and saw them both flat."

"Can we plug them?" I ask, trying to sound like I know something, but I remember a friend getting a tire plugged when we were teens back in Baddeck.

"Normally I'd say yes, but you have a long drive ahead of you and I don't want you breaking down on the road alone." I slowly walk down the steps and Beck's heat curls around me as I move closer to him. "Hop in," he says and opens the passenger side door of his Jeep. "We'll head to the station and get this fixed tonight."

"But it's closed."

"I called Ross on my way over here. We'll get this fixed for you tonight, so you can safely get on the road tomorrow."

He closes my door, and Dryden shoves his hands into his pants pockets looking somewhat left out and annoyed. "Anything I can do?"

"Nope." Beck slides in next to me, a frown on his face. He starts his car and turns to me. "Has anything like this ever happened before?"

"No, never." He scrubs his face and stares at Dryden as Dryden goes back in the house. My gaze goes back and forth between the two. "You don't think—"

"No, I'm not saying that. I mean, what reason would he have to flatten your tires."

It's a statement, but I sense it's a question too. "None."

"He's staying at the house tonight?"

"Yeah, I was actually just on my way to bed when he got back. It's been a long day. I was going to read and hit the road first thing tomorrow."

"You can still do that."

I nod, and stare at the sidewalk as he starts driving. He has something on his mind, something he doesn't seem to want to say, so I go quiet. If he's going to say he's not going back to Cape Breton and he likely won't see me after doing this favor, I'd rather not hear it. Maybe I'm living in a fantasy world, but I'd rather live there on my long drive home tomorrow.

Five minutes later, we're at the station and his boss Ross meets us there. After he greets us, they talk 'tires,' which goes right over my head and the next thing I know, we're back in my driveway and Beck is jacking up the car to put the new tires on. I never knew how sexy a guy could look doing mechanical work. Well, maybe that's not entirely true. Maybe I knew how sexy he looked in the snowstorm when I fell on his face.

It's dark by the time he's done and starts putting all the equipment back in his car. "I don't know how to thank you." I notice his greasy hands. I point toward the house. "Do you want to—

"Yes."

He's unusually quiet as we walk into the house and I hover in the hall as he washes his hands. Once he's finished, he comes back down the hall and walks into the living room to look out the window. I follow him. What is going on in that brain of his?

"You can head on up and read and sleep," he tells me, his body stiff as he glances out my front window.

"Okay, I'll walk you out."

He shakes his head, walks over to the sofa and plants himself on the cushions. "If it's okay with you, I'm going to stay right here tonight."

"Beck?"

"If anyone goes near your car again, I should be able to hear and see them from here."

I shake my head. Honest to God, if there was one thing he could have done to make me fall in love with him more, this was it...

"Get some sleep, Piper."

I nod, and dart up the stairs. I slip into my room, my heart beating a million miles an hour. I grab my e-reader and slide between my sheets, working very hard to calm myself so I can concentrate. Twenty minutes pass, and I snatch my phone from my nightstand when it pings. My heart beats faster and I put my hand over my mouth to stifle a laugh as I read Beck's message.

"Are you wearing your Sunday panties?

I laugh. I'm not, but as I think of the saying, Selfie Sunday,' I respond with, "Yes, why?"

"Selfie please..."

## 18

## BECKETT

It's been three long weeks since I fixed Piper's tires and she left for Cape Breton, and I've been working my ass off for vacation time, which—halle-freaking-lujah—is finally here. I don't regret the long, late hours at the repair shop, or the extra hours ones I picked up at the cafeteria, when the dorms opened to vacationers. I needed work to occupy my mind—I'm still convinced Dryden punctured Piper's tires on purpose—I just don't have any proof. I can only assume he did it so she couldn't go to Cape Breton and he could make his move. Who knew the guy was such a douche bag? Although I could be wrong. I'm just glad he's back in the Hamptons for the rest of the summer, and he'll be back at Storm House come fall.

I toss my clothes into my bag, anxious to get on the road. I've been going through the day to day motions these last few weeks, trying to keep a smile on my face, but dammit, I miss Piper and when I get home later today, I hope she still want to hang out. First things first, I need to see my family, and my buddy David wants to get drinks tonight.

I grab my phone and check for messages. The night I stayed at her place, before she left for home, I wasn't sure what the future held. That's why I asked her for a sexy selfie, just to let her know I didn't want things to end. We've been texting daily, although I've heard less and less from her lately. The tourist season is in full swing and she's crazy busy, so I'm not reading anything into it. I hope she's as excited to see me this week as I am to see her, although we haven't solidified anything. While we might not have rock solid plans, there's definitely something rock solid in my pants. But it's not just sex. I love hanging out with her. I'm pretty sure my buddy David is going to have a heart attack when he finds out what we've been up to.

I wave goodbye to Matt, Kennedy and Madelyn at the front door, and as I back out of the driveway and look at them, noting how big Madelyn is getting, I can't help but wonder if it's time I got my own place. They're not in a hurry for me to leave, but maybe I'm in need of more privacy. Hell, they don't even know about Piper and me, and if she hadn't left and we wanted to continue hanging out, we wouldn't have been able to do it without them knowing. While I'm actually okay with people knowing, I'm not sure Piper is, which once again reminds me how much her family hates me.

I go through the drive thru and grab a coffee before I hit the road, not stopping once on my long five-hour drive. I'm tired but excited as I turn off the road, and pull into our long drive-way, noting the mailbox is tilted again. Over the winter, the plow truck drivers love to see how many mailboxes they can take down with one swift swipe. I laugh. Some things never change. I stop my car and pick up a few fliers that had fallen out of the tilted box. There's no wind today, so it doesn't look like anything has blown away. I jump back in my car and head up the driveway, park behind Dad's truck and kill the ignition.

I take a moment to glance around the yard. I've missed this place. My brother is the first out the house, and he tugs open my door, practically dragging me from the seat before I even have a chance to get my seatbelt off.

"What the hell, Tanner," I laugh as I finally get free, and scramble to my feet. "Were you trying to strangle me?" Ignoring my somewhat playful outrage, he pulls me in for a hug and I can't believe how much he'd grown since I saw him at Christmas? "What are you eating?"

He laughs and when he stands back, I notice at seventeen years old, he might have an inch or two on me. My two younger sisters, Bethany and Lauren, come out after him, and they both give me hugs. My older brother Daniel doesn't live at home anymore, so I'll have to swing by his place, or the service station he runs. My brother and sisters talk nonstop about school, their friends, their lives and everything else under the sun as we all walk inside, and the second I see Mom and Dad standing back so my siblings can see me first, a sense of home and hearth comes over me.

They both smile at me, and I head straight for them and the three of us hug. My heart swells, and my mind goes to Piper. Does she get greeted this way when she gets home? Christ, I feel sorry for anyone who doesn't, and if she doesn't it sort of makes sense that she's reluctant to have her own family. Sadly though, she doesn't know what she's missing out on. I have a little niggling inside me though that our crash course on life while co-habituating and taking care of Madelyn might have her rethinking her future. What I don't know is, if I'm involved in that future.

I spend the next few hours with my family, and when my cell rings, I grab it from my pocket, not disappointed that it's my buddy David, but a little disappointed that it's not Piper. I let him know I'll meet him at Cabot Crow, and after catching up with my family, I grab my duffle bag and head to my bedroom. I glance around and grin. It looks the exact same, with my trophies still sitting on the shelf.

For a brief moment, my chest constricts, knowing how much my family saved and sacrificed to put me in hockey so I can move away and make something of myself. Most people who grew up in this small town stay in this small town and while I have fond memories, it's not economically viable for young people anymore, which means I need to get a good education, and make it to the NHL so I can help my siblings go to college, where they can make something of themselves. I walk up to my dresser and tug open my top drawer. I move a few pairs of socks and nod when I discover the little velvet box I was looking for. Yup, some things never change...and sometimes they do.

I shoot Piper a text, letting her know I'm home and I'll be meeting up with David tonight. I wait a few minutes for her response and when nothing comes, I chalk it up to her being busy. I'm disappointed sure, but hopefully I'll hear from her before the end of the night, and maybe we can meet up somewhere quickly. Yes, I'm dying to see her.

I head back downstairs, and my family is scattered, doing their own things as I go outside and jump into my car, ready to catch up with my childhood friend. I take in the gorgeous Cape Breton scenery, never tiring of the lush green rolling hills as I drive the short distance to the town's pub. The parking lot is full, which is to be expected on a Saturday night in our small town, and I check my phone one more time before I glance around, searching for David's car. I head toward the front doors, and find David standing outside, scrolling through his phone.

"Hey," I call out and a smile spreads across his face as his head lifts.

"Buddy!" He spreads his arms, and I go in for a hug. "How's my favorite soon to be NHL goalie?"

I laugh, and shake my head. "Living the dream," I joke. God, it's so good to see him. "How about you?" I stand back and smile at him, and he hasn't changed a bit since I saw him at Christmas.

"Kicking ass and taking numbers, my friend," he tells me. He too played hockey, but his goal was never the NHL.

"What's new?" I ask.

He eyes me like I might have a concussion. "It's Baddeck, Cape Breton. Same old, same old."

I laugh. He's right. Not much changes on the island, though next year, David will be heading to Halifax to go to law school. He chose University of Cape Breton over the academy for his undergraduate years, to stay back and help out his family. His father took sick a few years back, and like me, he comes from a big family and wanted to be there until his siblings were old enough to really take care of themselves.

"Except for maybe your beard." I angle my head to study it. "Did you finally hit puberty?"

He laughs and fake punches my gut. "Don't be jealous that you can't grow one, dude."

"I'll try not to be." He's not far off. I tried but mine just comes in all sparse. "Let's grab a beer, and shoot some pool."

He hesitates. "I was thinking maybe we'd go somewhere else."

Okay, that's strange.

I reach for the door handle. "Unless I'm mistaken, the Cabot Crow is the only pub in town."

"It's overrated." He gestures toward his car. "I thought we'd head to Breton Banks restaurant. Come on, I'll drive."

Okay, maybe I was wrong. Maybe a lot has changed since I've last been here. "I didn't realize you turned eighty," I tell him. He laughs and shakes his head, and I stand there and fold my arms, ready to get to the bottom of this. No one in Cape Breton goes to Breton Banks restaurant—unless you're over eighty and yes they check ID, not to see if you're of age, but to see if you get the senior discount. Hell, they pretty much stop serving dinner at six, because by that time of night their customers are home in bed. "What the fuck, David?"

He scrubs his beard and it makes a rustling sound, and that's when I see it—Piper's car, and her shiny new back tires. My heart speeds up, and my breathing changes as I stare at it, and David follows my gaze.

Why didn't she let me know she was going to be here tonight? Unease works its way through my veins, and David must sense it. Is she in there with some other guy, thinking I'd be with my family tonight?

David shifts from one foot to the other. "We should go."

"It's okay," I say and pat him on the back. Honestly, he's one of the good guys and is just looking out for me, and as I turn to him, I'm just not sure how much I should say—how much Piper would want me to say.

"Everyone's home for the summer," he says. "I didn't want your first day to start off with bad memories."

"Hey, we're not seventeen anymore."

He briefly closes his eyes and looks upward. "Thank fuck."

"Come on. Let me go take your money at pool." He laughs and slaps me on the back as I enter, and my gaze quickly catalogues the room, searching for Piper. I find her at the bar, sitting on her stool, her back to the bartender, and her eyes on me. My heart speeds up as she holds my gaze. If I had to guess, I'd say she was waiting for me, knowing I'd be hanging out with David tonight at our favorite spot.

She lowers her gaze, acting all demure, sweet and innocent and my dick twitches as it thinks about the way she followed every one of my commands in the bedroom. I stare for a second, until her friend Autumn—who I also went to school with—says something to her, and David nudges me to set me into motion.

"Forget about her," he murmurs, and we walk into the room with the pool table. I see a few of our old friends, and we all shake hands and spend a few minutes getting caught up before David grabs us a pool table and gestures the server to bring a couple of beers.

We both make a friendly bet of five dollars, laying our money on the table and I try to keep my focus on the game, which is hard to do, because every time I glance at Piper, I find her staring at me. I miss nearly every damn shot as David clears the table.

"What was that you said about taking my money?" David asks, as he sinks the eight ball and wins the game. I tell him to fuck off—playfully of course. He laughs, but it dies an abrupt death and he stiffens, his gaze on something over my shoulder. "Don't look now."

I spin and glance at the door as it opens and closes and my body tightens when none other than Noah Blackmore strides in like he owns the place. Hell, maybe he does. His father might be mayor, but his family owns a lot of businesses in the area. My gaze jerks to Piper, and she's staring at Noah every bit as much as I am. He walks up to the bar, and I grip my stick harder as he leans against it, and says something to Piper and Autumn.

I resist the urge to go say hello—with my fist.

I watch for a moment longer to see if Piper needs my help, but he steps away and goes to talk to some guys from our high school. I meet Piper's glance and she slides off the stool. So does Autumn. She crosses the room and comes toward me, and I almost forget to breathe as I watch her, note her ripped jean shorts and V-neck T-shirt that hugs her gorgeous breasts. My dick twitches.

Down boy.

"Are you okay?" David asks.

"Yeah," I murmur, my voice thick and deep as I fist my hands to stop myself from meeting her halfway and planting a hard, possessive kiss on her mouth to let everyone know she's mine.

*Is she though, Beck? Is she yours?*

Maybe not—not forever anyway—but for a little while longer, and I plan to draw it out the best I can.

I back up, and lean against the pool table as her hips sashay, and she closes the distance between us. David sucks in a breath beside me, and I don't need to turn to know he's watching me, gauging my reaction.

"Hey," I say, struggling to keep my cool as she walks up to me, sets her fruity drink on the table, and grabs a cue.

"Hey," she responds, and glances at the table. "What are you playing for?"

"Five bucks," I tell her.

"Hmm."

"What?"

"How about we play doubles." She takes a five from her purse. "Boys against girls." She lays the five on the table, and adds, "Winner takes all."

I grin at her. "You're on."

I walk over to the chalk, pick it up and swipe it over the end of my cue. David takes the chalk from me when I'm done and leans in and whispers, "What the fuck, Beck?"

"What?"

"When were you going to tell me?

I glance at him, even though it's hard to tear my gaze from Piper as she circles the table, pulls the balls from the pockets and rolls them across the table to Autumn, who is racking them. "Tell you what?"

"That you've been sleeping with Piper?"

## 19

## PIPER

It's crazy how fast my heart is racing, so happy to be here with Beck. The last few weeks didn't even seem so bad, knowing he was going to be home for vacation, and that I was going to see him. My parents, of course, think the smile that's been on my face since I've been home is because I'm happy to be back at the resort, but that's not the case at all. Just standing next to Beck now, and knowing what I have planned for later has heat and excitement racing through my body.

Beck says something to his friend David, something about me, no doubt, and David shakes his head, like he's completely dumfounded. I'm sure he is. The two of them spent years avoiding me and now Beck can't seem to take his eyes off me. I have to say though, I love the way he's looking at me. I'm not sure any other guy has ever looked at me with such hunger, such intensity.

"So, what do you say?" I pull the last ball from the pocket and turn to Beck. "Winner takes all?"

"If you want to lose five bucks, David and I don't mind taking it."

"No problem with that at all," David says and he's still looking at Beck, no doubt wanting all the details. They'll have to wait, because after this game, win or not—likely not—I plan on walking out of here with Beck. Not hand in hand, and we won't actually be walking together, but I plan to make up for the last three weeks apart.

We flip, and the guys win the break, and David takes it and sinks a low ball. I walk around the table slowly, studying all my shots, and Beck does the same. Each time we pass and our bodies touch, I'm sure we're shooting off enough sparks to keep the kitchen firing in a blackout.

The waitress comes with some mozzarella sticks that I ordered earlier, and she sets them on the table. David takes another shot and misses, and as he says something to Autumn, I grab a mozza stick and hold it out to Beck.

"Bite?"

"Sure, I'll bite," he says, like I'm baiting him, and I suppose I am. I love that I was able to surprise him tonight. I was purposely quiet all day, not texting him back and it damn near killed me. But his reaction when I asked to play was priceless.

I grin as he sinks his teeth into the cheese and leaves a long string of gooey mess as he pulls back. "Best thing I put in my mouth in a while," he says.

"Oh yeah?" My entire body tingles as I stare at his mouth, counting down the minutes until I can feel those lips on my body again. Yes, what I have planned comes with risk, and I can't even imagine my parents' reaction if they knew I was associating with Beck tonight, but I'm damned tired of being a rule follower. "Mmm, you're right. Best thing I've put in my mouth in a long time, too."

He leans into me, his breath hot on my neck. "What the hell are you up to, babe?"

God, I love when he calls me that. I blink innocently. "Up to? I'm not up to anything." I nudge against him, my hand lightly brushing his cock as I ask, "What are you up to?"

"Fuck me," he grumbles as I step around him and walk to the table.

"I think you're up," Autumn says, and I bite my lip to stop myself from laughing.

"Yeah, I think you're up, Beck."

He gives me a look that suggests I'm going to pay for this later, and if that's the case, I'm proud of myself. If I could, I'd pat myself on the back and say it's a job well done.

Beck walks funny as he steps up to the table, and bends over to take his shot. He misses, and I make a tsking sound. "I thought you were a better player than this."

"Show me what you got, then."

I bend over the table, take the shot and somehow, miraculously, sink the ball. I blow on the end of the stick. "Did I show you?"

He grins at me, and it's easy to tell he loves the way I'm playing with him. Well, mostly. I notice the way David's face tightens as he glances over my shoulder, and I angle my head to see what he's looking at. That's when my gaze lands on Noah. God, I couldn't believe it when he walked up to me earlier. Did he somehow forget he took my virginity and dissed me all those years ago and if I hear my mother tell me one more time that he's studying political science and could very well follow in his father's footsteps, I might vomit. If she's trying to play matchmaker, she can forget it, partly because I am not getting married—did they forget what kind of an example they set for marital bliss—and two, I don't like Noah.

I'm not sure he and Beck ever had a problem with one another, but if looks could kill, Beck's pool cue would be embedded in Noah's chest. Funny, up until recently, Dryden never gave me the time of day, and I've seen Noah every summer and it's only now he's talking to me. What's the common denominator here? That's right: Beck.

"What did he want?" Beck asks as he steps up to me and takes a drink of his beer.

I meet his gaze and instantly know he's talking about Noah. What I don't understand is why he looks like he might want to murder him. Sure, I told him Noah was my first and last, but that's all he knows. I shrug. "He just wanted to say hi. What's going on with you two, anyway?"

"Nothing." He takes another drink of beer, and turns to glare at Noah. Noah, just smirks and turns.

"Apparently, he wants to be mayor, like his father."

"He told you that?"

"No, my mother did."

He simply nods, and stares at the table, like it might have just caught on fire, but I don't want to talk or think about Noah or my mother, so I say, "It's really nice to see you, Beck."

He grins. "Yeah, nice to see you too, babe. Want to get out of here?"

"We have to finish the game first."

"Oh, why didn't you say?" I have no idea what he means, until he takes his shot and sinks all the balls, including the eight, cleaning the table. I grin. I guess with the right motivation, he really did show me what he's got—and I like it a lot.

Grinning after he wins, he takes the money off the table and splits it with David. "Catch up again tomorrow?" he asks.

David just shakes his head and pats Beck on the back. "Yeah, go, have fun, and tomorrow we're going to have a talk."

"You got it."

I look at Autumn, and she's racking the balls again. "I'm going to stay and have another game with David." She glances at David who's sipping his beer. "That is if you want to play."

"Sure," David agrees, and as I glance at the two of them, I can't help but think they'd be a cute couple. David moves to Halifax in the fall for law school, and Autumn is going there for med school. What a power couple they'd make. For a quick second, as I note the look they give each other, I wonder if they've been hooking up at university.

"Let's get out of here," Beck says, putting his mouth to my ear. A shiver goes through me, and once again I note that Noah is watching us.

I walk ahead of Beck, although it's likely clear to anyone watching closely that we're together, and once we're outside and alone, I spin and go up on my toes to put my arms around him.

"I fucking missed you," he murmurs, and the next thing I know his lips are on mine, devouring me like a man starved. A part of me registers that anyone could leave the pub and see us, the other part doesn't care. I rake my hands through his hair, my heart elated because I've missed him too.

The door opens and I break the kiss so fast, you'd think his lips were on fire. He wipes his mouth with the back of his hand, his eyes never leaving my face as a couple of patrons say hello and walk to their cars.

Once we're alone again, I nod toward my car. "Come with me."

He doesn't ask where, he just nods and follows me through the parking lot. He climbs into the passenger seat, moving the seat back as far as possible as his big body takes up all the space, and I try to settle my hands and my heart. I steal a fast glance at him, and he's tapping his thumb on his lap, staring straight ahead. I reach across and put my hand on his leg, and he keeps his eyes on the road, like an animal ready to take down prey as his big, warm palm closes over mine.

I flick my signal, and turn toward the resort and that's when he finally speaks. "Where are we going?"

"Do you remember that time—"

He cuts me off with, "I said we could sneak into one of the rooms and fuck all night." I turn and find intense eyes staring at me.

"Yeah, that."

"Are you sure about this?" His brow is furrowed with concern.

I love that he's worried about me, and what we're about to do is risky, but I think that's what I like most. No, I like Beck the most. "Here's what I'm sure about." He cocks his head waiting for me to expand my explanation. "I've worked every position at the resort." I pause and wait, and when he doesn't say anything, I add, "The only position I haven't worked is my body under yours and I'd love to rectify that."

His grin is slow and devilish and so damn sexy that my panties grow moist. "Bad ass," he teases. "I'm liking you more and more, Thorne."

It's sexy the way he uses my last name, so I respond with, "Right back at you, Moore." I drive along the long road and the resort rises up in the distance. It's magnificent really, situated on the shore, with a gorgeous golf course in the rear. There's one big main building that houses rooms, a restaurant, a pool, and a large viewing deck. We also have small cottages and chalets overlooking the ocean, and in the distance, there is an east lodge and a west lodge, with rows of rooms and a big outdoor pool. In the far distance, there's a ski hill, ski lifts and a lodge.

I drive to the end of the east lodge, and park away from the streetlights in the parking lot. I turn the car off, and take in Beck's silhouette. "Repairs are being done on this room. No one will be by until tomorrow. Tonight, it's all ours."

He gives a curt nod, and exits the car. My God, his body is tight and intense as he circles the front of my car, and opens my door. I grab my purse and slide out, and he puts his hand on my back and guides me to the door. I fish the keycard from my pocket and he takes it from me, and slides it through the lock. The light goes from red to green and he opens the door, and urges me in.

"God, I've fucking missed you," he says again, and pulls me into his arms after locking the door. His lips are soft, exploratory as he reacquaints his hands with my body and I moan as I sink into his kisses. He cups my ass and lifts me onto his hips. He carries me to the bed, sets me down and flicks on the light. His gaze races over the place, and he laughs when he sees his favorite ketchup potato chips, animal crackers, Garrison beer and some strawberries.

He laughs and picks up the box of crackers. "Animal crackers?"

"Don't think I haven't seen you sneaking Madelyn's."

"Wow, I can't get anything by you, can I? But I'll have you know..." He sighs and looks at the box of crackers. "Animal crackers were my first love." I smile and he shakes his head, and my heart fills with foreign emotions. "You've been planning this, huh?"

"Yeah."

"Does that mean you've been thinking of me?" He walks to the counter, grabs a beer and cracks the lid. He takes a big drink and hands it to me. I wet my dry mouth and set the can on the nightstand.

"Maybe," I reply working my best to sound coy.

His gaze falls over my body, the way my legs are parted, the ripped jean shorts high on my legs. "Did you maybe touch yourself while you were thinking of me?"

"You mean like this?" I ask, and slide a hand down my body, touching my breasts through my blouse and going lower. I reach between my legs, and move the fabric to the side to show him my panties before I slide a finger in.

"Fuck," he curses under his breath. "New panties?"

"Yeah."

"But I really like your other ones."

"I think you'll like these too."

He takes a deep breath. "Show me," he demands in the deep voice that raises my temperature from normal to inferno.

"You really want to see them?"

"Fuck yeah, I do."

I bite my lip. "Okay." Standing, I pop the button on my shorts and his hungry growl fuels the need inside me. Jeez, I love him like this. The hiss of my zipper cuts through the room. Earlier this week, when I was planning this, I knew I wanted new panties, even though he loves my other ones. At first I thought of something sexy, with either silk or lace. I quickly shut down that thought. I'm sure the girls he was with in the past all showed up in silk and lace.

I bend forward as I slide my shorts down my legs, hiding the saying on my pink panties. Honestly, I can't wait to see his reaction. I linger, taking my sweet time to get the shorts off my ankles and his growl is a good sign he's losing patience.

"Piper," he growls.

"Yes." I blink up at him, and continue to fuss with my shorts.

"Let me see."

I stand, and his gaze drops, and I wait for it...

Two seconds later, he starts laughing, his shining eyes meeting mine. As he looks at me with such adoration and amusement, I'm not sure I've ever seen such a wide smile on his face, I grin back. "Do you like them?"

"Puck me," he reads the words. "That's fucking funny, Piper."

"Oh, you think that's funny?" I say and slowly turn around so he can read the back.

He reads the words on the back of my panties. "The puck stops here."

I glance at him over my shoulder. "I know you're the goalie, not me, so I probably can't stop any puck from going in."

His nostrils flare, his entire body hard and tight and ready. "Do you want it to stop there?"

"Beck, I want to do everything with you."

His mouth is on mine in seconds, and his kisses are filled with need and hunger as he slides his hand into my panties, and pushes a finger high inside me. It feels so incredibly good, I close my eyes, knowing he's not going to make me wait to climax. He's going to give it to me hard and fast, and it's exactly how I want it. I missed this.

I missed him.

A keening cry catches in my throat as I claw at his shirt, wanting my hands on his bare body, but I don't want him to stop what he's doing to get his shirt off. I slide my hands under his clothes, and touch his trembling muscles, our mouths still entwined as he fucks me with his thick finger, knowing exactly how to touch me, exactly what my body needs.

He slides a second finger in, and presses his palm against my clit, and my body, having missed his touch, comes undone in record time. A pleasure filled gasp escapes from my throat as I come all over his fingers, and he murmurs into my mouth how much he loves it when I come. Or did he say he loves me?

Jesus, my orgasm is really messing with me, because he couldn't have said that, right?

I stop spasming around him and I'm a hot achy mess as he pulls his fingers from me, and licks them. "Fuck, I missed the taste of you."

"I missed the taste of you too." I drop to my knees—standing on shaky legs is a bit challenging anyway—and I open my mouth.

He tears into his jeans, and steps up to me, offering me his cock. I admire his hard length before it disappears into my mouth and I suck him like I've never sucked before, showing him exactly how much I missed him. He growls and groans, and the sounding rising in his throat thrill me. We're both a little frenzied making up for lost time, and while I want to taste his cum, he pulls out.

"I need you naked, and bent over the bed." We both strip, and once we're naked, I do as he says, and my heart leaps. Is he going to take me from behind? Will it hurt? I'm sure it will, but this is Beck and I'd never trust anyone with my body the way I trust him.

"Not this time," he murmurs, like he's reading my mind, as he sinks to his knees behind me. "But it will happen, Piper. You want it, you get it. Right now, though, my cock needs inside your hot pussy."

"Good, because my pussy needs your cock."

I expect him to plow into me, keeping up our frenzied momentum, but no, he sheathes himself quickly and slowly slides in, like he's treasuring every second, every inch as his cock sinks home. God, how did I live without this for these last few weeks? I don't know, but what I do know is I don't want to live without it—without Beck—for that long ever again.

He slides in and out of me, and lightly runs his fingers over my spine. Pleasure once again builds, and he bends forward and kisses me, and it's times like this, when he's so sweet with me, that it's impossible to keep my heart out of it. Do I tell him, and risk never seeing him again? But what if he feels the same way I do, and we can build something more. What the hell am I even thinking? My parents wouldn't allow him to come around, and next year, after our senior year, he'll be in the NHL, and I'll be moving back here permanently.

He groans and reaches around my body to stroke my clit, and once again I go off like a firecracker, squeezing around his beautiful, thick cock. God, this is so amazing with him.

"Babe, yes." He pushes once, twice and then comes inside me. His breath is hot on my flesh as he rests his chin on my back, and I spread my arms on the bed, exhausted, but so damn happy he's here with me.

He shifts behind me, gripping my hips and helping me to my feet. The next thing I know, I'm between the sheets and he gets rid of the condom and slides in beside me, adjusting the blankets to keep us warm. I smile, wanting to stay like this forever.

*Why the hell can't that be possible?*

He shifts to face me, going up on one elbow. "What are you doing tomorrow?" he asks.

"Work." But I'm not interested in thinking about tomorrow. I just want to bask in tonight.

He frowns and brushes my damp hair from my forehead. The tender intimacy in his touch, the closeness of his body, and the warmth in his voice, draw me in deeper, and I'm pretty sure I've never felt this close to Beck, or any other human before.

"You really work seven days a week here?"

"Always something to be done." He lightly runs the rough pad of his index finger over my kiss swollen bottom lip, before he rolls away and stands, like he has darker thoughts on his mind, I watch the play of his muscles as he walks to the window and tugs open the curtains, standing there stark naked.

"Beck!"

"What?" He turns and grins at me over his shoulder.

"Someone could see you."

"Nah, it's dark in here, now get your sweet, naked ass over here and come look at the moon with me."

"I didn't know you were a star gazer." I slide from the bed, but drag the sheet with me, tugging it around my shoulders. Beck takes one chair and positions it in front of the big window overlooking the ocean. I put my hands on my hips. "Where do I sit?"

He drops down, and drags me onto his lap. "Right here seems fine."

I lean against him, and we go silent as we take pleasure in the moonbeams dancing on the rippling waves.

"It's gorgeous here," he says quietly.

"It is."

His exhale is exaggerated before he continues with, "It's not where you belong, Piper."

I exhale a shaky breath right along with him, somehow knowing he was going to bring this up when he was home. I just didn't think it would be sooner, rather than later. "I know."

"You should get to do what you to do, follow your passion." I glance at him and frown. He brushes my hair back. "That's all I'm going to say about it."

"Okay."

I turn back to the water and a beat passes between us before he says, "Come to dinner tomorrow, at my parents' place."

His offer shocks me and I blurt out, "I don't think I can." My God, this is such a small town, news of me having dinner at the Moore's would spread like a brush fire, and my parents would lose their minds, and no doubt try to ground me.

*You're a grown-ass woman now, Piper.*

That's right. I *am* a grown-ass woman—one who can and should be making her own decisions on where she has dinner and who she has it with.

...and what the future might look like.

That thought circles my brain, filling me with a strange kind of bravado—or maybe it's rebellion—as Beck nods slowly and the disappointment on his face physically hurts my soul. I swallow against a painful throat, hating that I'm disappointing him.

He shrugs. "I know. I thought I'd ask anyway."

"Why do you want me to come?"

"I don't know." His hands tighten on my body, his warmth cocoons me and the feeling of safety and strength I get when he's wrapped around me, has me questioning...everything that has been my life. He gives a half laugh, half snort. "Maybe to see what it's like..."

"What do you mean?"

"You once told me you were jealous of what we have. Maybe I want you to experience it, just once."

"You want that for me?"

"I do."

I touch his face as my heart beats a little faster. God, he's the sweetest. "I don't think your parents will want me anywhere near your place...after..." I don't need to say 'after you were accused of vandalizing my car' for him to know what I'm talking about.

"I think you might be surprised." As I take in the genuine kindness on his face, my mind goes on a journey. What would it be like sitting around his table, with his parents and siblings? I bet they all tell stories and simply enjoy each other. I can't deny that I've been thinking more and more about that scenario, ever since we played house with Madelyn. A little bubble of excitement wells up inside of me, and I smile as I envision that kind of life for myself.

"You know," he begins, pulling my thoughts back. "Growing up, I was a little jealous of you, too. I used to think your life was perfect."

I snort and stare off into the distance, watching an anchored boat bob in the water. A quiver goes through me. "Sorry to disappoint."

His palm slides up and down my arm to warm me. "I don't think you can disappoint me, Piper.

"I guess my parents weren't the only great actors on the resort. I just...I want to let you know, Beck. I never, ever thought you were the one who vandalized my car."

"You're not your parents, Piper. You just do what you need to do to get by day to day, but underneath it all, you're not a snob."

Is that why he never went to my party? He thought I was a snob? "My seventeenth birthday party..." I begin.

"It's in the past," he says, and I close my mouth. If he wants to leave it in the past, I can too, which means I'll never know why he didn't come and then ignored me afterward.

"I know, you can't come and I'm not going to pressure you. Your decisions are yours." I smile, liking his understanding. "But if you do change your mind, just stop by. Dinner is usually around six, and Mom and Dad always cook too much, and like Mom always says when we have friends stop by, it's just another potato in the pot."

"Your mom sounds pretty nice."

"She is. You'd like her."

"Wait, she's only going to let me have a potato if I show up?" I tease.

He laughs. "I can share my meat with you."

I wiggle on his lap. "You mean again."

He puts both arms around me and stands. "Yeah, babe. Again, and this time," he murmurs, sliding a hand over my ass... "The puck does *not* stop here."

# 20

## BECKETT

I try to stifle a yawn as I set the dining room table for Sunday dinner, happy to be sitting around it with my family again. Mom glances at me, as she takes the silverware from the cabinet and I just smile at her. She knows I was out all night for a couple of reasons. One, I'm exhausted, and two, my bed was barely slept in. I'm sure she'd be surprised to hear I was with Piper—at her family's resort, no less—and while she might worry, she'd never judge, which I appreciate.

Jesus, last night was just about perfect. The only thing that could have made it better was the two of us waking up early and watching the sunrise. But we couldn't, because we shouldn't get caught together. So, after a few rounds of sex—my God, I still can't believe the things she wanted me to do to her body—we snuck out under the cover of darkness and she drove me back to my car at Cabot Crow.

At home, I went to my room, and spent my time thinking about the way I took her, everywhere, the way her body opened for me, accepted every inch. It was the most amazing night of my life, and I am so not ready for us to be over. Before the end of this week, before I leave for the city, we have to talk. We never wanted the same things before, but we're also not the same people we were before we began sharing a house.

Mom glances at the table, and it's ridiculous—I know Piper isn't coming—but I set a place for her just in case.

"Math still not your thing?" Mom teases, and I laugh, not telling her I do tons of math when I'm with Piper while trying to keep my shit together. She points to the extra setting and chair squeezed in next to where I sit. "You set one too many places. Last time I checked I only had five kids."

I set the drink cups on the table. "I'm hoping we have company." I try to act casual, playing it off, even though every nerve in my body is firing with hope. "Probably not, though. But just in case. But I doubt it."

*Jesus, get it together, dude.*

Mom wipes her hands on her apron. "David?" she asks, and it's a logical conclusion. Or at least it would be if I wasn't acting like a bumbling idiot.

"No, uh..." I pause and look at Mom. "Do you remember Piper Thorne?" I actually thought about wearing the clothes she made for me, but she's not going to show up here tonight, and I'd like to keep them clean in case we do something else that requires nice khaki pants and a dress shirt.

"You mean the girl who's always been a thorn in your ass?"

I snort. "Funny, Mom."

"I guess you know where you get your sense of humor," Dad says, coming into the room and throwing his arms around Mom from behind and kissing her on the neck.

I shake my head. "Get a room." They laugh and honestly, I'm glad they're still into each other. It's nice to see the love they have, and to know love can last the test of time.

"Speaking of room," Dad begins. "You didn't come home last night."

Leave it to Dad to state the obvious. Mom, she's a bit more subtle. "I was with a friend."

"Ah," they both say, that one word laced with so many suggestions—none of which they'd dare say out loud—and I roll my eyes at them.

"So, Piper," Mom begins. "You two are friends now?"

Okay, yeah, she's putting it together. "We are, actually. We shared a few classes at the academy, and we just took care of a friend's daughter for a week." I stand there, and realize Mom and Dad have fallen silent as I grin like an idiot. I shrug like it's nothing, but can't seem to stop talking about her. "Oh, and I..." I pause and laugh. "She needed this male model for her design class..."

"They have fashion design classes at the academy?" Dad asks.

I fuss with one of the placemats, even though it's already straight. "No, she goes to the local community college for that."

"Wow, that's a lot on her plate," Mom says.

"Yeah, she's pretty driven, and she's a great designer."

"What was this about you being a model?" Tanner asks, skidding into the room, his video game still buzzing from the living room.

Oh, God, what have I done?

"It was nothing."

Tanner backs up, and starts rubbing his chin, getting ready to raze me. "I don't know, Beck. With those chicken legs—"

I grab him and put him in a headlock, running my knuckles over his skull. He might be taller than me, but I'm older and have more body weight, which gives me the advantage—at least for this next week. He laughs and gut punches me, and when we finish, I find Mom and Dad just shaking their heads as they stare at us.

"Some things never change," Dad snorts.

"Some things do. Beck here is a model now," Tanner jibes.

"It was just to help her out. She made me khaki pants and a shirt. She did a great job."

Tanner starts walking beside the long dining room table, throwing his arm out and really hamming it up as he pretends to strut the catwalk.

"Keep it up, little brother."

"Maybe after dinner you can show us your moves, big brother, and hey, if the NHL doesn't work out..."

I glance at Mom and Dad. "How do you put up with him?"

They both laugh. "Did you forget what you were like at seventeen?"

My chest tightens. "Yeah, I remember seventeen." My thoughts rewind to last night. I'm pretty sure Piper was going to apologize about her party, but I stopped her. The past is the past and I want to leave it there. Besides, the more I get to know her and understand her, the more I realize the decision to leave me out had to be her parents'. They didn't want the kid from the wrong side of the tracks sullying up the joint.

Mom must realize what she said, and the memories it invoked in me, so she quickly pivots and says, "Well, Piper is welcome to come to dinner any time she likes. I would love to see her again, Beck."

"Thanks, Mom."

She touches my face. "Of course. Now, William, go find a nice bottle of wine, in case we do have company."

Mom and Dad disappear into the other room, dragging a still modeling Tanner with them, and my heart fills with gratitude as I watch them disperse. I really am a lucky son of a bitch to have them for my parents. I didn't need Piper to tell me that to know it. They've worked hard and sacrificed to get me to where I am today, and instead of questioning me on Piper, after everything we've been through, they trust me enough to know I'll make good decisions.

I hear my sisters' voices coming in through the back door. They seem to be talking to someone, but I don't know who—until the someone answers and I nearly bite off my tongue.

What the hell?

Mom keeps the wood floors waxed so I nearly slip and fall in my sock feet as I try to rush out of the room. I grip the wall, and work to gather my cool. I take a couple deep breaths, and try not to appear so thrilled, which I am. I straighten up to my full height and walk around the corner, coming face to face with Piper. A small, almost nervous smile teases the corners of her lips as our eyes meet. No wonder she's unsure, I'm staring at her like she's an alien.

"Are you just going to stand there, or are you going to say hello to your friend?" Mom asks as she comes around the corner.

"Hi, Piper."

"Hi, Beck."

"Piper was telling us about the new paddle boats at her resort," Lauren says. "How come we never go there?" she asks, turning her focus to Mom.

"We're busy, Lauren. You have music, and Bethany has horseback riding, and Tanner has debate classes."

Not knowing the history between our families, Lauren crinkles her nose. "Yeah, but—"

Mom gives her a stern look, one I'm far too familiar with. "Why don't you girls go get cleaned up for dinner?"

They grumble and stomp up the stairs, and I grin at Piper. "Teenagers."

She laughs. "I'm sure I was no better at their age."

Mom steps closer to Piper. "You didn't have to go through all the trouble," she says and that's when I realize Piper is holding a pie. Piper hands the pie over and Mom inhales the delicious aroma.

"No trouble. Well maybe a little trouble. I had to sneak it from the kitchen without the baker catching me. Last time I snuck something out, I nearly got a rolling pin to the back of the head."

Mom laughs. "Well, thanks for taking the risk."

"No problem, Mrs. Moore."

"Oh, please call me Rose. Now if you'll excuse me, I'll put this in the kitchen. Maybe you can help Beck finish setting up, and I have to say it's so nice that you're joining us for dinner. I want to hear all about fashion school."

Her eyes go wide as Mom disappears into the kitchen. I hold my hands out. "It's okay, she's not going to say anything."

"You...told her."

"Yeah. I'm sorry if I wasn't supposed to."

"No, I just...I think that's nice, actually." She smiles as she blinks up at me, something warm in her eyes.

I relax and step close, wanting to drag her into my arms and kiss her. I lightly touch her hand and our fingers play. "The table is set. I think that was just Mom's way of leaving us alone." I glance around. "Do you want me to show you around?"

"We could start with your room."

"Mom," I call out teasingly. "Can I have a girl in my room?"

"If he's allowed, then I want to be allowed too," Tanner calls out from the living room, where he's playing some video game now.

"Go on," Mom says. "Tanner, we'll discuss your privileges later."

I twine my fingers in Piper's and lead her up the stairs. We go into my room, and I close the door. From downstairs, I hear Tanner tattletale that we shut the bedroom door and it makes me laugh. God, I missed that kid.

Piper grins. "He's funny."

"If funny means pain in my ass, then yes, he's funny."

She laughs and steps into the room, running her hand over my desk, and chair and walking up to my window to look out at the tree nearby. "Is this how you snuck out at night when you were just a boy?"

I put my hand to my chest. "Me, sneak out? I'll have you know I was a good boy. A rule follower."

Her face flushes. "Yeah, well, I used to be a rule follower too." She walks up to me and pokes me in the chest. "Until I started hanging out with you."

"I'm a bad influence, huh?"

She grins, and I put my arm around her. "The worst."

I dip my head and kiss her sweet lips. She coils her hands around my neck and holds me tight. When we break apart, I tell her, "If my family wasn't downstairs, I'd fuck you on my childhood bed."

She arches a brow like she quite enjoys that idea. "How many girls did you sneak in here?"

"You really want to know?"

I take in the sexy curves of her body as she strolls around my room, stopping to look at my trophies and medals. "I want to know."

"Would you believe me if I told you that you are the first girl, outside of family, to ever be in this room?"

She turns to me, her eyes big, her mouth ajar. "You're lying."

I lean against my desk, and cross my legs. "When have I ever lied to you?"

Her brow puckers. "I don't think you ever have."

I shrug. "Then why would I now?"

She grins, clearly liking the idea that she's the first girl I've had in my childhood bedroom. "I guess you wouldn't." She touches my trophies. "You must stop a lot of pucks, huh?" Her chest rises and falls as she glances at me, and my dick twitches, thinking about her sexy panties from last night, and the pucks she didn't stop.

"I've stopped a few." She walks around the room for another second, and my eyes are glued to her. Honestly, I still can't quite believe she's here. Maybe I'm still asleep and dreaming —or fantasizing. I'd be lying if I said I never fantasized about her. "I'm glad you're here, Piper."

She stops in front of me, and leans into my body, her lush breasts against my chest as her warm sweet scent teases my senses. "I'm glad I came."

I run my hands up and down her soft arms. "How did you get away?"

She turns from me, but I catch something on her face before she hides it, something that looks like...guilt? What is it she doesn't want me to know...to see?

"Do your parents know you're here, at my place?"

She shakes her head. "No."

"Do they even know you're gone?"

"Yeah. I had to give tennis lessons at six-thirty, so I had to get out of them. They weren't very happy about that. I told them I had to go see an old friend, and it was strange, they seemed rather suspicious about that. I guess I can understand that. I've been home for weeks now, and I've seen all my old friends."

"Why don't they bring in extra staff for lessons?"

"They do, actually. But the guy didn't show, and now Dad has to give the lesson and his back isn't good." Sadness moves over her face. "Maybe I shouldn't have——"

"Hey, if you can't stay, I understand." I lightly run my hands up and down her arms.

"Do you...want me to stay?"

I already told her I was happy she was here. Does she need more convincing? "More than I want to eat that pie, and you know how much I love pie."

"And animal crackers," she adds, and my dick jumps up, remembering the animal crackers I ate last night—as well as the other things I put in my mouth.

"What do you want though, Piper?" I ask. I honestly hate the way her parents manipulate her, and does her father really have a sore back, or it is a way of keeping her under their eye?

"I want to be here." Under her breath, she adds, "We made a deal."

"A deal?"

Mom's voice sings out from downstairs. "Kids, time for dinner."

Before I can press, and ask about this deal—I really don't like the way she averted her gaze and hope it's not something too terrible for her—she opens my door. She obviously doesn't want to talk about it, so I leave it for now.

We head downstairs, and Tanner puts the last bowl on the table as everyone jumps into their seats. My brother Daniel comes in through the door, and for a split second he goes still when he sees Piper taking a seat next to me at the long oaken table. As my older brother, he knew what went on back in the day, so I can imagine this is quite confusing for him. I still owe David a phone call.

"Piper, right?" he asks, and takes his hat off.

"Yes, and you're Daniel, right?"

"The one and only," Daniel says and just like that, awkwardness averted.

He drops down. "Mom, this looks great."

"Hey." Dad glares at me as he opens a bottle of wine, which we never have at dinner and I assume it's because Piper is here. "I helped."

"Thanks, *Daddy*, this all looks great," Daniel teases, and Piper laughs at his comment.

Soon enough, bowls are being passed around and we load up on roast beef and all the fixings. Beside me, Piper is quiet, taking it all in, but there's also a gleam in her eyes, a genuine happiness about her and I love that.

"So, Piper," Mom begins. "Tell me more about this fashion design class. I've always loved to sew, but I'm not a fashion designer."

"Oh, I'd love to hear more," Lauren pipes in.

"Me too," Bethany adds.

"She will be an amazing fashion designer one day if she wants," I say, and Piper gives me a grateful smile.

Tanner nudges Daniel. "Did you hear? Beck is a male model now."

Daniel nearly drops his fork. "You're kidding me?"

"He was helping me out," Piper explains, and as we all eat, Piper talks about her course and her final assignment, which I helped her out with. Once she's done, she redirects the conversation and asks, "Now, who wants to tell me what Beck was like as a kid?"

Daniel grins, and rubs his hands together. "I do." I grip Piper's leg under the table, bracing for the embarrassing stories he's about to spill. His smile widens as his gaze goes from me to Piper.

"Do you remember that garbage can fire in the back of Sam's Convenience store a few years back...?"

Oh God, kill me now!

# 21

## PIPER

It's Saturday night and tomorrow will be one full week since I've had Sunday dinner with Beck and his family. I haven't stopped smiling since sitting down at the table with them. The stories his family told were hilarious, and simply drew me in deeper to a place I never had any intention of going. How could I not fall for him, though? He's sweet and kind and everything a girl could ask for. Honestly, why hasn't he been snatched up by now?

Oh, probably because he's been spending every spare moment with me, the two of us secretly sneaking around and falling into bed together every night at the resort. He leaves tomorrow morning to head back to the city, and there's no question about it—we need to talk before he goes. I mean, we've talked about everything under the sun except a couple of very important things. One, what I ever did to make him boycott my birthday party, and two, how we really feel about each other.

I smooth my hand over my pretty blue dress, and consider what I'll change into after dinner with my parents and their friends. My entire body flutters thinking about Beck, and the night we have planned together. Not that I'm in on the plans. He told me to leave it up to him, and I have no idea what he has in mind, only that I should expect the unexpected—whatever that means. Before we meet, however, I have to go to dinner with my parents, the mayor and his wife, and yes, their beloved son who took my virginity and walked away.

I don't want to go. Hell, it's the last thing in the world I want, but it was the only way I could sneak away last Sunday and have dinner with Beck and his family. My parents practically forced me to agree before they'd let me out of tennis lessons, and perhaps that's why I didn't feel too bad leaving them high and dry, and it's strange how Dad's back seems perfectly fine now.

As that thought rolls around in my brain, my stomach tightens. Jeez, that wasn't a very nice thing for me to think. They've worked long and hard to provide for me and I'm clearly just an ungrateful spoiled girl.

I leave our house and walk to the main lodge, the gorgeous evening sun high in the sky, lifting my spirits. It's only one dinner with one family and I'm sure with enough wine, I can get through it. I concentrate on what's happening afterward, and my imagination goes wild. What does Beck have planned? I honestly can't wait to find out.

Normally we'd have our fancy meals at the resort's high-end restaurant, but not tonight. I have no idea why Mom and Dad decided to go to Cabot Crow. I figured they'd choose Breton Banks restaurant over the popular pub, but no, that's where we're going. Maybe it was the mayor's idea. This way he can get out with his constituents and show them he's one of them. He's not. Like my parents, he comes from money and doesn't know what real life and real struggles are. Who am I to talk? I don't know either.

"Is that what you're wearing?" Mom asks as she comes into the main lobby, her gaze going up and down the length of me. I shift under her inspection, and flare my dress.

"Don't you like it?"

She stands back and examines me for a moment. "We're dining with the Mayor, Piper. Surely you can do better than that, and where are your pearls?"

I groan. Pearls are for people dining at Breton Banks restaurant, not Cabot Crow pub. "I think they're back at my apartment," I fib, and she tucks her hair behind her ear.

"What about that yellow dress we got last year?"

I eye Mom and take in her turquoise, form-fitting dress. She looks amazing, really, and it sort of breaks my heart that she's broken and sad beneath the façade. "The yellow dress that makes my skin look pale?"

"It makes you look trim and pretty."

"Unlike this floral blue one?" I ask and flare the skirt portion again.

"It looks a bit...slouchy."

Slouchy is her nice way of saying I look like a slob. I don't think I do, and the dress doesn't hang on me. In fact, it's a bit tighter than it was last year. Probably because I've been eating with Beck so much. That guy does love food, and we've been snacking as we stay up late to watch sunsets. You'd think I'd be burning calories with all the sex we've been having, though. Beck seems to love the extra weight, and I like that about him.

Dad comes into the lobby wearing a very expensive suit, looking as handsome as ever. "How are my girls?" he asks, bending to kiss Mom on the cheek. To those around us we look like the perfect family, but they can't see the way Mom flinched as Dad's lips grazed her cheek, or the way she so quickly, so carefully jumped back into character. She could totally give Sawyer a run for her money on the stage.

"Your dress is gorgeous, Piper," Dad comments as he straightens, smoothing his hand over his steel blue tie. I share a look with Mom, and she just gives a little shake of her head, like the matter has been put to rest and I can go out looking like a slob, in her eyes, if that's what I want.

"Shall we?" he asks, and puts his hands on our backs to guide us outside. I jump in the back of the vehicle, and the leather is warm beneath my backside. Snatching my phone from my purse, I grin as I read a message from Beck. We're meeting later at Cabot Crow, and I'm not worried about running into him while out with the mayor and his family. He's been busy setting up things for tonight. I'll of course explain to him what went down, and about my parents trying to set me up, but that conversation is for another time.

Beck: Three hours and counting.

Piper: What are we doing?

Beck: You know I'm not telling you.

Piper: That's right, you like to show instead of tell.

I giggle and put my hand over my mouth as Dad glances at me in the rearview mirror. No doubt wondering why I'm suddenly blushing. I just smile at him, and he goes back to driving along the curvy road.

Beck: Babe, you're making me hard.

I stifle a giggle this time as heat and need flare through me. Honest to God, three hours until I see him again is three hours too long. At least it will give me something to look forward to and help me get through this meal.

Piper: Do I need to bring anything?

Beck: I've got everything covered.

Piper: Animal crackers?

Beck: No babe, the only thing I want to put in my mouth tonight is you.

I close my eyes and can almost see the hungry, needy look on his face as he texts me. God, I am in so deep with this man. I exhale as my nipples tighten and moisture grows between my legs. My lids flicker open and once again I catch the way Dad is watching me in the mirror. Mom notices it too, and she shifts in her seat. Her gaze goes from me to my phone back to me.

"Who are you texting with?"

I flip my hand like it's nothing. "Oh, just an old friend."

Her gaze narrows in on me. "Is this the friend you went to see instead of giving tennis lessons last week?"

"Yes," is all I say and tuck my phone back into my purse. I stare at the lush trees as Dad drives, and when we cross the bridge where we used to gather as kids, and jump into the river, I smile. Back then, when we were all in our early teens, things like whose parents had money, and whose didn't, never seemed to matter. It was in high school when my family became a little more pretentious, wanting to separate the haves from the have nots. Then again, it might have been before that and I didn't notice. They always did try to steer me toward boys who came from 'proper' families as they put it.

Dad pulls into a parking spot at Cabot Crow and I slide out and smooth my hand over my dress. I actually can't wait to get out of it. I would have preferred to wear one I made, but then I'd have an inquisition to look forward to. No way would they understand me taking design courses, because in no way would they help me run a successful resort.

"Now you be nice to Noah," Mom says.

Warning bells jangle in my brain. "Mom, you said this wasn't about trying to set me up." I stare at her, my throat tight.

"One little date isn't going to hurt."

"Ohmigod, this is a date?"

Keeping a smile on her face, for the sake of those watching, she says, "I'm just trying to show you that you two have a lot in common."

"Like what?"

She frowns at me, and I glance around, debating how far I could run in my heels before Dad hunted me down with his car and made me act like a proper young lady.

"You're both from the area, you're both in college, and you're both following in your parents' footsteps."

When I think about it, Beck checks two of those boxes. But he's carving his own path in life—doing what he loves to do because his family has his back—and I really admire that about the Moore's.

"I've been hearing things about you hanging around that Moore boy." I pale. Honestly, how could she not have heard.

It's a small town with a big rumor mill. "That has to stop now, Piper. Now straighten your shoulders, they're here."

I slouch as a car pulls into the lot, and I'm not sure how I'm going to eat now. My stomach is tight, and my God, is Noah what my parents want for me? Do they not want me to be happy, in a loving relationship, not one that's for show only? Does Mom not want me to be happy? How can she spend her life miserable like this?

"Piper," Noah greets, his disgusting, hungry gaze taking in my dress. As he examines me, a hard quake wracks my body and I sure as hell hope he doesn't take it for anything other than repulsion.

*Three hours, Piper. Three hours until you're in Beck's arms. You've got this.*

After we all exchange pleasantries, we head inside and I hang back, and walk slowly. Noah falls in step with me, and gives me a grin.

"I haven't seen you around much."

"Been busy," I tell him and it's not a lie.

"Saw you playing pool with Beck a bit back. What's up with that loser?"

I stiffen. "Don't call him that. You don't know him."

"Are you saying you do?"

"We go to the same college, so yes, I do." Coming to his defense, I add, "He happens to be the star goalie of the championship team. That's impressive don't you think?"

"Yeah, I heard he fucks anything with a skirt at the academy."

I swallow, hard. While that might have been true, it's not true anymore. But I'm not about to get into a debate with Noah. I will be pleasant and get this meal over with.

"I've had a few classes with David," he tells me.

I glance up at him. Where is he going with this? I'm not sure I want to know, but there's a part of me that wants to hear what he has to say.

"David's a nice guy," I say. "He's going into law next year."

"You seem to know a lot about him too."

I shrug. "He's Beck's best friend."

"Did you ever stop to think Beck is just fucking around with you, Piper?" he asks, his voice taking on a hard edge.

Our parents enter the restaurant and I stop and turn to Noah, my heart pounding a thousand miles an hour. "What are you talking about?"

"He fucked your car up because you didn't invite him to your party when we were kids."

"He didn't fuck my car up," I say, mostly to myself. Everyone believes he did it and I'm not going to argue this with Noah. "And he was invited...he just didn't come."

"He's always hated me, you know."

I shake my head. "Why would he hate you?"

"Because of who my dad is, and that I come from money. That's why he hates you too. Maybe that night he saw us fucking—"

"Don't be so disgusting—"

I glance into the restaurant and meet Mom's gaze as she takes a seat. She smiles, like she's pleased I'm having quiet time with Noah. Oh, if she only knew.

He steps closer and puts his hand on my arm. I flinch it off. "All I'm saying is, he's not a good guy. Definitely not who you think he is. He's a liar, who will say anything to get what he wants." His brows rise. "He's not saying things to you to get what he wants is he?"

"What goes on between Beck and me is none of your business."

He hisses. "So, you are fucking him."

"It's not—"

"Careful, Piper. He's never gotten over not being invited to your party, or the fact that you and I fucked—"

"He didn't know that back then."

He leans closer and it throws me off. "Are you saying he knows it now?"

"I just...I'm not...I mean..." Flustered, I blow out a breath. "What do you want, Noah?"

"I want you."

"You were the one who slept with me and disappeared, remember?"

"Beckett told me to never set eyes on you again, or else." He slices across his neck with his index finger.

I gulp, hardly able to believe what I'm hearing. "You're lying. Why would he do that?"

"Because he hated you—and me—so much he wanted us to be miserable. I guess he figured he could achieve that by breaking us up. Ask him. Ask him if he told me to never go near you again or he'd make my life a living hell. Ask him." He pauses for a second.

"You said he was a liar. Why would he tell the truth about that then?"

He shrugs. "You're right. But ask David. He was there when Beck threatened me." When I don't answer he continues with, "Look, Beck comes from a tough family of coal miners, Piper. I wasn't going to mess with that all those years ago, and I guess I always figured someday we'd find our way back together." His voice softens as he adds, "He should have been run out of town after he fucked with your car...and before he could fuck with you." He gestures toward our families inside. "But let's forget about him and talk about us. They want this for us, too. We'd make a power couple and you'd look really good on my arm when I'm running for politics."

My stomach cramps so hard I'm sure I'm going to be sick. With my mind still on Beck, I ask. "Why are you saying these things about Beckett?"

"Because I think he's putting his dick in you as some sort of weird revenge plot, and I have no idea what he'll do if he sees us together again—or sees just how good we're together. He's jealous, babe. He never wanted us happy, and I think it's time to put him in our past, don't you?"

My legs go weak as my brain rattles around inside my head, but I refuse to believe anything coming out of Noah's mouth. He's the liar, not Beck. I shake my head. Why do so many people not want us together?

"I need to sit down." I falter backward, and sink onto one of the benches outside the restaurant. A familiar sound reaches my ears, and I glance up to see Beck's Jeep easing into a spot in the parking lot.

"Ohmigod," I whisper under my breath as Noah takes a seat next to me and puts his arm around my body. I try to shake him off but can't.

Beck jumps from his vehicle and hurries to the doors, but his steps slow and his face hardness when he sees Noah holding me.

He stops in front of us, and I can't even imagine what's going through his head. I'm about to speak, and tell him it's not what he thinks when he talks first. "What are you doing here, Piper? You said you had dinner plans with your parents."

"I do…"

Everything about him is hard…intense. "Then what are you doing with Noah?"

"We're on a date," Noah says puffing his chest out.

A beat of silence, and then Beck speaks. "Oh yeah, is that true, Piper?"

"No…well yes, but…"

"No, you're not on a date?" he asks, his voice an octave deeper, and completely sober. "Or yes you are on a date?"

"I said we're on a date," Noah pipes in and stands.

As the two guys face one another, I open my mouth and even though I'm certain what Noah is saying is a lie, I ask meekly, "Did you…threaten Noah's life, after my seventeenth birthday party?"

He stares at me long and hard, and I'm not sure what's going through his head. Maybe that's for the better, because I'm guessing it has everything to do with me, and it would probably gut me to hear it. Oh God, was Noah, right?

His body is stiff, his blue eyes arctic cold when he answers with, "Yes."

My chest contracts and Noah leans in and sneers, "Told you."

Beck doesn't take his eyes off me. "Why don't you ask him why, Piper? Ask him why I threatened him."

I glance at Noah, that question dancing in my eyes. "I told you," Noah answers quickly. "He was jealous and hated us because we had more than he did. He's a nobody and even he knows it. He's just having fun, fucking you over." Noah laughs. "Just tell me you didn't fall for him. That was likely his plan, get you to fall for him so he could fuck you over even harder."

"Is that what you believe?" Beck asks me.

I consider how he boycotted my party, and went out of his way to avoid me afterward. "Tell me it's not true." There's a desperation about me, that spills out in my voice.

A long pause and then, "I shouldn't have to tell you." His chest rises and falls erratically, and I've never seen this murderous look on his face before, never seen this kind of darkness. It frightens me. "You should know."

"She knows all she needs to know." Noah drops down and puts his arm around my shaking body.

"Careful, Piper." Beck takes a step closer, and Noah holds his hand out to keep him back. Although, judging by deadly look in Beck's eyes, if he wanted to get his hands on Noah, not even his team's defensive line up could keep him back. "He's not who you think he is."

Noah snorts. "I could say the same about you."

Beck's head angles, his gaze on Noah. "No, she knows who I am."

As I stare at him, my heart stops beating. My God, as I look at him now, really look at him, look past the pain and hurt... the vulnerability, it occurs to me that Noah hit on something dark and deep inside of Beck, and with me throwing an accusation at him, I've taunted those lurking demons, and provoked his biggest insecurities. As my world closes in on me, one question dances in my brain: how can a man like Beck, a legend on the hockey team, harbor fears of not being good enough? Honestly how could he not, I've been sneaking around and hiding him like he was a dirty secret.

"Wait!" Noah practically yells as my brain and body go on an emotional rollercoaster ride. "What the fuck are you wearing, dude?" Noah laughs, hard, and that's when I realize Beck is wearing the clothes I made for my final assignment, and he so kindly modeled for me. "Dude, you don't belong in clothes like that, unless you're headed to the resort, and I'm guessing you're not."

"No, maybe you're right." Beck scrubs his face and glances around. "Maybe I don't."

I finally find my voice. "Beck—"

I'm about to reach for him when the door opens and my father walks out, his features hard as he glares at Beck. "Is there a problem here?"

Beck stares at me, waiting for me to answer and I try to formulate a response, and while I'd like to say my words are lodged in my throat, the truth is I'm a chickenshit. My parents have been so good to me, providing me with a top-notch education, and handing over a business—even though I don't want it.

*Beck has been so good to you, too.*

"No, no problem here," Beck says as I continue to stall. "See you around, Piper."

My heart drops into my stomach, his words hard and final, and everything inside me knows, I've hurt this man, and chances are he'll never talk to me again.

Noah leans into me. "I told you, once a loser always a loser."

"Beck!" I yell. He turns to me and the hurt in his eyes steals my breath. I want to make this right. I want to do something, anything to fix this, but the only words I can get out are, "Don't hate me."

"Hate," Beck says, and scrubs his chin with his palm. "I don't hate you, Piper. I've never hated you. But I once said you could never disappoint me. I was wrong."

# 22

# BECKETT

I wake up early after a very restless sleep and the first thing I do is check my phone. Nothing from Piper. Why I thought she might have texted is beyond me. She was just on a goddamn date with the douche bag that took her virginity and wrote shit about her on her car because she was nothing but a conquest to him and he felt the need to shame her for it. God, we live in a fucked-up world.

Really though, I have no idea what his problem is, other than his huge ego, which I'd like to take down a couple notches with my fist. Maybe I should have told Piper everything when we were teenagers—or even last night. Why didn't I? Oh, I guess because I hoped, after we spent so much time together that she would see that I wasn't the kind of guy who'd do something like that. That I didn't need to outright tell her I wasn't a worthless loser from the wrong side of the tracks. That she would have known there was more to me, but no, she had to ask, and because she had to, it made me feel like shit and I goddamn well refused to answer, much to Noah's delight.

I scoff as last night's ordeal races through my mind. To think that douche bag is going into politics. I guess it shouldn't surprise me. Like father, like son. Even if David and I had given Noah's name to the cops all those years ago, his daddy would have somehow brushed it under the rug and I can only guess Noah wants Piper now because his daddy thinks she'll look good on his arm.

Fuck them all.

But seriously, I'm in love with Piper, and no matter what, and no matter who she thinks I am, or that I'm not good enough for her, I don't want anything bad to happen to her. I just hope she heeds my warning.

I kick the blankets off and push to my feet, my body tired, loaded down more than it's been in a long time. I glance out the window and note the dark clouds. Looks like I'll be driving home in the rain today. I shove all my clothes back into my bag, make a quick trip to the bathroom and once I'm done, I pack my toothbrush. I'm leaving a bit earlier than expected, but I was also scheduled to leave today, so no one should be the wiser that something horrible went down last night.

I'll have to call David later. He spent hours helping me set up the yurt in the clearing—a wide open spot far back in the woods behind our house. My friends and I spent hours there as kids, fishing, swimming, laying beneath the stars and sleeping in tents. While the area is gorgeous, I wanted to make it a little more upscale for Piper, hence the rental of the yurt with the skylight in the middle of the dome so we could fall asleep to moonlight and wake up to sunshine. I'd dressed up in preparation—thinking she'd get a kick out of me wearing the clothes she made—and gone to Cabot Crow to get take-out for us to munch on later. Little did I expect to find her on a date with Noah. I guess all the work and planning was all for nothing now.

Downstairs, I find Bethany and Lauren eating cereal in front of the TV. I give them both hugs and, in the kitchen, I pull Mom into my arms.

There's concern in her eyes as she asks, "Leaving so soon?"

I don't want to talk about Piper, so I say, "Looks like rain. I thought I'd better hit the road."

"Not staying for Sunday dinner?" Dad asks, stepping into the kitchen. "Piper is welcome to join us."

I must pale at the sound of her name as Mom angles her head to examine me, but I can't get into this right now.

"Wish I could, but I have to hit the road." Needing a reprieve from Mom's probing eyes, I jerk my thumb over my shoulder. "I'll go say goodbye to Tanner." They both nod and I dart up the steps. I sneak into his room, sit on the side of his bed and give him a little shake.

"Dude, what the fuck?"

I laugh. "I'm taking off. Give me a hug."

"Fine," he grumbles and my heart aches with the love I have for my kid brother as he throws his arms around me. It also aches for Piper. She doesn't know this kind of love, and while I hope someday she finds out, I don't think she's going to find it with Noah, or here in Cape Breton. I hope for her sake that I'm wrong.

"Come see me in the city sometime," I say to him. "Lots of pretty girls there."

He laughs. "Yeah, then why didn't you find yourself one there?

"What?"

He runs his fingers through his mussed hair. "The girl you found is right here, from Cape Breton. You didn't need to go to the city at all."

He's not wrong.

I nod, and exhale as my heart cracks a tiny bit more, and I struggle with everything in me not to let it shatter completely.

"We're not together. Not anymore."

He sits up a bit. "Why the fuck not?"

"Don't swear."

"Okay, why the hell not?"

I glare at him. "We're different people from different worlds, kiddo."

He shakes his head, and his brow furrows. "Dude, you can't be fucking serious."

"Tanner—"

"Is it because she was with that douche bag Noah last night?"

My head jerks back, my gaze moving over his face. "How the fuck do you know that?"

Now it's his turn to give me a warning look about my language. "Small town, bro."

"Fuck."

His hand touches my arm. "For what it's worth, Beck, I saw the way she looked at you. She really likes you."

I laugh. "Out of the mouths of babes."

"Say what you want, but I have two eyes, and I can also see that you're really sad. I'm sorry, Beck."

"I'm okay."

He adjusts his pillow as he sits up straighter, like this conversation is about to get very serious, and I'm not sure I can handle that. "Maybe you should talk to her."

"I have to go, Tanner." I stand. Honestly, I don't think she'd want to talk to me even if I tried. I basically called her out on her shit.

"Beck."

"Yeah, bud." I turn to him when I reach the door.

"I really liked this girl. Her name is Cora. A bunch of us were going to the drive-in. I couldn't wait to see her there. I thought she liked me too."

"And...?" I ask. Where is he going with this?

"She got in trouble at home and her parents took her phone away for the night. She didn't show, and didn't text anyone. I guess I figured I was wrong, and she didn't like me."

"I'm sorry, Tanner."

"I did something really stupid."

"Like what?"

"I made out with Cassidy."

I cringe. "Shit. Not smart, dude."

"Yeah, I know, right? I really liked Cora. I fucked everything up."

"You're telling me this why?"

"Maybe there's something going on with Piper that you don't know. Maybe there's a reason she was with that douche bag, just like there was a reason Cora didn't come to the drive-in."

When did my little brother get so smart? "That's smart, little buddy."

"You have a long drive ahead of you, so you'd better think about that."

A half laugh, half snort crawls out of my throat. Is it that simple? We're not teens, we're grown adults with futures to figure out. Then again, maybe it is that simple and I'm blowing shit up in my head because old demons still lurk inside me, warning I'll never be good enough.

"Thanks, buddy, I will." I give him a wave goodbye, but his words are stuck in my brain as I head downstairs, give everyone another hug, and head out to my vehicle. I wave to Mom and Dad standing in the doorway watching me, and drive down the long driveway. I glance at the tilted mailbox, a few flyers looking like they're about to spill out, and point my car toward home.

I drive for a long time, Piper on my mind. Tanner's words on my mind. Everything that happened over the last couple of months on my mind. Up until last night things were going so good with Piper and me. Sure, she wasn't ready to tell her parents we were together, wasn't ready to tell them she didn't want to run the resort, but I felt she was warming to both ideas. Was I so wrong about her?

How could I be?

She got out of giving tennis lessons to come to Sunday dinner, and it was clear to everyone at the table how happy she was to be there—with me. To some it might sound like she simply changed her schedule to have dinner with us, but to me, I realize it was like moving mountains.

Why the fuck would she go on a date with Noah?

My phone rings and my heart jumps into my throat. I snatch it from the seat. It's David, not Piper and I hit talk, putting him on speaker. He deserves to hear what happened from me. Then again, maybe he already knows, considering Tanner had heard.

"Hey David, what's up?"

"You tell me."

Yup, okay, he knows.

"I guess you heard, huh?"

"I was with Autumn last night. Piper called and told her you showed up when she was on a dinner date with Noah."

*Dinner date. Fuck.*

"Yup, she actually went on a date with that douche."

"She should know it was Noah who fucked with her car, Beck."

"Maybe, but not knowing it was him, still shouldn't mean she doesn't trust me, right?"

"I know what you're saying...Anyway last night, we met up with Piper, and Autumn thought you two needed to talk so we went to the clearing, but you weren't there. Piper cried when she saw what you had planned for the night. Like cried hard, so hard we could hardly understand what she was saying, but she was mumbling something about a deal. Does that mean anything to you?"

I speed up to pass a car, my mind spinning faster than my wheels as I try to figure out what David is telling me. "I don't know, man."

"I'm going to talk to Autumn again, and see if she knows what's going on."

I shake my head, not sure he should be involving himself. "The yurt—"

"Yeah, I'll take care of it."

My heart warms. I can always count on my buddy. I would have taken it back myself today, but one look at it would simply remind me that my life is a mess.

"Drive safe, and call me when you get home."

"Okay," I say as the word home bounces around inside my brain. Fuck, Piper and I had made a home at Kennedy and Matt's place—at least for a week. But it felt good and felt right and it made me want to get a place of my own, so we could start on a real home for the two of us.

I continue to drive, and my stomach grumbles, but I don't want to stop for food or coffee. I just want to figure out what Piper was talking about when she mumbled something about a deal to my best friend.

I drive for hours, until I'm almost home. On the side of the road, all the familiar billboards come into view, and I laugh. You know you're always approaching the city when they start plastering billboards with restaurants and hotels. As I haphazardly look at one for a local hotel chain, a big slice of apple pie being served in the restaurant, my heart jumps into my throat, and my foot eases off the gas.

Holy fuck!

As my car slows, and other cars pass me, my world spins on its axis.

Pie.

Deal.

My mind races and then slows and I'm practically a hazard on the highway when the tumblers all fall into place. I press on the gas, getting my car back up to speed as everything begins to make sense.

The only way she could come to my place for Sunday dinner was by making a deal and everything in my gut tells me that going to dinner with Noah was the price she had to pay to spend Sunday at my place.

Motherfucker.

I didn't even give her a chance to explain. As old insecurities took hold, I jumped to conclusions—that I wasn't good enough, would never be good enough for Piper. My little brother was right, and things weren't as they seemed, and now, I'm pretty sure I fucked up any chance of a future. I finally arrive home, pull into the driveway, and hurry up the front steps.

Before I can put my hand on the knob, the door flings open. Kennedy's smile falls from her face when she takes one look at my sorry ass. "Oh, Beck," she says quietly before pulling me in for a much-needed hug.

"I know, everything is fucked up."

# 23

# PIPER

I sit outside the resort, my hands tight on my steering wheel as I watch happy guests stroll the golf course. My gaze wanders to the water, and the boats, and while everything about this place screams happiness, I'm miserable inside. I take a breath and try to push back the sadness—heck, Kennedy is having a birthday party for me tonight—but I can't even seem to fill my lungs.

I'm completely miserable inside, yet I can't cancel this Hawaiian luau on her. She's been planning it for months and it's more than just my birthday celebration. It's a way for us all to get together again during summer break. Before we know it, we'll all be buried in classes and sports. I steal a glance at myself in the mirror and swipe at my face as tears threaten to drip.

God, the way Beck and I parted...it was horrific. The way he looked at me, the sadness on his face. I made him feel horrible about himself. In my heart, I know he didn't do that to my car, yet I asked him anyway, proving to him that I am no better than my judgmental parents—that I think I'm better than the boy from the other side of the tracks.

I pretty much couldn't hate myself anymore, and my God, after I called Autumn and she and David took me to the clearing to see the yurt...let's just say it devastated me, and for the last week, I've been a walking zombie, barely speaking or functioning as I went from day to day, considering my life, my future, what I want—and what I lost. But Beck was right. I can't stay at the resort and spend my life dying a slow and painful death.

I check my phone for the millionth time, and there's nothing from Beck. I've been too scared to message him, to afraid that he'll tell me what he really thinks of me, and the truth is, I totally deserve it. Why didn't I defend him? Why didn't I come right out and tell my father that Beck and I were seeing each other, when he interrupted us at Cabot Crow?

*Because you are so messed up, girl.*

I'd messaged Kennedy and even though I hadn't told her what was going on or asked about Beck, she told me he was looking for a new place. Probably because he didn't want to see me coming around.

Knuckles rap on my window and I damn near jump through my sunroof. I turn and spot David standing there, looking lost, forlorn, and maybe a little frightened. I roll my window down.

"You scared me."

"Can I get in?"

I nod and hit the unlock button as he circles the car and slides into the passenger seat. He pulls his door shut, and the air conditioning ruffles his hair. I wait for him to talk, but he stares straight ahead for a long time, like he's waging a war inside his head.

"David?"

"Beck's a good guy."

"I know."

He slowly turns my way, our eyes locking. "Do you?"

Those two words fill me with pain and take the breath from my lungs. The truth is, I do know, and that's why my heart aches. I never meant to hurt him. "I do."

"I need to tell you something."

My throat tightens. I have no idea what's going on here, only that it's not good. "Is Beck okay?"

"No, not really, but that's not what I want to talk to you about."

I grip the steering wheel and squeeze until my hand hurts. "Okay."

"It's true, Beck did threaten Noah."

"He told me."

"What he didn't tell you was why."

"I asked Noah why, and he basically said Beck was jealous."

A groan full of disgust and anger reverberates in David's throat. "I don't want to hurt you. I never wanted to hurt you and neither did Beck." Oh, God, what is going on here? "But you need to know, it was Noah who fucked your car up that night, not Beck." My heart lurches, and the world goes a bit black around me. "I know you thought it was Beck, but—"

"No, actually, I never thought it was Beck. My parents did, but I didn't. He was always so sweet and kind to everyone, and I just...well, he stopped talking to me after the party."

"Yeah, no wonder."

"What?"

"Nothing. Look, the past is the past, and I've seen you two together so I know how you both feel about each other. I think you guys need to have a talk."

I shake my head, and my cheeks grow damp as tears fall. "He hates me, David. He won't talk to me."

"Oh, okay." He shrugs. "I thought you knew him. I guess you don't."

I stare at him. He's being an asshole, and David is never an asshole. I guess maybe he thinks I need a bit of tough love, and maybe he's right.

"You know what? You're right." I pick up my phone, and with shaky fingers, I shoot a text off to Beck about tonight.

Me: Hey, will you be at my party tonight?

I stare as three dots instantly appear and I hold my breath as I turn my phone to David. He nods and we both wait.

Beck: Do you want me there?

. . .

I nearly sob like a damn baby as he responds and I quickly run my fingers over my phone. Tears blur my vision and auto-correct kicks in.

Me: Yes, I'd love it if we could talk.

I set my phone down and a plan forms in the back of my mind. I reach across the seat and give David's hand a squeeze. "Thank you."

He nods. "Okay, happy birthday. Have a safe drive." He exits my car and a new sense of hope flows through my body. I back out of the parking lot and try to calm myself down for the long drive back to the city.

I don't bother stopping, and even though I'm tired—I haven't slept well in forever—I'm jittery, anxious to see Beck again. I drive straight to my house, and go still when I pull into the driveway and find the front door open. I stare, my heart beating a bit faster. Was the place broken into or is Alysha back already?

I unhook my seatbelt and fire her off a text. She instantly responds, informing me that Dryden is still here, and she sends numerous apologies. I climb from my car, stretch my legs out and head up the steps. I really don't want to spend the weekend here if Dryden is still hanging around, and why the hell didn't he go home, anyway?

"Hello," I call out as I enter, tossing my keys onto the side table.

"Hey, you're back," Dryden says, coming into the hall with nothing on but his running shorts.

"What are you still doing here?" I ask.

He shrugs, like it's nothing. "I figured no one was here this summer, so why not stay?"

Shouldn't he be back in the Hamptons working or something? "Did you think to ask me if you could stay?"

He shrugs off my question. "It's July, no sense in going home now. Training starts next month. You're back for the birthday party?"

I stiffen. "How do you know about that?"

"Alysha told me."

I nod and pick up my bag. "Yes, and if you'll excuse me, I need to get ready."

He reaches out to take my bag from me, and I jerk it back. "I got this."

"Okay." He laughs and holds his hands up. "Gotta love an independent woman. Hey, maybe I can come by the party tonight."

I still on the stairs. "I think Kennedy just invited close friends."

"I'm close friends with Beck. He'll be there, right?"

I'm not sure why, but there's something in his voice, a change of sorts at the mention of Beck and I think his question goes deeper than simple curiosity.

"Yes, he'll be there. We're friends. But Kennedy is putting on the party, not Beck."

"Still just friends, huh?" he asks, hearing only what he wants.

You know what, I'm sick of being a chickenshit. I turn to him and smile. "After tonight, I hope Beck and I are more."

His face falls flat, his lips turning white as his nostrils flare like a bull about to take down the matador. The hairs on the back of my neck stand up straight, as he goes deathly still. I have no idea what his problem is, but maybe I'll ask Kennedy if I can stay at her place tonight. I'm also going to message Alysha and tell her I don't want Dryden staying here.

I dart to my room, shut and lock the door, and send a text to Alysha. I know this puts her in an awkward situation, and while I love the girl, it's my name on the lease. She messages back, apologizes again, and tells me she'll talk to him. Okay, I don't know who this assertive, take charge Piper is, but I kind of like her. With that done, I gather some clean clothes and head to the shower. I hear Dryden's phone ring as I close the door and turn on the shower. I block everything out, and turn my thoughts to Beck, and what I want to say to him tonight.

I finish showering and go back to my room to rest and hang out as I wait for the sun to set. Once it does, I dress in a fun, Hawaiian print floral dress with sandals, and tip toe through the house, not wanting to run in to Dryden before I head to Kennedy's. There are lots of cars on the street, and music blares from the backyard as I circle around the house and find a gorgeously decorated backyard. I grin as I take in the blow-up palm trees, the lights, the food and the punch bowl. My heart swells as I see all the people who've come out to celebrate my birthday, but the one guy I was really looking forward to seeing isn't here.

"Piper," Kennedy calls out and runs up to hug me. "It's so good to see you."

I put on a big smile. "It's so good to see you too." I wave to a few friends who turn my way, and I spot Daisy at the punch bowl chatting with Brandon and Chase. It's so good to see the three of them together. They've all been friends since childhood and it's nice to see how they're all still so close.

"Come on, let's get you a drink."

I nod as she loops her arm in mine and guides me to the punch bowl. She fills my cup and the fruity scent of pineapple reaches my nose. I glance around, and Kennedy puts the cup in my hand and says, "He's probably working late at the service station. He's been working a lot this last while. I guess he's trying to save up for his own place."

I bite my bottom lip, as worry wells up inside me. "You think he'll show?"

"Are you guys, okay?" Kennedy asks quietly, as I swirl the punch around inside my glass.

"I don't know." I turn to her. "We're going to talk tonight." She nods, and I angle my head. "Kennedy?"

"Yeah?"

"When you asked me to help Beck take care of Madelyn, were you trying to hook us up?" Her chest expands as she takes a deep breath and exhales. "I thought so," I say with a laugh.

"Are you mad?"

"No, I just wonder why you did it. You guys, heck everyone here..." I glance around and try not to feel anxious when I don't see Beck. "...you all knew we avoided each other, because we didn't really get along."

She nods slowly, and gives me a small smile. "There's a fine line between love and hate."

"I never hated him." He never hated me either, he told me so, but I did disappoint him and I think that might be worse. My phone rings, and I reach into my purse, hoping it's Beck explaining why he's not here, although I don't recognize the number. Maybe he's calling from the service station.

"Hello."

"Is this Piper Thorne?"

"Yes, who's this?" I ask and glance at Kennedy who has a questioning expression on her face.

"This is campus security. You need to get down to the sport-splex right away. There's something you need to see." I swallow as the call ends, and I frown as I glance at Kennedy.

"Something is going on at the sportsplex. They want me to come down, right now."

She takes my drink from my hand and sets it on the table. "Okay, I'll go with you."

"What's going on?" Matt asks, and Kennedy quickly explains. "Okay, let's go."

"You guys are having a party, you can't just leave," I say but they're already rushing me out the door to their SUV. "What do you think is going on?" I ask tentatively as I climb into the back seat.

Matt shoots off a text, before he backs out of the driveway, and casts me a glance in the mirror. "No idea."

"Have you heard from Beck?" I ask. Was that who he was texting?

Matt shakes his head. "I texted him a few times, but nothing." He must read my worried expression because he adds, "I'm sure he's just stuck at work."

*Or he changed his mind about talking to me.*

Matt parks in front of the pool and my heart jumps into my throat as I spot two police cars already there. "What is going on?"

We all climb from the vehicle and I hurry into the building. I come to a dead stop when my gaze goes to the walls, to take in the splashes of red spray-paint that spell out horrible, hateful slurs...about me....

I nearly drop to my knees as my hands fly to my mouth, old hurts from the damage done to my car coming back to haunt me.

"Are you Ms. Thorne?" an officer asks as he comes up to me as Kennedy and Matt flank me, shock and horror on their faces.

"Piper!"

I turn at the sound of Beck's voice, and nearly sink to my knees, so grateful for his strength and presence as he hurries toward me. He slides in next to me, and puts his arm around my back, murder on his face as he reads the walls.

"Beck," I murmur and he holds me tighter.

"This place was locked down today," the officer tells me. "Whoever did this had a key." He zeroes in on me. "We understand you have your own key and don't need to sign in."

"That's...that's right," I say, unable to calm my brain and figure out where he's going with this. "Who...who would do this?"

The other officer, the younger one, looks at his notepad and that's when I realize who he is. Dustin Harding, from Cape Breton. His father was a police officer back in our hometown. I heard Dustin was going into policing, but I didn't know he worked in the city. He was older than us, but Mom and Dad were quite fond of his family. My God could this situation be any more fucked up. But maybe because he knows us, he'll know Beck didn't do this. Then again, like Noah, he always thought he was better than those on the other side of the tracks.

"Do you know someone by the name of Beckett Moore?" he asks with a grin, because of course I know Beck. He knows Beck, too. Why the hell is he acting like he doesn't? Does this give him some kind of sick pleasure?

"Yes." Beck's arm on my back tightens.

"You know who I am," Beck pushes out between clenched teeth.

"Has he ever had access to your key?" Dustin questions me.

I lean toward the rock-solid man beside me. "You know Beckett and you can't think—"

Dustin cuts me off. "Has he ever had access to your key?" he asks again.

I shake my head. "No, I mean yes, he opened the door when he was with me."

Dustin looks rather pleased with himself when he concludes, "Looks like he opened it again, when he wasn't with you."

I shake my head so hard my brain rattles inside, spinning out of control, unable to keep up with what's going on around me. "No, he couldn't have. He didn't."

Dustin angles his head and gives me a sympathetic look. "You, as well as I, know this isn't the first time he's done something like this."

"No," I say, my blood draining to my feet. I glance at Beck, take in the strained look on his face and that's when I notice the red on his shirt. Is that...blood? "Where...were you?" I ask, but as soon as the words leave my mouth, I realize how horrible and accusing they sound, but that's simply because I'm flustered, and nothing is coming out right and I'm worried he might be hurt. "I mean—"

"We have a witness. He even captured it on camera." The officer puts his hands on Beck's shoulder, and the world as I know it tilts on its axis. "Beckett, if you'll come with us."

God no, this can't be happening...not again. My phone rings, and I pull it from my purse. Any ounce of blood left in my face drains to my toes as I glance up at Kennedy. "It's my parents." I shake my head. "They've already heard. They're on their way here to bring me back home."

## 24

## BECKETT

I dip my sponge into the bucket of soapy water, and scrub it over the hateful words written on the pool wall. I have no idea what I did in a past life, I can only assume I was a real douche, like whoever really did this to the wall, and while I have a gut feeling, I have no proof. The video footage did look like me, and we all know there's only one other guy on campus—with a little creative camera work —who could pull that off. The police are looking into it, but what I don't understand is why Dryden would do something like this. Fuck, how did he even know this was something I was accused of when we were kids?

I listen to music as I scrub, but getting the paint off the wall proves harder than I anticipated. I don't care how long it takes, though. No way do I want anyone seeing the things said about Piper, even though she thinks I did this. We were so close, I could feel it in my bones, so close to making things right between us. Then this shit happens. How fucked up is my life anyway?

A tap on my shoulder scares the shit out of me, and I angle my head. My heart stops beating when I find Piper standing there, her eyes so big and so full of sorrow, it nearly brings tears to my own eyes.

I tug my earbuds out and let them dangle around my neck. "I thought you left town," I say. She flinches, and wraps her arms around herself. Dammit, that came out cold and harsh, and I know things aren't good between us and she thinks I did this, for some reason, but I love her, and can't stand to see her hurting.

"I know..." Her words fall off as she takes in my soapy sponge.

"How did you know where I was?"

"Kennedy told me. You didn't have to do this." Her breathing is erratic as she looks at the wall.

"I know. I wanted to."

Her throat sounds rough and scratchy as she swallows and that's when I notice her puffy eyes. Looks like she got about as much sleep as I did last night. At least I didn't have to spend the night in lock-up.

"Beck," she begins softly, and glances at my bare feet. "I know you don't want to talk to me, or listen to anything I have to say, so I was hoping you'd let me show you something..."

"Wait, is that what you think?" Her head lifts, tired eyes locking on mine. "You think I don't want to talk to you or listen to anything you have to say?"

A little sparkle of hope lights her eyes. "Are you saying you do?"

I drop the sponge into the bucket and wipe my hands on my sweatpants. "Of course, I do."

"But...you didn't show up at my party...either time," she adds under her breath. "So, I just assumed..."

I stare at her. What the hell is she talking about? "And you think I didn't show up because I was doing this?"

"No," she snaps so quickly my head jerks back. "No, Beck. I never thought that. I know you didn't do this."

"Then why did you ask me where I was?"

"You...had blood on your shirt." Tears pool in her eyes and it takes all my strength not to wrap my arms around her and tell her everything is going to be all right—that we're going to be all right, but I have no idea how we can move past her not trusting me.

Wait, did she say blood...and not paint?

"I was worried you were hurt," she whispers softly.

My heart crawls into my throat, making speech difficult. "You were worried about me?" She nods. "I'm okay. The blood wasn't mine." She blinks, her eyes full of questions. I'm about to explain but she cuts me off.

"You don't have to tell me, or explain anything."

"Oh, so you know then."

"All I know is I went to the police station this morning, first chance I got, to tell them it wasn't you." She closes her eyes, like she's completely embarrassed. "I actually told them it was me."

"You did what?"

Her laugh is tortured. "I knew you didn't do it, and I told them I dressed up like you and pretended to be you because we had a fight." She shakes her head and groans. "They looked at me like I sprouted a second head."

I'm not sure whether to laugh or cry. "I can't believe you did that."

"Yeah, then I went to see Coach Jameson. I was worried about you getting kicked off the team."

"I was worried about that too." Christ, the thought of getting booted out scared the living shit out of me. I have a family counting on me, and I don't want to let them down.

"He said everything was straightened out."

I nod and look down. "You did all those things after you found out I had an alibi, huh?" Yeah, we definitely don't have a future if I have to keep proving myself to her.

"No. I have no idea where you were last night. I still don't know, and you don't have to tell me anything for me to believe you didn't do this."

My head jerks up, my breath coming quicker. "Are you serious?"

"I never believed you did that to my car either, Beck."

"Just so you know, last night—"

"Nope." She holds her hand up to cut me off.

"I think you'll want to know this." Her brow furrows, and I continue with. "Do you remember Gerard, the homeless man who hangs around outside the service station?" Panic invades her face.

"Yes, is he okay?"

"He got hit by a car, and the car took off. I was just finished up at the station, and was about to head to your party when I heard the crash. I found him on the road bleeding. I couldn't even think straight. I just reacted, got him into my Jeep and took him to the hospital. I was in such a hurry, I left my phone at the service station, and by the time I got back, there was a text from Matt to meet him at the sportsplex."

Her hand touches mine, and her warmth curls around my heart, making it just a little bit harder to breathe. "My God, Beck. Thank God you were there. Is he going to be okay?"

I nod. "He's banged up, and I'm going to go by to see him later."

"Can I come?"

I can't help but smile. "If you want."

"I'll get him a hamburger." That makes me laugh and she looks down, but not before I catch a hint of embarrassment. "That's silly, isn't it."

"No, it's not. It's thoughtful." I touch her chin and lift it until her eyes are on me. "What's silly is you trying to take the rap for this." Her hands fall and dangle at her sides. I reach out and capture one of her hands. Her breath flitters. "You could have gotten kicked out of the academy."

She closes her eyes, takes a big breath and lets it out slowly as her lids flicker open. "I guess you should know, I'm leaving the academy."

The pool deck closes in on me, and for a second I feel like I'm drowning. Piper is leaving the academy? No way, no how. She can't do that, not because of me. "What the fuck, Piper?"

"My parents showed up last night to take me home. I didn't go, obviously, but we talked all night. That's why I couldn't get to the police station to straighten this out until morning, even though I guess it was already straightened out."

"You can't leave the academy."

"Yeah, actually I can. I'm going to enroll in community college full time, and get a degree in fashion design."

My jaw drops. I'm so incredibly happy for her, I can't help but throw my arms around her and give her a big hug. I set her down, keeping our bodies close and she continues with, "I told them everything. That I don't want to do a business degree. That I don't want to go back to Cape Breton and run the resort, and especially that I don't want to marry Noah Blackmore." Her body physically quakes in disgust.

I stare at her, my eyes full of questions and she answers with, "I don't know what the future holds, I only know I want it to be with you."

My throat constricts as I swallow and congratulate her. "I'm so happy for you, Piper and I don't know what the future holds either, I only know I want it to be with you." My lips find hers, and I kiss her softly, tenderly, my heart so full of love I'm sure it's going to burst. I inch back and press my forehead to hers, giddy inside. I shake my head. "I can't believe you were going to take the rap for me."

"I was going to take the rap for us."

"But wait, who did this?"

"I think we both know."

I nod. "Dryden, but why?"

"I called Alysha. Apparently, his parents are assholes." She shakes her head. "They put a ton of pressure on him, to be the number one goalie, or they'd stop supporting him. He had access to my keys when I left them at my place when he was staying there, and of course he was the one with the video footage. It was all staged."

"Fuck."

"I guess maybe he thought getting close to me would throw you off your game or something."

"If I didn't want to punch him in the face, I'd kind of feel sorry for him."

"I know." She angles her head and looks at me. "There's one thing I don't know, though."

"What's that?"

"Why you never went to my seventeenth birthday party."

Now it's my turn to look at her like she sprouted another head. "Because you never invited me."

"But I did invite you, Beck."

I shake my head as my brain dredges up painful memories. "No, you never gave me an invitation. If you had, I definitely would have been there. You see, I liked you." Tears fill her eyes and my heart stalls. "What?"

"We've lost so much time together," she murmurs.

While I agree, I still don't understand. I lightly touch her arm. "What are you talking about?"

"I put the invitation in your mailbox. All this time, I thought you got it, and didn't come because you hated me."

I glance upward, as an epiphany strikes. "Jesus Christ, that fucking mailbox."

"What about it?"

"Every year the plow truck driver does a number on it. You must have put it in before we fixed it, and it must have fallen out and blown away."

"I gave you one, Beck. I hope you believe me, and I really hope you don't hate me for what you thought I did then, and for how I acted—then and now."

"I never hated you. In fact, I've always liked you, Thorne."

My heart crashes as I step closer to her, and throw my arms around her, even though I'm full of soap. She hugs me back, her warm sweet scent curling around me and hugging tight.

"I like you too, Moore. No that's a lie." I go perfectly still as a grin plays with her lips. "I love you," she whispers.

I grin as my heart takes flight. "I love you too, Piper." I scoop her up, and plant a big wet kiss on her mouth as we laugh and hug. After a minute, I set her down, and press my forehead to hers. "I can't believe it's taken so long for us to get here."

She laughs. "What is it about you, Beck? Everyone has it out for you."

"I don't know. I'm a nice guy."

"Yeah, you are a nice guy." She pokes me in the chest. "A nice guy who likes cookies on Thursdays, and selfies on Sundays."

I smile, and then turn serious again. "Wait, when you showed up and didn't think I would talk to you, you said you had something to show me. What is it?"

"I thought you'd never ask." She takes my hand and leads me into the women's change room. "I don't think I'm supposed to be in..." She lifts her skirt, showing me her panties, which say, *I'm sorry*."

"Fuck me," I murmur.

"You know, I remember when Kennedy and Matt made up, you said something about make-up sex being the best sex. Is that true?"

I drag her to me and put my lips to hers. "Yeah, it's true, babe, and I'm going to prove that to, right here, right now, over and over and over again. But first this."

"What is it?"

I pull back, leaving cold where there was once heat, as Piper stares up at me, curiosity dancing in her beautiful eyes. I root through my front pocket and pull out a box. I open it and show her the jewelry inside. "This is for you."

Confusion moves into her eyes. "Beck."

I grin and pull the necklace from the box. I unclasp it and put it around her neck. "I've had this since we were seventeen, Piper."

Tears fill her eyes. "You were going to give it to me for my seventeenth birthday."

"I was," I tell her. "Then I was going to give it to you last night, but well, shit kind of hit the fan."

We both chuckle at that, even though there's nothing funny in what went down. She touches it. "It's beautiful." She smiles up at me. "A palm tree."

"Because you've always wanted to go to Hawaii."

"You knew that..."

"Yeah, and someday, when I put a diamond on your finger and ask you to marry me, maybe we can go there for our honeymoon."

Her eyes widen. "Beck, are you serious?"

"My love for you exceeds animal crackers, Piper. I've always known I wanted to marry you." I kiss her deeply, and she returns it with such tenderness and love, I could sob with happiness. I break the kiss, sure my heart is going to burst. "Now let's talk about this *sorry* written on your panties..."

She glances around. "Maybe we should go somewhere private."

I capture her hand. "You're right. The last thing I need is to get arrested again."

Laughing, we both run from the building, our hearts full of love and understanding as we leave the past behind and hurry toward our very bright future.

# EPILOGUE

Piper

I take a deep breath, breathing in the unusually warm fall air. Come October, the weather is normally a lot colder, the trees turning gorgeous colors, but this weekend, we've been having a heat wave, which is great for our Hawaiian luau—take two.

That thought makes me laugh. But since our last party was a bust, like a real bust, with Beck getting arrested and all, Kennedy insisted we have a do-over and I'm glad she did. We're deep into fall semester and we've all been so busy, we've barely seen each other and of course I'm no longer at the academy, so I rarely see anyone.

I glance around her backyard as everyone chats and enjoys the food and punch. But today isn't just a birthday celebration for me, it's also an engagement party for Beck and me—I lift my ring finger to examine the gorgeous diamond—and it's also a celebration for Daisy. She passed her medical school entrance exams, which she spent all summer studying for, and now she's just waiting to hear if she's been accepted to Dalhousie Medical School here in the city.

Speaking of Daisy.

She seeks me out in the crowd and waves to me. I gesture her over, and she weaves her way through our friends, and comes my way. There's a girl I've yet to meet following her over. That's just like Daisy though, always watching out for others, and making everyone feel like they belong. She'll be a great doctor.

I slip off the stool I'm sitting on and give Daisy a hug. "Congratulations, Daisy. I'm so happy for you."

Daisy takes my hand and if I'm not mistaken, I'm pretty sure that's a look of longing on her face as she glances at my ring. For a girl who claims she's never getting married, she sure is looking at my diamond with wonderment in her eyes.

She lets my hand go, and introduces us. "Piper, this is Naomi." She pulls Naomi closer. "We met last month when we interviewed for medical school."

I smile at Naomi, who is inches taller than Daisy, with dark hair, and gorgeous tanned skin. With Daisy's wild blonde curls that have a mind of their own, and her light skin, Naomi is the antithesis of my friend. "So nice to meet you, Naomi. When do you guys hear if you're accepted to med school?"

Daisy crosses her fingers and glances upward, like she's tossing up a prayer, but with her volunteering, sports and grades, she doesn't need it. "In a couple of weeks."

"You'll both get in." I nod and tap my head. "I know these things."

Daisy laughs. "I hope you're right."

Brandon steps up to her, putting his hands on Daisy's shoulders like he's done a million times before, giving her muscles a squeeze. "What's up, Duke?"

What the hell?

Did Daisy just suck in a breath, and is that pink hue spreading across her cheeks from Brandon's touch? My God, I have to be mistaken. Those two, as well as Chase, go way back. Friends since they were born. Besides, Daisy, who is on the women's hockey team, doesn't date hockey players. She's made that clear to everyone—a million times.

Why then are her cheeks flushing?

Despite the flush, her voice is casual as she answers, "What's up, B?"

I think the nicknames they have for each other are cute, although I have no idea why Brandon calls her Duke. His hands drop from her shoulders and I note the way he keeps casting glances at Naomi—and it's obvious he's about to turn on his boyish charm.

As if picking up on his interest, Daisy introduces them, and wow, even though Naomi is friendly, it's clear she isn't interested. Strange, because Brandon can have his pick of girls. But maybe like Daisy, Naomi doesn't date hockey players. Naomi excuses herself to go get another refill of punch. Daisy takes one look at Brandon and laughs.

"No way, B. She's out of your league, dude." She punches him on the shoulder and he feigns pain.

"Come on, she's cute." He holds his shoulder. "We'd make a good couple, don't you think?"

"Like being a couple is what you're interested in." Daisy gives an unladylike snort before taking a big gulp of punch from her cup. "Trust me, she's too smart to date a guy like you."

He blinks dark lashes over those dark, puppy dog eyes of his. "You could say nice things about me."

"Like what? Oh, I know, I could tell her about that time you nearly drowned me at Wautauga Beach, or the time you made me eat dirt. Oh wait, even better. I could tell her about the time you tricked me into touching a fish's eyeball after you caught it in the river. I might have been a tomboy, but touching fish's eyeball..." A shiver goes through her. "That's just disgusting, Brandon."

He laughs. "You don't remember anything nice?"

"No," she says blatantly, and I grin as I watch the exchange. There's something more going on here, I feel it in every fiber of my body, and I have to say, I'm intrigued.

"How about this then, you pretend to be my girl and show her that hockey players aren't all bad."

She lifts her chin an inch. "Lie, then?"

"Come on, Daisy. Are you forgetting I covered for you that night you drank at the beach and got sick? I told your parents we ate bad pepperoni on the pizza and even stuck my fingers down my throat so I would get sick too, just to convince them."

She groans. "Really, B? You're playing that card? Now?"

"If we pretend to be a thing, maybe it will pique her interest." Brandon gestures toward me. "Remember how Dryden was suddenly interested in Piper when he found out she was with Beck."

"Yeah, and look how well that turned out for him," I pipe in. "Life is not a romantic comedy."

"Okay, true," Brandon agrees. He nudges Daisy. "Will you think about it, though? Tell me you'll think about it, buttercup."

"Right after I solve world hunger, sure." She groans and finishes the contents in her cup. "I need a drink."

Brandon takes her cup from her, like he's trying to soften her up, and smiles. "Let me help you."

"I can get my own...Brandon!" Ignoring her protest, he takes off and she runs after him.

I jump back on my stool and laugh as I watch them go. My God, life is funny and complicated and wonderful and I don't think I've ever been happier. To think last year, I was a miserable business student and now I'm a full-time design student, and while my parents still aren't pleased with me, we're talking again, and they've come to accept the fact that I want to live my own life. They'll keep running the resort for now, and I honestly hope they find happiness again, either with each other, or with new partners. They deserve all the good things life has to offer.

Talking about good things...

My heart beats a little faster as Beck comes toward me, looking like a big goof in his flashy Hawaiian shorts. It's crazy to think our lives were on a crash course, and now, I'm pretty sure I couldn't love him more. But that's a lie, because I know tomorrow, when we wake up together in bed —yes, he moved in with me—I'll love him more than I did today.

"There you are," he says, and pushes my legs open to slide in between. His hands slide around my back, and I absorb his warmth. Will I ever get used to him being mine?

"I was here all along," I whisper and wet my lips.

He kisses me deeply, and someone, I think it might be Brandon, yells, "Get a room." We both grin, and Beck presses his forehead to mine. "God, I can't wait for you to be my wife."

"I can't wait either."

We haven't solidified any plans, not with him getting drafted to Tampa along with Matt. We don't have Dryden to worry about anymore. After the investigation and being charged with mischief, he moved back home to the Hamptons. But I don't want to think about that. I have too many happy things going on in my life, and I'm so proud of Beck, and he's proud of me.

We'll have a wedding when the time is right, and for our honeymoon, we'll be celebrating at a real luau in Hawaii. It might not be as great as this one, though. Beck also wants to wait to give my parents time to warm to the idea of him being their son-in-law. He's a wonderful, kind, forgiving man like that and he wants my parents to be a part of our lives—our kids' lives when we have them—despite everything. His parents couldn't have been happier when we told them, and they all openly accepted me into their home and lives. It's a wonderful feeling.

I grin as I watch Daisy jump and try to take her cup out of Brandon's hands. He's much taller than her so he can easily keep it from her. What is it about Daisy and hockey players? What does she have against them? You'd think she'd love them, considering her dad was in the NHL, and Brandon and Chase, her best friends since childhood, are also on their way to great things. Then again, while tons of guys want to date her, she declines them all. What is her story? I shake my head, a grin pulling at my lips. While I don't know what it is, I'd love to find out.

Daisy throws her arms around Brandon and practically tackles him to the ground, and as soon as I watch them fall together, I know it—they were meant to be.

"What's so funny?" Beck asks and turns to see what I'm looking at.

"Daisy and Brandon. I think they're both in for a wild, but fun ride."

"Really?" Beck's gaze moves over my face, and I cup his cheeks and kiss him.

"Yeah, really, and I can't wait to see the mess they make of things, and how it all shakes out in the end..."

\* \* \*

Thank you so much for reading Piper and Beck's story. I hope you enjoyed it. The fourth book in the series, **Home Advantage (Rebels)** releases November 8, 2022. Please read on for an excerpt.

## Home Advantage (Rebels)
### Daisy

Do I believe for one small second that Brandon Cannon, right winger extraordinaire and my very best friend since childhood, is ready to give up the puck bunnies and settle down with a soon to be medical school student?

Uh, how about no, with a capital N.

Which raises the question: why the hell did I agree to be his wingman so I can show my good friend Naomi Sanders that he's a real catch and she should give the well-known player a chance?

Brain tumor?

Honestly, is there any other explanation? Okay, maybe there's one, and I can't even believe I'm admitting this to myself after all these long and painful years of doing 'buddy' things with Brandon. But I, Daisy Reed of sound mind and memory, have been in love with none other than Brandon Cannon, my best friend since childhood, for as long as I can remember.

Okay, there I said it, and the next thing I need to do is go for a brain scan. I mean come on, we're talking about a guy who made me eat dirt, a guy who tricked me into touching a fish's eyeball. A FISH'S EYEBALL for God's sake!

Yeah, he did those things when we were kids. But you know what, he also did good things...great things even. Like when we were teens, he pretended to be sick right along with me— saying we both ate bad pepperoni on our pizza—claiming it gave us food poisoning. He saved my ass the night I went to a party when we were all on vacation at Wautauga Beach, in Washington, where all our parents have cottages. I wasn't allowed to go to the rowdy party at Sebastian Wilson's house, at the end of the beach, but I snuck away and did it anyway. When I drank too much, I called Brandon for help. He took me home, and fortunately my parents bought the bad pepperoni story. Brandon stayed in the spare room that night, and kept checking on me every few hours. How could I not love him, right?

So I guess I owe him this, and despite how much it's going to break my heart to see him with my friend, Brandon and I don't stand a chance at a future. You see, he friend zoned me a long time ago. I was the only girl allowed in the tree house, or the blanket tent, and while I thought it was cool back then, I realize now, the guys all thought of me as one of them. The boobs and the hips that came along later, they didn't faze them one bit.

So here we are many years later, sitting at the campus Tap Room, after my kick ass hockey game, where I scored two goals, and the guys—my buddies—are all ruffling my hair and telling me I did a great job. I keep scanning the place for Naomi. She had to run home after the game and said she'd meet me here later. Little does she know I'm Brandon's wingman and I'm going to try to set them up. Does that make me a bad friend? I guess not, especially if they end up married with kids.

Why does that thought bring pain to my stomach? Oh right... because I love him and never in this lifetime will he be mine.

As I swallow, hard, my friend Alysha nudges me. "Are you okay? You're quiet tonight."

I snort. I get it. I'm never quiet. "Just tired," I tell my new roommate. Alysha moved out of our friend Piper's place and in with me, after Piper and Beck got together and Beck moved in with her. She came here from The Hampton's to study dance, and I like her a lot. She doesn't date, and is practically engaged to a boy back home. Although she never talks about him, which I find a bit weird.

"I can imagine you're tired." Alysha raises her beer glass and I click mine to it. "You kicked ass tonight, girlfriend."

I smile. While I do love hockey, heck my dad was in the NHL but a future in the sport isn't for me. I spent all summer studying and it was just last month I wrote a six hour medical entrance exam. It's no wonder I'm exhausted. But it was worth it because I passed. Now I, along with Naomi, wait for the results of our interviews, and I'm nervous as hell. I hold my hands out and examine my nails, which are faring worse than my nerves. I bring my fingers to my mouth and, catching me by surprise, my hand is slapped away from my face.

"What the—"

I look up and find Brandon shoving everyone away so he can sit next to me. "Stop biting your damn nails," he warns, for the millionth time, and plunks down next to me, like a damn bull in a China shop. I shove him, but it does nothing to nudge his powerful body, as his hard thigh squishes the side of mine.

I shove him again. I realize it's futile, and can't help but think I'm doing it just to touch him. Yes, my friends, I am that pathetic. "Move."

He shifts, and scrubs his hand over his face, and I try to ignore the little shivers rushing over my skin as his scruff of a beard makes that little rustling sound that vibrates through me. It's a familiar habit and I wish I didn't like it so much?

"Hey, Duke."

"B," I respond. We've been calling each other by our nick-names for as long as I can remember. I'm still not sure why he calls me Duke. Maybe it's because he simply sees me as one of the guys, and Daisy is too flowery a name for me. Yeah, we'll never be an item.

But I can't think about that right now, not when he's practically sitting on me, and I like it. I take a fast breath at his closeness and try to pull off casual, but his warm familiar scent of fresh soap and something uniquely Brandon curls around me and messes with my hormones. Good lord, when I'm around him I'm like a dim-witted moth. Not that he'd notice and maybe I'd be horribly embarrassed if he did. When push comes to shove the last thing in the world I want is to risk losing his friendship. He means the world to me.

"Why are you chewing your nails again?" He takes my hand in his, and his stupid warmth invades my skin and curls around my heart. "I told you, you'll get into medical school." I nod, and he goes quiet, thoughtful before adding, "Want to do something next Wednesday? Go shopping or something? Grab dinner?"

My throat tightens. God, he can be so damn sweet. Next Wednesday is when the interview results come in and I find out if I got into Dalhousie Medical School here in Halifax. I hadn't mentioned it to him in ages, I don't want to think about it, but he didn't forget the date.

"Yeah, that sounds good," I reply casually. "But you might be on a date with Naomi that day."

His face lights up. "So she said yes, she'll go out with me?"

"I'm still working on it. You have a reputation that can only be cleaned up by a professional PR firm with years to spare, and you gave me, who knows nothing about PR, one week to do it." It was at Piper's birthday celebration that Brandon set eyes on Naomi, and I foolishly agreed to help set them up. Not because I don't think they'll be good together, but because maybe he is ready to settle down, and they might be a great couple. Could I be any more of a masochist?

He takes a swig of beer and a juicy drop clings to his bottom lip. He swipes it away with the back of his hand and I try not to stare at his mouth or think about how many times I wondered what it would be like to kiss him—on his lips. Yes, he cheek kisses me all the time. We're pals like that.

"She's not into hookups, B." I stare at him, gauging his reaction, and for a moment he seems like he's a million miles away. "B?"

"Yeah."

"She'll want to go nice places—places that aren't your bedroom."

"Are you saying my bedroom isn't nice?"

"It's disgusting, but that's another story."

He toys with the label on his beer bottle, his big fingers tugging at the label and I try not to imagine them toying with my panties in much the same manner.

He arches a brow looking totally offended. "Then you're saying you think I don't know how to treat a girl."

"Fish eyeballs!" I shoot back.

He laughs. "Well, okay, maybe you're right. I guess it's good that I have you. To get insider information, so I don't mess this up."

"Insider information?"

He shrugs. "Yeah, find out what she likes, what she doesn't... things like that."

"You've really never been on a real date before?" I ask even though I already know he hasn't. He shakes his head. "The first thing you need to know is that on a real date, with a girl you like you have to put the real work in B. It doesn't just come to you. I realize you had it easy, girls throwing themselves at you, but this is different. Naomi isn't a puck bunny, infatuated with you." How crazy is it that I'm giving advice when I've not been on a real date either? But I'm a girl, who doesn't sleep with hockey players, and I know how I'd want to be treated, so maybe I can be of value to him.

He nods this time and when a plate of cheesy fries is set on the table, he snags one. I try not to stare at his mouth as he takes a bite, and holds the cheesiest part out for me. I open my mouth and he feeds it to me.

"You never did tell me what you wanted in return for helping," he reminds me.

The only thing I want in return is him and I can't have it. I sigh, and say, "To see you happy, B." He smiles at me, and while this might sound cliché, the truth is, it truly takes my breath away. His hand goes to his temple and he rubs slightly and I narrow my eyes, as he frowns. "Are you okay?"

He plasters on a smile, and while it looks genuine, I know him well enough to know something is bothering him. Is he worried about making it into the NHL? Most of the guys are, but most of the guys don't have the kind of pressure Brandon does. His father was one of the greatest and Brandon is expected to follow in his footsteps.

"I'm fine," he says cheerily, and leans into me again. "What about you?" I'm fully aware of the way he's changing the subject and I'm about to call him on it until he shifts ever so closer and my brain nearly shuts down. Geez, I wish he'd cut it out—I think. "What can I do to make you happy?"

God, if he only knew.

"Naomi is here," I say instead of answering and I lift my hand to wave her over. She comes toward me, dressed in a long pantsuit that looks amazing on her lithe body. Her hair is loose, framing her pretty face, and her makeup is absolutely on point. Everything about her reminds me I have no game—outside of the rink. I do, however get asked out a lot, but I'm beginning to believe it's a competition between the guys now. I shove Brandon. "Go. I can't say nice things about you if you're sitting right here."

He leans in and gives me a friendly kiss on the cheek. "Thanks Daisy."

"Yeah, yeah, now go."

He stands and everyone grumbles and pushes him as he stumbles his way from the booth. He heads to the bar, where our friend Ryan Potter is sitting, and Naomi moves in beside me to take Brandon's place.

"Great game tonight," she tells me, and I grab the pitcher on the table, fill an empty glass with beer, and set it in front of her. "Did I scare Brandon off or something?" she asks.

I laugh at that. "No, he needed to talk to Ryan."

"He's cute huh?"

Okay, maybe this will be easier than I thought. At the birthday party she didn't seem to have the time of day for Brandon. I guess maybe she's changed her mind. I've yet to meet a girl who wasn't interested.

"Yeah, he's cute."

"You going to go for it then?" she asks me, and judging from the confused look on her face, I should probably pick my jaw up from the table.

"Me, go for it?"

"You two are always together, and it's easy to see how comfortable you are around one another."

I take a big gulp of beer, like a huge gulp, hoping I don't say something crazy and give myself away. I set my glass on the table. "We're friends. We go way back." I hold both hands up. "Trust me, there is nothing between Brandon and me." She eyes me, her head angling. She's far from stupid which makes me want to babble on, and say more to convince her, but she who protests too much...

"Oh, I just thought you liked him."

"I do like him. He's one of my best friends, and I'm so not his type. I mean I'm a tomboy and he's into girly girls, you know." *Stop rambling, Daisy*. I take a breath and go for it. "Actually, it's you he likes."

Her big dark eyes stare at me in disbelief. "Me?"

"Yeah, he's been asking me about you."

She lifts her head and turns to look at Brandon, who is looking back. "I don't think I'm his type either, Daisy. I mean, his reputation..."

"Yeah, apparently, he's played out, and is looking for a nice girl...like you."

She puckers her lips and runs her finger over the rim of her glass, as she considers my words. "He really told you that?"

"Yup."

She stares at him for another second. "I don't do hook-ups."

"He's not looking for one. You know underneath it all, he's a pretty great guy."

"Didn't he make you touch a fish's eyeball?"

I can't help but laugh as my mind goes back to that day on the lake. We were sixteen, out on the boat, and he caught a speckled trout. He wanted me to touch the scales and when I did the boat moved and I ended up poking the eyeball, and got so freaked out I jumped up and fell into the water. He abandoned—and lost—the fish when he dove in to save me, and it only solidified my love for him.

I snort. "The story isn't as bad as it sounds."

She turns to me. "I trust you, Daisy. If you think I should go on a date with him, then I will."

I angle my head, catch Brandon's gaze, and if I'm not mistaken, I'm sure he's a little wobbly on his feet. Was he drinking before he came to the pub? I'm not sure, but something is off about him. Heck, maybe he's in love with Naomi or something and it's messing with him. Lord knows it's messing with me.

"Yeah, I think you should," I say. Just because I mean it, doesn't mean I don't hate everything about it.

"Okay, I'm free tomorrow. Next week, I'm away for reading week." She leans into me, and her warm vanilla scent fills my senses. "You're a good friend, always helping others. You're a real caregiver, Daisy."

"Yeah, that's me." If I'm thinking about others, I don't have to think about myself, or how I was abandoned as a baby—so my real mother could snag herself a hockey player. The simple fact is, people use me to get what they want—just like Brandon is doing. But he's not all to blame. I agreed to this, because deep down I have horrible abandonment issues, and I'm terrified of losing him. One thought dances around inside my brain as I fill my glass up again, wanting to drown out the emotions rising in me.

When it comes to setting up Brandon, I'm damned if I do, and I'm damned if I don't.

If you want to find out what kind of trouble Daisy and Brandon get into in Home Advantage check it out here.
**Home Advantage (Rebels)**

# ALSO BY CATHRYN FOX

**Hands On**

**Hands On**

**Body Contact**

**Full Exposure**

**Dossier**

**Private Reserve**

**House Rules**

**Under Pressure**

**Big Catch**

**Brazilian Fantasy**

**Improper Proposal**

**Boys of Beachville**

**Good at Being Bad**

**Igniting the Bad Boy**

**Bad Girl Therapy**

**Stone Cliff Series:**

Crashing Down

Wasted Summer

Love Lessons

Wrapped Up

**Eternal Pleasure Series**

**Instinctive**

**Impulsive**

**Indulgent**

**Sun Stroked Series**

**Seaside Seduction**

**Deep Desire**

**Private Pleasure**

**Captured and Claimed Series:**

Yours to Take

Yours to Teach

Yours to Keep

**Firefighter Heat Series**

Fever

Siren

Flash Fire

**Playing For Keeps Series**

Slow Ride

Wild Ride

Sweet Ride

**Breaking the Rules:**

Hold Me Down Hard

Pin Me Up Proper

Tie Me Down Tight

**Stand Alone Title:**

Hands on with the CEO

Torn Between Two Brothers

Holiday Spirit

Unleashed

Knocking on Demon's Door

Web of Desire

# ABOUT CATHRYN

*New York Times* and *USA today* Bestselling author, Cathryn is a wife, mom, sister, daughter, and friend. She loves dogs, sunny weather, anything chocolate (she never says no to a brownie) pizza and red wine. She has two teenagers who keep her busy with their never ending activities, and a husband who is convinced he can turn her into a mixed martial arts fan. Cathryn can never find balance in her life, is always trying to find time to go to the gym, can never keep up with emails, Facebook or Twitter and tries to write page-turning books that her readers will love.

Connect with Cathryn:
Newsletter https://app.mailerlite.com/webforms/landing/cif8ni
Twitter: https://twitter.com/writercatfox
Facebook: https://www.facebook.com/AuthorCathrynFox?ref=hl
Blog: http://cathrynfox.com/blog/
Goodreads: https://www.goodreads.com/author/show/91799.Cathryn_Fox

Pinterest http://www.pinterest.com/catkalen/

Printed in Great Britain
by Amazon

22865297R00179